RULE BRITANNIA

A Drabble and Harris Thriller

ALEC MARSH

Published by Accent Press Ltd 2019

www.accentpress.co.uk

Accent Press Ltd
Octavo House
West Bute Street
Cardiff
CF10 5LR

ISBN 9781786157188
eISBN 9781786157195

Printed and bound in Great Britain by Clays Ltd,
Elcograf S.p.A

For
John and Lynn

CHAPTER ONE

London, December 1936

A fog of tobacco all but concealed the strutting satyrs, winged cherubs, and nude dancing nymphs that adorned the low ceiling of the Granville Club's Long Bar. The cloud floated over a noisy, bobbing, gas-lit landscape of gentlemen patrons, lounging in the deep leather armchairs, standing chatting in groups or propped at the bar, spirals of smoke ascending from their pipes, cigars, and cigarettes. There was a lone chromatic renegade among the uniform landscape of black and grey cloth – Ernest Drabble, dressed in a country suit of green herringbone tweed, finished off with a muted yellow waistcoat, and a blue and silver striped tie; this of his college, Sidney Sussex, Cambridge. He was thirty years of age, and in the prime of life.

'It's busy for a Monday,' he remarked, as he pressed his stomach against the bar to allow another patron to pass. Drabble's companion, Percival Harris, dismissed this comment with a shake of the head.

'You've been hiding away in your ivory tower for too long, Ernest. I've warned you about this before.' Harris lifted his silver tankard above head height and wagged it jauntily, 'Let's have another.'

A moment or two later, the two men raised refreshed pints to their lips. They complimented the brew. Harris nudged Drabble's elbow.

1

'See the chubby chap at the end of the bar?'

Drabble scanned the crowd.

'Over there,' said Harris, pointing brazenly with his tankard. 'Barrel-chested fellow just ordering now.' Drabble peered along the bar and saw him.

'Reckon if he shaved his hair off, he'd be a spit for Mussolini.'

Drabble laughed; the stranger certainly had the rubbery pout and the bulging eyes of the Italian leader, not to mention the tan.

'Look,' continued Harris, 'even waves his ruddy arms about like *Il Duce*.'

Drabble smiled. 'You don't suppose he's actually one of his doubles?'

'Or the man himself?' Harris shrugged. 'Dictators have to have holidays, too.' He looked back over. 'I really ought to find out who he is; it might make something for the column. People just die for lookalikes, especially of Latin tyrants; they can't get enough of them.'

Drabble chuckled; Harris was never off-duty. Evidently deep in thought, he watched Harris grope in his jacket pocket and take out his pipe, knock it on the bar and then remove a rectangular tin from his other pocket. Gritting his teeth about the stem of the pipe, he pressed a pinch of tobacco into its small bowl, struck a match, and dipped the flaming tip in – all achieved in a rather graceful, sweeping action. A plume of smoke erupted from it, followed by a second, then a third. Each billowed heavenward and Drabble watched them blend into the nicotine congestion above; for a moment, he saw the slender arm of a nymph and the primed bow of a cherub.

2

Then Harris broke the silence.

'So where are you off to again – Devon?'

'Cornwall,' corrected Drabble. He had been dreading this topic.

'What's the drill?'

'Oh,' he replied casually, 'just a bit of research.'

'Research of course, but *what*?'

'Same old stuff.' Drabble looked down at his drink. 'More Cromwell - nothing to interest your readers, I'm afraid.'

Harris arched an eyebrow at him.

'Why don't I believe you, Professor?'

'Because you never do, Harris,' he sighed wearily. Drabble remembered the several times before when Harris had used information supplied by him journalistically, rarely with his blessing. They eyed each other for a moment.

'Come on,' said Harris. 'Spill the beans.'

Drabble felt his resolve weaken; the truth was he liked his friend more than he always trusted him, but he also knew resistance was a waste of time. Harris had a way of getting it out of you in the end. Drabble set down his tankard and cleared his throat: 'Well, since you *asked*,' he paused, finding the words. 'I confess… it's all a touch morbid.'

'Morbid?' Harris' eyes lit up. '*Morbid in what way?*'

'Promise you won't breathe a word of it?'

Harris' hand went to his chest and he frowned as though the mildest suggestion of indiscretion was a grievous insult.

'You have my word,' he declared, with the solemnity

3

of an archbishop officiating at a state funeral. Drabble contemplated his friend's face doubtfully one last time, and lowered his voice. He did a quick look left and right, and then announced: 'I'm going to inspect the head of Oliver Cromwell.'

Harris recoiled in disgust.

'Good God –'

'I know,' sighed Drabble. 'It sounds too good to be true, doesn't it?'

Harris' eyes narrowed.

'It *sounds* bloody grotesque, old man. Christ alive. And you're really positive that this is the *actual* bonce of the Lord Protector?'

'That's what I'll find out.'

He grinned.

'And suppose it is. What can this sensational artefact actually tell you, over and above what we already know?'

Drabble eyed him sharply. 'Well, that remains to be seen. The fact is that no one has seen it for hundreds of years.' He saw Harris' nostrils flare and regretted this revelation. He cleared his throat, and tempered his enthusiasm: 'The *primary reason* is simply to verify that it really is what this chap Wilkinson holds it to be - *i.e.* the decapitated cranium of Oliver Cromwell. But, as it happens, my next piece of research is going to be on the Restoration of 1660, and that was when they dug him up and everything else, so it'll be interesting to see what marks there are on the skull, what bits are missing - you never know.' He could feel his pulse beginning to quicken at the prospect but he caught his breath, and gave a grudging grimace as though it was a serious chore after

4

all. 'It might even lead to further avenues of academic endeavour,' he concluded, in what he hoped was an especially boring-sounding voice.

'What you really mean, Ernest, is that you just want to see it.'

The accusation stood a moment. Then Drabble broke into nervous laughter.

'I don't know,' said Harris, shaking his head. 'You grotesque so-and-so.'

'Come off it!'

'Come off it yourself,' countered Harris, chuckling amiably. His tankard hovered at his mouth – a pose Drabble recognised as being preliminary to his draining its contents. 'So, a question,' the drink remained poised. 'Or rather two questions: what is Cromwell's head doing in Cornwall, and where the dickens is the rest of him?'

***

'What we think we know is that Oliver Cromwell's body was – and remains to this day – buried in the mass grave at Tyburn, underneath what is now the Regal Cinema at Marble Arch.'

'Never did much like that place,' Harris announced thoughtfully. 'But if Oliver is under the Regal, what's his head doing two hundred miles away in Cornwall?'

'I'm coming to that.' Drabble placed his glass on the bar and took out his pipe. 'As I'm sure you can remember from dear Mr James' lessons at school, Oliver Cromwell died in 1658 and his son, Richard, succeeded as Lord Protector.'

'Tumbledown Dick.'

'That's right. Anyhow, he was a bit of a numpty and the British people saw it in their wisdom to return the monarchy. Hence the Restoration.'

'Charles the Second,' interjected Harris. 'Lots of bastards. Loved spaniels. Good egg.'

'Well, as you might very well imagine, the King and his supporters were still pretty miffed about the execution eleven years before of the King's beloved father, Charles the First.'

'Perfectly reasonable.'

'And, of course, the man they blamed more than any other for this was Cromwell. The tiny problem was, while they could torture and hang some of the other chaps responsible for killing old Charlie, Cromwell was dead already.'

'That old chestnut.'

'Precisely, so they did the next best thing: they dug him up from his resting place in Westminster Abbey, along with two other Parliamentarians, one of whom – fellow by the name of Bradshaw – had only died the year before and hadn't been embalmed terribly well, to say the least.' Drabble cleared his throat.

'Still a bit saucy, was he?' said Harris, with a wince.

'It gets better,' Drabble leaned in. 'Cromwell's corpse spent the night under guard in the Red Lion at Holborn, hence the legend about it being haunted by his ghost.'

'Is that so?' Harris looked up from his pipe, grinning with all his white teeth. 'That'll explain the beer.'

'At dawn the following morning the bodies were carted up to Tyburn, which is where they did all the public

6

executions in the capital in those days, and hanged by the neck, next to one another on a three-armed gibbet. Then in the afternoon, in front of crowds of onlookers, they were cut down – and beheaded at sword-point. It is said that Cromwell's head took eight blows to hack off, which goes to prove what a tough old boot he really was.'

Harris chuckled.

'No joke,' added Drabble. 'Bradshaw only needed six.'

'What a pushover.'

'The corpses, minus the heads, were then dumped into the communal grave beneath the Tyburn Tree – but a final ghoulish punishment awaited the severed heads. Those were taken to Westminster Hall and stuck up on high poles of oak, tipped in iron. There Cromwell's head resided for twenty-five years – a grim reminder to all and sundry of what happens if you have the temerity to mess with the monarchy. It wasn't until about 1685 that during a particularly violent storm it blew off, bounced down the slate roof, and landed in the guttering, where it was found by a sentry, who decided to keep it for himself.'

'Well, naturally,' said Harris, smirking, 'what else would you do with the embalmed skull of the late dictator? One for the mantelpiece, surely.'

'In point of fact, he hid it in his chimney for a further twenty years.'

'In his chimney?' Harris nudged his elbow. 'Seems a rather *cavalier* thing to do!'

Drabble acknowledged Harris' rejoinder with a friendly nod and cleared his throat: 'On his death the sentry bequeathed it to his daughter, who sold it, and a

7

little later the head ended up in a travelling circus as the chief freakish exhibit, you know, taking top billing over the bearded ladies, three-headed pigs, and ventriloquist ponies. It changed hands again and reappeared about the same time as the French Revolution, when it was bought by three chaps and put on display – people queued around the block to see it, sixpence a time. But then the head was lost – I mean, literally, it vanished, until the other day when I got a letter from this doctor saying he had it. Like everyone else, I'd assumed it was gone for ever. If it is what he claims it to be, then this is going to be a major breakthrough.'

'Seriously?' The light that had gone out in Harris' eyes suddenly returned. 'How major?'

'It's hard to say, but I promise you'll be the first to know. For now, I'll repeat, the owner says he doesn't want people to know about it, so keep it under your hat.'

'Blimey,' said Harris, scratching his chin. 'If heads could speak.'

'But a touch morbid.' Drabble shrugged and raised his glass. 'Cheers.'

'Cheers.'

They sank their drinks.

'Righty-ho.' Harris plonked the empty vessel onto the bar and thrust his pipe into his mouth. 'I've a man to see about a dog,' he nodded his head in the direction of Mussolini's double, 'and you've a date with a skull.'

CHAPTER TWO

Drabble emerged from the Granville Club into the teeth of a decided drizzle, one as strenuous as it was unremitting if the new deep, broad puddles were anything to go by. Why he had entrusted his Cromwellian secret to Harris, who, let's face it, had never proven himself so very reliable over the years, could only be guessed at. A Freudian analyst would no doubt have ascribed it to some unexpiated, infantile confessional impulse.

He was still pondering this as he climbed into a taxi and the bright gas lanterns outside the doorway of the club faded from view as they jolted and juddered along the cobbled thoroughfare of Pall Mall and then turned up onto St James'. It was sheer childish excitement. There could be no other explanation; that sense that only at the threshold of a journey does the excitement of its impending reality take hold. Until then it is but a mere apparition. Now it is real. He would just have to hope that, for once, Harris could be trusted to act honourably.

Drabble looked out; through the raindrop-flecked windows he saw dense avenues of long winter coats capped with umbrellas, illuminated by the glittering shop-fronts either side. There were festive garlands and bunting in the bright windows – it was a world away from the poverty in the provinces, let alone his life at Cambridge. The traffic queued to get onto Piccadilly and he could make out the distinctive stage-lights of the Ritz up the hill on the corner. He rubbed the misted-up glass and looked

9

out; there was a lad selling the *Evening Standard* sheltering beneath a hotel's arcade. Drabble rolled down the window and called out to him.

The boy, his teeth chattering from cold, looked over and then up at the rain. He pulled down his broad cloth cap – roughly half as wide again as his head – and trotted over, jumping some of the larger puddles on the way. He shoved the damp folded newspaper through the gap, and snatched the waiting coin in one rapid movement, concluded with a polite brush of his dripping peak before scampering back to the covered pavement. The taxi moved on. Drabble unfolded the newspaper and held it in the light:

'LET KING MARRY WOMAN HE LOVES' – PLEADS CHURCHILL

AMID angry exchanges in the Commons this afternoon Mr Winston Churchill called upon the Prime Minister, Mr Stanley Baldwin, to clarify the precise Constitutional position concerning the marriage of His Majesty to Mrs Wallis
Simpson, before any 'irrevocable' step was taken.

The traffic eased as the taxi approached Hyde Park Corner. Suddenly they braked hard and the driver swore. Through the windscreen Drabble saw the flank of a horse, with bridle and tack, pass in front, followed by the coachwork of the number 23 tram. The driver leaned out of his window and bellowed. Drabble held the newspaper up to the window and the light:

Mr Churchill was shouted down on all sides of the House and
failed to pass a motion calling on the National Government to do so.
He accused Ministers of forcing the King's hand before being silenced
by the Speaker. At this the whole House cheered and Mr Churchill
was obliged to take his seat.

They passed Apsley House, squat, grand, rain-stained and streaked in soot, and were soon speeding northwards along Park Lane; the great open space to their left an infinite black void. On the right, there were crowds in evening wear – men in silk top hats and capes, and ladies in long coats – massed under dripping umbrellas, queuing at the entrance of the Dorchester.

'Excuse me, guv.'

Drabble saw the driver strain his face around to address him; he had a spiky white moustache that bristled as the words emerged from the corner of his mouth. 'You look familiar; ain't you that mountaineer – what was it? Oh yes, the "Bouncing Don"?'

Drabble lowered the newspaper and forced a smile.

'That's right,' he said.

'How's the arm?'

'Much better, thanks.' He lifted his elbow up and down in a peculiar, half-embarrassed demonstration of its recovery.

'Honour to have you on board, sir.'

Drabble nodded his thanks, mentally cursing Harris,

11

and returned to the newspaper.

'And if you ask me, sir,' the driver continued, 'you should have another go, now you're back on your feet.'

Drabble gave the driver a thumbs-up and picked up his newspaper; his eye retraced the main headline again. What business was it of Stanley Baldwin's, or anyone else's for that matter, whom the King married? Mrs Simpson was certainly not everyone's cup of tea, that was clear, but she clearly floated the top man's boat so that was settled. Apart from a dozen or so all-but-fossilised bishops, who cared if she'd been divorced? It was 1936, not the bloody Dark Ages. And you couldn't exactly say that there was no constitutional precedent entirely – Henry VIII was divorced at least twice... Mind you, that was at least two dynasties ago. Drabble's thoughts trailed off. He noticed a smaller headline down in the corner:

'Grievous Blow to Monarchy'

English-speaking South Africans are deeply uneasy over the mounting Empire Crisis. Whether or not the King now marries Mrs Simpson he has undermined the standing of the Monarch and damaged the prestige of the Empire.

Christ alive. The 'Empire'. 'Prestige'. It would take a damned sight more than Mrs Simpson to undermine the prestige, if such a thing existed, of the Empire. Drabble snatched open the next page and saw another two pages dedicated to the affair; at the top of each the words

'Constitutional Crisis' were printed in bold type. His eye caught a headline about a fascist rally against the government, which sealed his contempt. He tossed the newspaper onto the seat. It wasn't going to happen. British kings didn't abdicate: that's what they did on the Continent – everyone knew that. Plus the Windsors were too clever by half. Review the evidence; they and their Germanic forebears had withstood terrible wars, an industrial revolution, domestic upheavals, the loss of the Americas, and at least one well-documented case of actual lunacy – and none of them had abdicated. Any one of those would have been enough to dispense with a French, Austrian, or Russian head of state. They'd be damned if they were going to let an American divorcee beat them, whatever English-speaking South Africans might think.

The taxi made a left at Marble Arch, leaving the tall Portland stone facade of the Regal Cinema – and probable location of the Tyburn mass grave – to their right, and they drove across the top of the park, the carriage rocking gently from side to side as they clattered along. He glanced at his watch and nodded satisfactorily. The taxi crossed over the Bayswater Road and up into Paddington proper, along Sussex Gardens, with its proud pillared mansions.

'Excuse me, guv?'

He looked up to see the driver's moustached mouth in the light.

'Do you reckon he'll go, sir?'

'Who?'

'The *King*, sir,' the driver said, straining to be heard over the engine and traffic noise.

'Oh, I shouldn't think so.'

'They say Baldwin's got it in for him.'

Drabble shrugged.

'As far as I can tell, Baldwin's got it in for everyone.'

The driver nodded. Through the side window Drabble glimpsed a drinks party in full swing under electric lights in one of the grand houses.

'But if he does go, won't that mean the Duke of York becomes king?'

Drabble sat forward so he didn't have to shout.

'I suppose so.'

'But that's crackers –' the driver's contempt was captured in the corner of the mouth by a passing headlamp: 'Nice enough bloke, don't get me wrong, but he can't even ask for the bog without making a meal of it.' Drabble saw the head in front of him shake in dismay. 'Why can't Edward marry this Simpson? So she's been married!' The driver shrugged, 'Who cares?' He glared malignantly at Drabble: 'We know they're all at it, anyway.'

***

From the bar, Harris watched Drabble weave through the crowd, and exit through the wooden door of the saloon. He shook his head gently. Oliver Cromwell - now that *was* a story if ever there was one, not that he wanted to let Ernest realise it. Found after being missing for – what was it, 150-odd years? Fantastic. He tugged out his pocket watch. Ten past eight. There was still time to get a paragraph or two in for the morning's paper. The 'return of the Lord Protector'… He grinned. It could be a ruddy good yarn, oh yes. He felt in his coat pocket for his pencil, located his discreetly slim notebook, and caught the barman's eye before evincing the tiniest of nods towards his empty glass.

'While you're there, Harris,' announced a voice from behind. 'I'd die for a whisky and soda.'

Harris nodded again to the barman to approve the exhortation, and turned on the voice: 'Grubby Howse!' he declared, shaking the proffered hand of the Right Honourable Member for Kensington South. 'As always, you show impeccable timing.'

Grubby beamed, his open mouth revealing tombstone teeth.

'Come, come, Harris, you know as well as I do that I'd be shirking my public duty if I didn't rescue a constituent – even an incorrigible denizen of Fleet Street such as yourself – from the appalling vice of drinking alone,' he furrowed his brow with mock sincerity and nodded significantly. 'Striving to rehabilitate society's waifs and strays is an important part of an MP's vocation, you know.'

'Well, I'll drink to that -' Harris raised his brew, 'and I'll take this opportunity,' he looked down at Grubby's drink, 'to pay homage to your ceaseless dedication in this matter.'

'Cheers,' said Grubby.

'Cheers.' Harris glanced towards the doors and the row of telephone booths that lay beyond; there was still time to make the first edition, masses of it, but he couldn't afford to be complacent. 'You know what, Grubbs, I've just heard the most remarkable thing – and I've got to tell someone before I ruddy well burst. You can be trusted to keep something under your hat, can't you; well at least 'til the morning?'

***

The taxi pulled away and Drabble trudged up the covered incline leading to the entrance of Paddington Station. The domed crescent latticework was filled with smoke, its zenith lost to the night, and the air was heavy with the faintly sweet smell of coal dust and soot. Three locomotives, their coaches beyond, stood to the right, steam hissing from the flexing muscles of the engines. People shouted orders and called out; passengers and porters hurried back and forth; there was the blast of a whistle, and Drabble saw a conductress wave to a fireman. The engine on the far platform moved off and its carriages emitted a collective rasp. The iron hands of the station clock pointed to eight forty-nine.

He consulted the board and confirmed the platform number for the Penzance sleeper, then picked his way through the crowd, pausing only to permit a woman in a long fur coat to pass by with her four dachshunds, each tugging in different directions on their leather leads. He was soon walking along the platform by the distinctive chocolate and cream livery of the Great Western Railway, the colour scheme reminding him of his childhood days during the Great War, when the coaches were full of khaki and the conflicting smells of gun oil, soldiers, and damp kit, during those long summer vacations down with

16

his aunts in Yeovil.

At the sleeper car, he was greeted by the steward who led him to his cabin, demonstrating the technique for lowering the folding bunk from the wall.

'Begging your pardon, sir, I shan't put it away, as you're in luck tonight,' the steward said in a broad Devon accent. 'You've got the compartment all to yourself.' He moved towards the door, rattling the bunch of keys in his pocket. 'And just to let you know, I'll be doing the rounds at six and twenty with the tea.'

'Six twenty? I hope your tea is strong.'

'That's right, sir.' The man paused by the door, still looping his bunch of keys around his finger. 'The dining car will be open a few minutes after we depart. I should get in early, sir. They never have enough lamb chops.'

The steward pulled the door shut as he left. Drabble pushed his bag into the luggage rack and heard the whistle go. He checked his watch. Nine on the nail. A moment passed and then the carriage moved gently and they started to ease away. The train gradually built up pace and left the station behind. Through the window, blackened high brick bulwarks sped past. He hung his brown trilby on the brass hook and wearily removed his overcoat before falling back into the seat, his eyes shut, listening to the faint sound of the locomotive all those carriages ahead. It was like a man rhythmically hammering a box in a distant room. He yawned. It was time for dinner, followed by the best sleep that Great Western Railways could offer.

Drabble made his way along the narrow passageway of the swaying carriage, steadying himself with his hands against the jarring, rocking motion of the train. In the restaurant car, the waiter sat him at one of the last free tables.

Drabble settled in and ordered a champagne cocktail. There was no need to slum it; this was on the college. Then, after glancing at the menu, he laid it down on the starched white table cloth. *Lamb chops it is.*

He unfolded his napkin and tried to remember the last time he had been in a restaurant car in Britain. In alignment with the external livery, the palette was borrowed from an Edwardian aunt's dress: all heavy browns and sober beiges, touched off with racy fawns, occasional flourishes of lace, and a dangling red tassel or two. These jiggling adornments fringed the silken lampshades of the individual table lights and edged the cream brocade curtains. His fellow diners talked in low voices or ate in silence, reserving their attention for their food rather than their companions. This was promising for a hungry traveller such as Drabble. It meant that the carriage was dominated by the diligent scraping of cutlery as well as the jingle of glassware and crockery as the rolling stock passed from rail to rail.

Three tables down, two young men, travelling salesmen judging by the look of their suits, were just now ordering another bottle of claret. The complexion of the chap Drabble could see most clearly was well on its way to a rich crimson tone already.

His waiter, dressed like the others in a cut-down beige jacket, returned and with a flourish presented the cocktail from a silver tray. Drabble ordered the soup without worrying the waiter as to what it was, followed by the chops, relying on the steward's inside knowledge, and a half a bottle of your best GWR claret. It can only help, he thought, as he slotted the menu card into the bracket.

Drabble smiled privately and looked out of the window; the blackened brickwork of an embankment gave way to the rear of a row of grimy terraced houses, their windows caked in soot. He lifted his eyebrows in wonder. What must it be like to live in one of those – barely twelve feet from the principal westward line out of London; scores of trains passing each hour – what? – 20 hours a day? He turned his glass between his fingertips and resumed his contemplation of the carriage. The fellows down the way were already refreshing their glasses. They'd be in Cornwall in no time at all at that rate.

At the adjacent table across the aisle was an erect young woman dining alone. Dressed in a powder blue hat and matching suit, she was probing a fluted vase-like dish of salad leaves with a long spoon. Unmistakably pretty, she had pale, almost colourless eyes which gave her an almost vampiric quality. They lent her beauty a doubtful quality.

'Mind if I join you?'

Drabble looked up; a meek smile poked out from under the broad, grey, and ever-so-slightly waxed moustache of a bank-managerish-looking man on the far side of middle age. Drabble gestured towards the seat opposite and the corners of the moustache lifted in thanks. But before the man could seat himself, the carriage jarred, and he lurched forward, breaking his fall on the table and crashing into the seat opposite. A wine glass smashed and the tablecloth was hauled in his direction, taking most of everything with it. Drabble snatched up his drink just in time.

The waiter was over gathering up the broken glass and resetting the table immediately as the man apologised profusely, loudly sucking at a finger that had caught on the broken glass and generally making protestations of disbelief at the commotion. 'Ruddy buffoon,' he hissed at himself again. 'I'm really very sorry,' he repeated, this time addressing Drabble. After a minute or two, when the final evidence of the accident had been removed and fresh places laid, the man's embarrassment seemed to diminish. He plucked up the menu, and had just begun to give it his attention, when he looked up at Drabble, a quizzical frown on his face.

'I say, do we know each other?'

Right on cue. Drabble cursed Harris. Again.

'*Yes*,' continued the man, a renewed certainty in his voice. 'I *definitely* recognise you.' He stared hard. Several seconds passed... Drabble couldn't bear it any longer.

'Let me put you out of your misery –' he paused as the waiter arrived with his soup. 'You might just have seen me on the Pathé news. Mind if I start?' He picked up his spoon.

'That's right –' the stranger's face brightened with a broad grin of resolution: 'You're the "Bouncing Don"!' He chuckled triumphantly.

'That's me,' replied Drabble, adding a weary smile. He mentally thanked Harris and awaited the inevitable follow-up topic.

'Bad luck about the Eiger,' said the man, who now

surveyed the menu card. 'You nearly cracked it.'

Drabble checked his enthusiasm with a sharp look.

'It very nearly cracked my skull.' *And poor Hubertus wasn't anywhere near so lucky*. He tasted the pea soup. *Salty.*

'I'm sure you're not wrong,' the man added, his mind half on whatever he was going to eat. He put the menu away. 'It was a sensational fall.'

Drabble smiled kindly. 'A hundred and twenty-eight feet of sensation, to be precise.'

'It's a miracle you survived.' The man's eyebrows knitted sympathetically. 'I was sorry to read about your climbing partner. Austrian fellow, wasn't he?'

Drabble nodded. Hubertus was one of the most courageous and resourceful climbers he'd ever known. He was also a good friend.

After a respectful pause, the newcomer engaged the waiter to order, at which point Drabble noticed his tie. Wide diagonal stripes of blue and red, separated by narrow white lines, yielded to a neat, tightly knotted regular triangle at the collar. For some reason the design, plainly military, was familiar, but as Drabble returned to his soup, he couldn't place it. He mulled on it as he dusted the surface of his soup in black pepper. But what was it?

Then it came to him: Indian Army. Of course it was. Drabble looked at the face above it, noticing signs of sun damage on the cheek bones and on the forehead. Suddenly he imagined the man in khaki with a Sam Brown, vindictively reprimanding some poor sepoy or flogging an elephant...

'I'll have the same as Professor Drabble, here,' he

heard the man say to the waiter.

'Gosh,' said Drabble, as the waiter moved off. 'You've a memory for names.'

'Nonsense, you're a national hero. I tell you, if we had more young men like you out there, the world would be a better place.'

Drabble laughed politely as he wondered quite how that would be, and glanced over at the girl on the adjacent table. She was peering at the menu through a delicate pair of spectacles which she held close to her eyes, like opera glasses. He wondered if she was short-sighted. 'Tell me,' Drabble began, searching for something to say and remembering the tie. 'What's your line?'

'Work? Insurance. I'm at Lloyd's.'

'Lloyd's?' Drabble's eye reverted to the tight triangle at the man's throat. 'How interesting.'

'I know,' the man said wearily. 'The good news is it's as lucrative as it is boring.' He laughed hard.

'Well, your good health,' said Drabble, raising his glass. 'Whatever else can be said, the world is more in need of insuring than ever.'

'More than you know,' nodded the stranger sagely. They touched glasses. 'These are dangerous times.'

There was a note of seriousness which Drabble could not miss in this remark, one that stole the jollity from the moment. Drabble cleared his throat.

'You seem to be enduring the lunches better that some of my acquaintances in the field.'

'The secret,' chuckled the stranger, 'is to skip pudding.'

'Ah.' Drabble felt they were on safer ground here.

22

'That's not an affliction singular to your profession. You should see the treacle sponge at college. It piles years onto the youngest of research fellows in a matter of weeks.'

The waiter served the man's soup and gathered up Drabble's empty bowl.

'So tell me, *Mister*?'

'Forgive me; Thompson.'

'What area of insurance do you specialise in?'

'Apart from the lunches?' Thompson smiled. 'Political risk overseas, industrial combines in the main.' He picked up his spoon and stroked the top of the soup.

'So, oil wells in Latin America?' said Drabble gamely. 'Shipyards on the Rhine? Textile factories on the Subcontinent?'

'That's right.' Thompson proceeded to carpet his soup with salt. 'All sorts of odds and sods.'

'Out of interest, Mr Thompson,' Drabble looked up; a white plate with three chops and vegetables hoved into view, 'what's the most expensive thing you insure?'

Thompson stroked the edge of his moustache with his napkin.

'I'm afraid I'm not permitted to go into details,' his voice adopted a stage whisper and he leaned in. 'But we certainly have several of the sorts of installations that you refer to on our books, with a commensurate liability running to several millions in pounds sterling.'

'Several millions in pounds sterling,' repeated Drabble. 'Goodness.'

The girl in the powder blue hat looked over.

Thompson efficiently dispatched his soup and chased away the dregs with his spoon by tilting the bowl this way and that. 'Now,' he said, making eye contact momentarily, 'rather more importantly, what brings the "Bouncing Don" to the south-west? I don't remember Cornwall having any mountains!'

'None that I know of,' Drabble said lightly. He frowned. 'Actually, I've not climbed since the accident. No, what brings me to Cornwall is just work, I'm afraid. Boring old research – no escaping it.' He smiled a little too hard.

Thompson was about to reply then stopped abruptly and looked at him hard, then clicked his fingers, 'that's it, *history's* your thing, isn't it.'

'Yes,' sighed Drabble. 'The papers had some fun about it.'

Thompson smiled. 'Didn't they just.'

Damn that Harris, thought Drabble. Yet again.

'I'm rather partial to a bit of history,' volunteered Thompson. 'What's your area?'

Drabble watched the waiter switch Thompson's bowl for a plate of lamb chops, as he decided on how much detail to go into.

'Seventeenth-century British,' he said at last. 'In the main.' He looked up to see Thompson spooning mint sauce lavishly onto his lamb. 'The English Civil War, the Interregnum, et cetera…'

'Yes, yes, how fascinating,' said Thompson, looking up from the plate. 'And what's down here - some cobwebby archive?'

'Ah, well.' Drabble permitted himself a smile. 'I wouldn't want to put you off your lovely chops. But –' He glanced low at the next table and saw a black leather boot and the hem of the powder blue skirt. 'I'm actually going down to inspect a *rather* important exhibit that's recently come to light.'

The man grinned encouragingly.

'Alas, I'm afraid I'm not really at liberty to say more than that, if you don't mind...' - the eager corners of Thompson's moustache fell – 'it's a sensitive matter.' Drabble lowered his voice: 'Put it this way, it's not so much an "it" as it is a "who" –' He noticed the girl at the next table looking over and stopped himself from further indiscretion.

Thompson took note and jumped in. 'Well, well, well, by Jove –' he took a good gulp of his wine, his eyes gleaming. 'I quite understand. But "who" could it be?' He sawed the flesh from the second of his chops. Drabble smiled apologetically. 'I look forward to reading about it one of these days,' he flashed a grin across the table. 'You never know, maybe I'll be able to insure it – or him!'

Drabble laid his napkin on the table and sat back. When Thompson introduced the food to his mouth, he inserted the fork much further than was normal. He also ate at pace. At that precise moment he hurriedly carved off and stabbed at another piece of meat while he chewed, before stacking the fork steeply with potato and vegetables in readiness for the precise millisecond that enough space in his mouth became available, or at least more available, at which point it disappeared inside. Drabble looked down at the stem of his glass. What *was* he hoping to glean from the visit, precisely? Should he reveal the purpose of his visit? Wilkinson had asked him to keep it confidential, but what would it matter?

Thompson was clearly unlikely to do anything with the information.

'Quite possibly,' he said at last in response to Thompson's last comment. 'About the insurance, I mean.' He thought for a moment. 'Whatever happens, I dare say it should keep me busy for an hour or two.' He smiled and raised his wine glass.

Thompson grinned back, and gave his wine a swift bob, drinking mid-chew. Then, with his jaws still working hard, he pinioned the narrow bone of the chop with his fork and severed the last ribbon of fat from it. He jammed this into his mouth and pushed his knife and fork together and nodded to the waiter to remove his plate. He wiped his mouth as the man arranged the load of plates and cutlery and ordered cheese.

'Port, Professor?' Thompson implored, looking over gamely. 'A glass or two won't hurt.'

Drabble looked at his watch. 'One, perhaps,' he said. He might need a strong stomach for the morning.

'You're a gentleman, Professor. It would be cruel to make me eat my cheese alone – and you can't have cheese without port, what?' Thompson addressed the waiter. 'We'll take a decanter.'

The cheese was a finger of cheddar, a sliver of gouda, and a virtually bottle-green triangular wedge of Stilton, dressed with three browning grapes. Thompson dived in heartily. Despite the grapes, Drabble thought it didn't look too bad, even if the Stilton was a little far gone for his tastes. He sipped his port. It was a young ruby; blunt in flavour, warming and sweet like a child's medicine. He should have opted for the whisky, though it too would probably have been of an inferior quality. The waiter paused at the table next to them and Drabble saw the girl reach for her handbag. After a moment, he saw her boots turn towards the aisle and begin to move along the carriage to the far door. Drabble turned his thoughts to his co-diner.

A lump of Stilton was caught in the thick hair of Thompson's moustache. Next his gaze settled on the broken skin of Thompson's bottom lip, and at the fine white scars that criss-crossed it. That was a lip that had been cut many times, he thought. The nose had been broken too, now he came to think of it.

'You a rugby man, Mr Thompson?'

'Me? No.' He turned his mouth upside down. 'Played a bit of soccer as a boy.'

A boxer, perhaps.

'Forgive me,' continued Drabble. He topped up their glasses. 'Most of us have a sporting passion. I boxed a bit a school. Have you boxed at all?'

Thompson eyed him, almost as if he was uncertain as to the direction of the conversation.

'Not really,' he added. 'I suppose my greatest sporting passion these days is the turf.'

Drabble nodded graciously. A gambling man; that fitted with insurance.

'And where did you grow up?'

'Surbiton.'

'Ah.' Drabble took a sip of port. 'Have you been following this abdication business?' he asked absently.

Thompson stopped chewing and looked at him directly.

'Yes,' he said. 'A very bad situation.'

'Do you think the King will go?'

Thompson resumed his chewing – but now slowly, almost thoughtfully. Drabble was beginning to regret raising the topic: it tended to end conversations badly, when Thompson piped up.

'He shouldn't do,' he said at last, stroking his moustached mouth with the napkin. 'In my view the King should stick to his guns.'

'And if Mr Baldwin threatens to resign?'

'Good riddance to him.'

'But who'll run the country?'

Thompson raised his glass.

'There's always someone who'll do it,' he said, nodding importantly.

'But who?'

Thompson cut a thin slice off the end of the Stilton, pressed it onto a water biscuit and pushed it into his mouth. He ate, his eyes roving between the plate of cheese, his port glass, and the tablecloth. The muscles in his cheeks swelled. If he knew the answer – not something that Drabble thought likely – then he clearly wasn't prepared to divulge it.

Drabble yawned and checked his watch discreetly; it was just coming up to half past ten. In the background, the waiter was laying the tables for breakfast, and an elderly diner snored alone in his seat at the last table but one, his wine-stained napkin still stuffed in his collar.

The decanter was all but finished. Drabble announced his departure.

'My bunk is calling me – and it's most insistent.'

Thompson looked like he going to protest but instead outstretched his hand.

'Best of British, Professor.' They shook hands; Thompson's grip was strong and took Drabble by surprise. 'I do hope your trip is everything you want it to be.'

'Thank you,' replied Drabble, producing a polite smile and trying to work out if Thompson had just winked at him. 'And good luck you, with all your oil wells – and the horses.'

He bade Thompson a final farewell, and made his way into the next carriage, tottering along the narrow passage, guiding himself with his hands between the wall and the rail, and finding himself a mite unsteady on his feet. That would be the port; beastly the way it crept up on you like that. He proceeded slowly. Depending on how it went, the ruby might deliver him a deeper sleep for the hours ahead.

***

Drabble finally arrived at the car which contained his compartment. The steward, now without his stiff collar and in his shirt and waistcoat, unlocked the door to his cabin, and Drabble closed the door behind him, locked it and put the chain across. Thompson *was* an oddball – no doubt about that. But then life was full of oddballs – and doubtless the world of insurance was no different in that regard from his own field of academia, which was also exceptionally well-supplied with oddities. Doubtless he had served in India prior to moving into insurance – after all, he was advertising the fact proudly around his neck.

And it was a common enough route, and explained the sun-damage. It would explain the man's politics, too. Drabble hung up his jacket and undid his college tie, which he looped around the coat hanger. He loosened his shirt; really, he *had* drunk too much.

Lastly, he switched off the light and lay on the bunk, dragging the blanket over him. I'll pay for it in the morning, he thought. If not sooner.

At first the room was pitch black, but as his eyes adjusted he could make out dim shapes above. The ceiling of the narrow compartment started to spin... forming a series of distorted oval patterns, like the revolving forms of a kaleidoscope that turned in time with the rhythmic movement of the train. Soon his thoughts receded and he found himself concentrating on the regular beat of the rolling stock, catching the breaks in the line.

There was a gentle knock at the door and Drabble awoke with a start. The door opened and the restraining chain became taut. Drabble stared into the darkness.

'What is it?'

'It's the steward,' replied that Devonian voice. 'Apologies for waking you, sir, just thought I'd let you know we'll be late in the morning. There's trouble at Exeter, I gather. So I'll wake you at seven, if you please, sir.'

The railwayman retired, locking the door after him from outside: there was an audible 'click' as the bolt located. Lord, he *was* tired. Drabble gave a huge yawn. He should remove his shoes. The sound of the train grew louder as he felt his body becoming weightless and he started to fall asleep. *Not to worry.* Then his thoughts vanished and all he could hear was the sound of the tracks.

CHAPTER THREE

In the darkness, just for a second, Drabble thought he was dreaming.

Stilton. Yes, he could positively smell Stilton.

His eyes blinked open: a black shape moved above him.

'Hey!'

He tore back the covers and started from the bunk – but the dark silhouette fell on him, a strong pair of hands gripping his throat tightly. He threw his hands at his attacker's face and there – *there* was the waxy moustache. Thompson reared his head back, evading Drabble's grasp and simultaneously pressed onto his neck with his longer reach, bracing his arms and leaning in with his body. Drabble yanked at Thompson's wrists, but they were locked. He struck at the insides of his elbows but these were rigid, too. Drabble's eyes widened. His windpipe was in agony. *One thousand... Two thousand... Three thousand...*

He imagined he saw a grin develop beneath the moustache. Thompson pushed on him harder. Drabble pulled again at the wrists and then picked at the fingers, attempting to prize them off his throat. But they were solid.

Five thousand... six thousand...

Drabble's chest tightened. This was it, he thought. *This is it.* He struck out again at Thompson's face, but could not reach. He gripped one of the wrists with both his

32

hands but could not wrench the hand away. Then he remembered the Indian Army tie -

Suddenly there was a loud crack and the bunk buckled, springing them onto the floor. Thompson went over first but he kept his hold tight and dragged Drabble on top of him. The distance between them broke. Drabble stabbed with his thumbs at Thompson's eyes. Thompson growled and snatched at Drabble's spiteful hands.

Drabble breathed in.

He hurled his fist down at Thompson's moustache; then a second down on the left eye. But now Thompson's strong hands were back at his neck, the tips of his fingers just scratching at the smarting skin of his throat. They almost got a grip, but Drabble ducked sideways. Given any chance Thompson would be throttling him once again soon. He wasn't just trying to frighten me, realised Drabble. This was the whole deal. Drabble brought his right fist back, and powered it squarely into Thompson's nose. It collapsed and there was a sound like someone cracking their knuckles. Blood pulsed from it immediately. Thompson went for his throat but Drabble lunged forward with his open hands at Thompson's neck. He grabbed – and *squeezed*. In the darkness he saw Thompson's eyes widen. They bulged. His hands pawed at Drabble's straining wrists but Drabble was locked on. This was like the moment he clung on to the North Face of the Eiger, all over again, waiting hours for rescue. He felt Thompson's warm blood run over his fingers and gather in the crevices formed by his hands against the man's throat. Thompson coughed, causing his head to jerk. Blood flecked Drabble's face. Drabble squeezed and braced his arms. Thompson's Adam's apple cut into the fleshy base of his thumb. He pressed on. The blood now trickled over the backs of his hands. Thompson raised his leg, levering it between them, but Drabble knocked it back and rammed the man's groin with his knee. His forearms were in agony. Keep squeezing, he told himself, *keep squeezing*.

He felt Thompson go limp, but couldn't be sure. Then a passing light from outside danced across Thompson's face, showing the blood-soaked jaw fall slack. Drabble froze.

Good God, he thought. The rest of humanity and the world suddenly came crashing down around him. What have I done? Drabble fled his grip and edged backwards, bumping into his Gladstone bag which was open and on the floor. He leaned back, almost pressing himself against the wall and stared over at the body. I've bloody well murdered him, he thought. I've done the bugger in, like a common criminal. Christ alive. Drabble looked down and saw his shaking hands. He raised his gaze to the window. He saw the glowing moon, perfectly gibbous, through the glass. It cast light across the still body, showing the full scene of horror; the broken features, the unnatural pose of the body and limbs. What have I done? thought Drabble.

He gave Thompson's leg a shove and watched it roll back, lifeless, to its original position. Outside the tree-line thickened and the moon vanished, plunging the compartment back into darkness. Drabble grasped his trembling hands together and raised them to his chin in silent prayer, panic rising in him. 'Dear God,' he hissed, squeezing his eyes shut, 'dear Lord…'

There was a roar – Drabble looked up, and crashed sideways into the wall. He opened his eyes: Thompson was over him and landed a sharp blow to his kidneys – and then another, and another. Drabble coughed hard, choking, retreating, fleeing as another blow landed. Thompson got to his feet and dragged Drabble up by his shirt and pinned him by the throat to the wall.

'Now, you're going to die,' he growled, bloody spittle spraying Drabble's face. A blade glinted at his chin.

'What do you want?' pleaded Drabble. 'Please...'

Thompson smiled and drew the knife back.

Drabble cried out and slammed his hands at Thompson's chest. The grip on Drabble's throat broke free and Thompson stumbled back, arms flailing, the knife clattering against the far wall. Drabble hurled himself forward and they crashed down onto the broken bunk. Thompson cried out sharply, and Drabble felt his body go limp, then tense, and he reached out with his hand formed in a claw before letting it drop. Breathing hard, Drabble stepped back; he saw the corner of Thompson's moustache lift – and then go flat, as the mouth fell open.

The light played against the face for several seconds. There was no movement. Drabble leaned against the wall, his heart thumping against his chest. Thompson did not stir. *He was definitely not moving.* Drabble shut his eyes and listened to the beat of the wheels on the iron rails. Still no movement. He swallowed and rubbed his throat. His fingers were tacky with blood and his neck raw.

He mopped the blood from his face and surveyed the body. Was Thompson actually dead? He might just be knocked out, as he was before. Drabble needed to make

35

sure. He got to his knees and returned to where the body lay. He wasn't moving. Drabble inched closer: still no signs of life. He swallowed and leaning over Thompson, he braced himself: he lifted his arm. It was heavy, much heavier than he had imagined and entirely limp. He pushed the cuffs of the jacket and shirt up the arm and pressed his forefinger against the wrist.

After a moment, he laid the limb down.

His eyes ran the length of the twisted body. So what had actually killed him? Did he hit his head when he landed? For a moment Drabble gazed at the dead, frowning face. He sighed with something of a mixture of relief and despair, and stroked the eyelids shut. It probably didn't matter. The man was dead; that was all.

But why was he trying to kill me in the first place? That was the question: Drabble frowned down at the body. The Indian Army tie had been yanked loose in the fight. In a peculiar mark of respect Drabble straightened it and pulled it tight. What were you hoping to achieve, Mr Thompson?

He unbuttoned Thompson's jacket and slipped his flattened hand into his breast pocket, finding the metallic surface of a flask. This contained whisky, and he laid it on the floor to one side. Pushing his hand into the other pocket he found a long leather wallet, which he took out and searched. Taking a swig of Thompson's whisky – waste not want not – he flicked on the light.

The main section of the wallet contained a folded five-pound note and a one-way-ticket to Plymouth. In a side pocket there was a dry cleaner's chit, and a black and brown membership card for the British Union of Fascists, held in the name of 'T. W. Woolley'. In the other side were several blue business cards. They said, *Major T. Woolley (Ret'd), Insurance Broker*. He put the wallet back in, presumably, Woolley's pocket, not Thompson's, and sat back, resting against the wall. He picked up the flask and tilted it to his lips. He looked over at the lifeless man now named Woolley. So you're a ruddy fascist, he thought. A ruddy fascist with a smashed-in face... and a blood-stained face, neck and chest.

He replaced the wallet, and contemplated his next move. He couldn't very well leave Woolley here, after all. Not unless he wanted to add a possible manslaughter charge – or something worse – and probable conviction to his curriculum vitae. Spending a fortnight, let alone the rest of his days, at Wormwood Scrubs didn't appeal either. That's if he escaped the noose. Christ, he thought. Of course, it wouldn't come to that. No. That's what the system was there for, to protect innocent victims of crime such as himself. This was a simple case of self-defence. But how could he be sure?

He couldn't.

The doubt ate away in the back of Drabble's mind as looked over at the body; he came to a resolution. That he also experienced a strong and rising sense of nausea rising from within, also helped. Whatever the rights or wrongs of it, and the way it seemed to him, mainly rights, he knew he needed to put some distance between himself and Thompson-Woolley's mortal remains. And fast.

If he knew the man's compartment - if he actually had one - then Drabble could, conceivably, return him. But he had to think. Drabble shut his eyes and massaged his forehead. Once again the sound of the hurtling iron beneath him overtook his mind. Things like this never happened at Sidney Sussex. But he knew what he had to do.

He eased open the door and looked out into the narrow passageway. It was in darkness and he couldn't see, or hear anyone, save for the peaceful sound of heavy breathing. He returned to the body and seized Woolley's ankles, hauling him into the draughty corridor. Drabble got most of him out, with his legs twisted unnaturally to one side. Then, with his hands gripping Woolley's belt, he yanked the rest of the torso into the passage. The wristwatch on Woolley's left arm snagged on the cabin door and slammed it shut. Drabble leaned back and heaved. Come on, you bugger, he thought, feeling like a horse hauling a recalcitrant plough. He passed the next cabin. The sound of snoring intensified, as did Drabble's anxiety.

Suddenly, Woolley's left shoe slipped off and the foot clonked onto the floor. Drabble stumbled backwards but caught himself. He looked over his shoulder. There was the faint outline of the end of the corridor in the darkness: *it was miles away*. He leaned down on his knees, bent forward. He was breathing hard and sweat ran from his face. He turned around and gathered up the feet. Pulling Woolley's shins under his armpits, he dragged him like a horse before a cart. He passed the next cabin.

At the end of the corridor, there was another bend. He heaved Woolley's legs around first and then pulled the trunk of the body around after; the man's leather belt straining under the pressure. He laid the body down and

38

turned the handle of the lavatory door. It was locked – his hand sprang away from the handle and there was a sharp cough from within. He looked down at Woolley and saw the moonlight fall across his face. *Why did you want to kill me?* The shaft of light crossed the floor and led his eyes to the window. He heard another cough from inside the lavatory compartment, and then the *whoosh* of the flush.

Drabble looked around: from the loo door, back along the passage, to the door of the carriage, to the window –

His heart racing, he slid down the window – filling the passageway with the wild clattering of the wheels grinding on the tracks and a turbulent, howling maelstrom of air. It instantly chilled the sweat on his face and shivering, he bent down, hauled Woolley's torso upright. He then hooked his arms around his chest and stood, heaving Woolley up. Drabble's left knee wobbled violently but he braced it. Now they were both up, he pushed Woolley forward so that his head and shoulders protruded through the open window into the swirling void. He then grabbed Woolley's shins and lifted; the man pivoted onto his chest. Drabble leaned and shunted, wheelbarrowing Woolley forward, clear through the window. For a moment he saw Woolley's hair play in the wind and then the body tumbled away, down the cutting, its legs and arms flailing wildly. He slung the loose shoe out after him and pulled the window shut.

The door to the lavatory cabin opened; yellow electric light cracked into the carriage and a man in a striped dressing gown, newspaper folded under his arm, stepped out. As he closed the door behind him he noticed Drabble standing in the shadows in the last of the light.

He cleared his throat.

'Good morning,' he said.

Drabble nodded a reply as the door shut. For a moment they stood in silence, and then the man departed in the direction of the adjacent carriage.

CHAPTER FOUR

There was a discreet cough from the other side of the door, followed by a double knock, and Drabble lifted himself from the bunk, now propped up on his Gladstone. He reached over and slid the bolt across. The door opened and a cup of tea, a digestive biscuit slotted in the saucer, was introduced into the cabin through the gap. He wished the steward a good morning.

'And good morning to you, sir,' returned the railwayman. 'Hope you slept well.'

'Like a log. Thank you.' Drabble said, receiving the vessel. He had changed into his clean spare shirt and donned a scarf to cover his neck.

'It's five after seven, sir, if you're setting your watch,' he added, before closing the door after him.

Drabble lowered himself onto the bunk, and watched the dark shapes of early morning speed past outside.

He sighed and looked down at his feet as his mind turned to the subject that had dogged him since whenever it was that Thompson/Woolley had attacked him.

What was it all about? The man did not seem to be a psychopath or unhinged in the sense that one would normally appreciate it. But clearly something was there all along: his memory of Drabble was really rather too good, and that made what happened later feel all the more premeditated – the meeting in the dining car, the whole shooting match, it was all planned. It was true that all sorts of snippets of information are wont to lodge themselves in people's minds, particularly in light of the fact that thanks to Harris – and poor Hubertus' tragic death – everyone in the world had had the opportunity to know it. But Woolley didn't make sense. Not entirely.

Drabble shut his eyes: Woolley's lifeless face appeared before him, the bloody trickle from the gaping mouth – something was wrong about the whole set-up and he didn't for the life of him have a clue as to what it was.

He felt the rising steam from the tea linger against his face and he crunched down some of the digestive biscuit.

If it comes to it, he told himself, I'll just have to explain that it was self-defence and that I panicked about the body. It was a moment of horror; that was all. He stared at the dirty wooden floor, noticing a fresh scuff-mark, perhaps created by Woolley's knife. His situation didn't look good, though. 'Surely, sir, if you were completely innocent and had nothing to hide, you would not have seen fit to dispose of the corpse in such a cynical fashion?' He drained his tea cup. No, it didn't look good. Lord. Drabble closed his eyes: I've been bloody foolish.

Bloody foolish. Now *there* was a word for it.

***

As the train pulled in to Plymouth North Road station, Drabble was waiting by the carriage door, the very same door through the window of which he had dispatched Woolley just hours before. He tried not to dwell on this fact, and unhurriedly slid down that same window, reaching outside to open the door with the handle, and stepped free from the train just as it was coming to a final halt. Calm on the outside, Drabble's heart, however, thumped in his chest. And he felt a tumult of emotions – from guilt to relief to something approaching fear: including a hardly conscious sense that what Woolley had been aiming to achieve might now be the ambition of others. Dozens of doors all along the train sprang open around him and passengers stepped down and took out their baggage. Porters moved nimbly to and fro with their trolleys, speeding trunks and suitcases this way and that. Drabble did not look back.

Inside the station building there was a cafe, its glass windows condensed with steam, and a stall with bundles of newspapers and racks of weeklies and periodicals. The newsagent, a pipe smoking in his mouth, was stacking them lethargically onto his counter. By the door Drabble spied a row of three wooden telephone booths. He noticed the girl from the restaurant carriage already in the middle box, talking urgently into the mouthpiece. She saw Drabble and turned away.

Outside, he saw a pair of taxis drive from the forecourt, luggage stacked on their racks. A stately navy Talbot was parked up, its engine running. There was a dog-cart in front; a man in an overcoat and hat was lifting a child to the waiting hands of a woman. The dog-cart's driver, meanwhile, sat at the reins, wrapped up in a thick grey blanket, hunched over with his eyes closed. Drabble raised his hat and called up to the driver.

'Don't suppose you're going anywhere near Stoke Climsland?'

A watery eye opened sleepily. He yawned and the second eye followed the first.

43

'You wantin' the village?'

'That's right.'

'Other way,' said the man, shaking his head. 'But I oughtn't be long – p'rhaps an hour? Bit less.' A glance told him that his passengers were all aboard and he flicked the leather reins; the horse nodded its head, tossing its mane. 'Have a cup of tea,' he called as the big front wheel turned. 'I'll find thee in the station.'

Drabble stepped back and watched the cart leave the forecourt and turn the corner.

That was irritating. Still – he referred to his wristwatch – it was early; not yet seven thirty. And he could do with a cup of tea, and some breakfast, now that he thought about it. He shuddered and pulled his lapel up around his neck. It would be cold on the cart, he reasoned, and it wouldn't do to arrive too early. He turned towards the station and almost bumped into the woman from the restaurant car; she rushed straight into the back of the waiting Talbot. A chauffeur in grey uniform closed the door after her and smartly went around to the front. The Talbot drove off at pace.

An intense rush of hot, damp air and the squeal of a kettle greeted him in the café; clouds of steam billowed from the lid of a chrome urn. A wide woman, her red face glistening, stood smoking in a broad apron beyond the counter, mistress of all she surveyed. She removed the cigarette from her mouth and stubbed it out as Drabble approached. He ordered a cup of tea, paid, and waited while she prepared the brew. He looked towards the door, and then took his tea over to a table in the corner, where he sat hunched over, his hat pulled forward, stirring the

44

tea moodily. A cluster of small white bubbles on the surface clung to the shaft of the spoon. He eyed the four or five empty tables and glanced again over at the door.

He pushed the small bubbles around the cup, and then closed his eyes; endeavouring to drive away the mental image of Woolley lying on the floor of the sleeper cabin. Alas, it felt like Woolley was as persistent in death as in life. Drabble glanced again at the door, then snatched up the sugar and poured a good slug of it into his tea. He stirred the brew and gave it a taste.

The door sprang open – causing him to look over sharply – and there was the tinkle of a bell: followed by a gust of cool air.

'Morning, my bonny Holly!' boomed the rotund newcomer, pulling off his railwayman's cap as though he were revealing some prize concealed beneath it on the top of his head. The mistress of the establishment cackled gleefully in reply and they began to converse in loud theatrical voices, although their actual words were rendered indistinct by the sounds of various apparatus. Drabble looked back down at the surface of his tea and felt a bead of sweat run down his arm. He closed his eyes, trying again to drive the mental image of Woolley away. Christ alive, was that Stilton he could smell? He brought the hot rim of the teacup against his cold lips and drank. When he placed the cup back into the saucer he saw his hand was trembling. Good God. He swallowed and squeezed his eyes shut. He saw Woolley's dead face, the mouth limply open before him – the arm raising up. At the time he seemed to be making a last desperate bid to seize him; now Drabble wondered if it was an appeal for mercy.

45

Was it mercy, after all? What had he done? He tipped more sugar into his tea and took a swig. Woolley's dead eyelids creased open... Drabble pressed his hand against his forehead, rubbing the skin, pushing it hard. His breathing was becoming fast and he could see that his chest was heaving. It was no good. He drained his cup of tea and snatched up his bag.

He didn't stop until he had reached the spot in the forecourt where he had conversed with the cart driver. He was aware that he was breathing rapidly and his hands were shaking. He knew what this was - he had seen people lose their nerve on climbs - but this was different: it was happening to him. He took out his handkerchief and dabbed his brow. He'd killed a man. It was in self-defence and it had been inadvertent – the fall, not a blow, had brought about Woolley's demise – but it was undeniable. At best it could be considered a deliberate, tragic accidental act of self-defence. That wasn't quite right, either. He shook his head. It was simple: the man had tried to kill him – and come unstuck in the process. He stared down at the cobbles. There was a price to pay for the horror of such self-defence, he reasoned.

Drabble resolved to push Woolley from his mind and looked up to see the cart turn into the station forecourt. The elderly driver gave him a nod as he drew up next to him. The horse pitched its head, steam coming from its mouth and nostrils.

'Stoke Climsland, you said?'

'That's right,' replied Drabble. 'Dr Wilkinson's place. Don't suppose you know it?'

The man nodded, and moved across to make room for

him. Drabble put his foot on the step and pulled himself up onto the leather seat. The driver flicked the reins and they moved off. The sky was now light, though there was still no sign of the sun. Drabble shivered and rubbed his hands together for warmth.

'Is it far?'

'About an hour,' said the driver.

Drabble pulled the lapels of his tweed overcoat up around his ears.

'Down from London?'

'That's right.'

The driver nodded gently.

They soon left the city streets and the tall buildings of Plymouth behind and were trotting along the Bodmin Road. The houses and hedgerows gave way to tightly packed market gardens, then trees and scraps of steep fields. At a crossroads, they went left and then in a break in the trees, Drabble saw the wide green inlet of the River Tamar. The surface of the water was smooth, green and peppered with wispy clouds of fog. A small clinker-hulled yacht sat perfectly still at anchor.

They passed through a village and then turned at the green, following a road signposted *Gunnislake*. The highway was steep and double-backed through a series of narrow turns as it ascended onto the moor. The temperature dropped noticeably and the horse gave off great clouds of breath as the cart climbed.

***

It was a little after nine when they arrived at Dr

Wilkinson's, leaving a lane and turning into a anonymous, rutted driveway. The broad wooden gate, greened by age and elements, didn't look like it had moved for a while, and boasted a fair amount of foliage growing through it.

'Is this it?' asked Drabble doubtfully.

The driver nodded.

Either side were thick dark copses, and Drabble saw a fox trot across the drive ahead. It glanced over.

The house came into view. It was stone, two-storeys, and possessed a tall, steeply thatched roof with deep, angular eaves evocative of Germanic architecture. Downstairs the lights were on. Drabble was relieved to find someone at home.

The trees to the left receded and he saw the village, with the sun, now in evidence, reaching a good height beyond. There was a stone church with a square tower, and a wood-beamed market hall with a flag flying above it. Drabble smiled, feeling the weak sun and cool breeze on his face. The horror of the attack and the death of Woolley now felt further behind him.

To the right of the house, he saw a barn. One of the pairs of tall wooden doors was open and inside he saw the gleaming chrome grille and large circular headlights of a red car, which he recognised to be a new Alvis Speed Twenty. He approached. Low-slung, light and lean, a spare wheel sat in front of the passenger door, slotted into the dramatic curve of the running board. His eye followed the line of the bonnet, arriving at the glittering spread eagle mascot and descending to the number plate, AVC 80. What a beauty, he thought, and exceptionally fast.

The driver dropped him a little way from the front

door and he watched the cart drive away, before turning back to the house, and the appointment before him. In that moment Drabble couldn't see any figures moving in the lit rooms, and in the silence, he heard the serrated cry of a crow. Then there was nothing except for the low rustle of the leaves moving in the wind. He smiled: any minute now, he would have in hands before him the head of Oliver Cromwell. The actual head.

It was only now, after everything that had just happened, that he found himself being genuinely pleased, thrilled by that prospect. This is it, he thought, as he adjusted his cap, and approached the house.

A lady's bicycle was propped against the low stone wall just in front. There was a newspaper, the *Western Morning News*, and a fresh loaf of bread in the bike's basket. Next he saw that the front door was ajar and he announced his arrival with the black cast iron knocker. Then Drabble called through the gap, 'Hello?'

There was no reply. He waited and called out again.

Gingerly, he touched the door, pushing it open and looked in.

'Hello?'

He saw a spacious hallway, with an even stone floor, interrupted occasionally by a rug or animal skin. The walls were decorated with the mounted contents of someone's game book; above an opening to the right he saw the webbed brown antlers of something large, possibly a moose, which were flanked by those of a pair of stags. Ahead, an imposing staircase led up to the galleried upper storey. To the right of the opening was a settle with leather cushions in the window by a slate fireplace, which was made up ready with rolled-up newspaper, coal and kindling, and was guarded by a pair of matching chairs. There was a gold-framed mirror over the mantelpiece. A homely corner, he thought. Warm in the winter.

He removed his hat, wiped his feet on the doormat, and advanced to the foot of the stairs. Through the antlered aperture he saw a polished oak dining table, four chairs either side and carvers at each end. In the middle was a glinting silver ornament, like a punch bowl. Arranged along the far wall was a row of hunting scenes – he could just make out their titles, *Breaking Cover*, *The Cry*, *The Death* - and in the far corner, an open doorway concluded in a dark passage.

A draught stroked his cheek. Stepping to the side, he saw beyond the staircase a dark oak-panelled corridor. At its end was another room, through which he could see daylight in the windows. On the floor, the three-pointed broad amber leaf of a maple danced towards him. He watched it perform a pirouette and then fall flat, before another gust launched it into the air.

'Hello?'

He moved along the corridor with his head cocked to one side.

'Anyone there? It's Ernest Drabble.'

He trod closer, placing each foot with care. Through the gap in the doorframe he saw a page of newsprint sliding across the green carpet, its edge undulating in the draught like a creature of the deep. The tip of a black umbrella was pinched between the carpet and the foot of the door, jamming it ajar. He released it and opened the door.

In the centre of the room he saw a wide mahogany desk, its drawers partly or fully yanked out, and left at crooked angles. Likewise, the drawers of a filing cabinet had been forced open and pulled out, one entirely free. Box files had been opened and their contents scattered. Above the tiled Victorian fireplace, a small oil painting of a horse race was askew and the mantelpiece was bare. Drabble saw a pair of brass candlesticks, the candles and a greetings card strewn on the floor by the coal scuttle. The grate was empty. His eye went back to the painting: the horses, their legs stretched out forward and back, appeared to float above the ground – a trick, he guessed, that was not intended by the artist. He peered closer at it and thought for a moment. He clicked his tongue and shook his head – his gaze continuing to rove around the room. In the wall next to the fire, he saw a safe, its thick door wide open, and its disturbed contents – documents and other items. By the desk, a substantial leather office chair rested on its side like a boat forgotten by the tide. A black telephone lay on its side on the floor, the receiver next to it. The place has been pulled to pieces, he thought.

Drabble righted the chair and sat down. Swivelling around, his gaze revisited the fire, the hearth, the safe, and the newsprint by the door. He looked down and saw the wastepaper basket was over-turned, its litter sprayed across the floor, along with pens, envelopes, and yet more leaves. On the far side of the desk, looking out of the wide windows, he saw the garden and felt confident that if he stood up he would be able to see the village low in the distance. The middle window was open.

51

Silence. He shut his eyes and felt the gentle breeze brush his face. He listened. The only sound was the intermittent rasp of a piece of typing paper, trapped under a glass paperweight, flicking back and forth. Had the burglars gone? He looked down and noticed an assortment of paperclips on the carpet. Had they found what they were looking for – presupposing they had something in mind?

Standing, he pushed the chair up to the desk. The wicker basket caught his eye. He bent down and groped towards it – stopping dead.

Through the gap of the desk and the chair, on the floor beyond, he saw a hand. He set the bin down, and pushed the chair to one side. A forearm and head came into view.

He swallowed.

'Dr Wilkinson?'

An orange leaf somersaulted slowly past the figure, briefly brushing the fabric of the jacket.

'*Dr Wilkinson*?'

He rose and edged around to the back of the desk. Stepping over the discarded filing cabinet drawer, he saw a man, lying on his front, his arms spread out and his head turned awkwardly to the right. The silver hair on the back of his head was stained with blood. The eyes were fixed open and lips drawn back just enough to reveal teeth clenched on the tip of the tongue. Drabble knelt down beside him and picked up his wrist. Several seconds passed. He rested it back down. The man's knitted burgundy tie was adrift, and extended like an aviator's scarf. Beneath it Drabble saw the ruffled corner of a piece of cream-coloured paper. He reached down and gently

52

lifted the body, easing it from under him. It was a telegram.

It read:

December 7 1936.
Time: 7.15 am
Addressed to: Dr. H Wilkinson, Spring Farm, Stoke Climsland

IMPERATIVE BRING ITEM TO LONDON IN PERSON.
DO NOT DELAY. SINCERE REGARDS.
CHURCHILL.

Drabble lowered the telegram, and looked over at the corpse. The man had not been dead long, he thought. Reading this telegram might have been the last thing he ever did. Drabble glanced over his shoulder at the doorway, and then back down at the right arm. The skin had been just warm on the wrist and the flesh was still soft, malleable to slight pressure. Quite possibly, Dr Wilkinson might only have been dead for a matter of minutes. Drabble's eye fell on the creased note. Churchill? As in, *the* Winston Churchill? It wasn't likely. He picked up the telephone, put the receiver to his ear, listened for a moment and dialled.

'Hello, operator? Westminster 2188 please.'

There was a hiss and a 'click'. The line started to ring. Drabble looked over his shoulder at the door. Come on, he thought, as it rang again. He reread the telegram and his focus hovered on the surname in capitals. There was another peal of bells and then - 'ding' –

53

'*Yeaoowh,*' blurted the voice on the line. 'What bally time do you call this?'

'Harris,' Drabble hissed, in a hushed tone intended to communicate urgency, 'it's me. Look – it's an emergency.'

'Ernest? An emergency –'

'Look,' Drabble cut in. 'Something's going on. Someone tried to kill me on the train –'

'By Jingo...'

'And now I've arrived at Wilkinson's place in Cornwall and he's dead -'

'Dead? Who, what... who's *Wilkinson*?'

'The man who had the head of Oliver Cromwell. He's been murdered. I've just got here and he's flat out on the rug.'

'Are you sure?'

Drabble looked over at the doctor's body: 'I'm no expert, Harris, but you don't have to be Miss Marple to know this wasn't a tragic accident.'

'But why would someone do it?'

Drabble eyed the doorway, suddenly aware that this phone call might not be an efficient use of time.

'There's this telegram, too.'

'A telegram?'

'From a man called Churchill.'

'What? *Winston* Churchill?'

'I've no idea, but how many Churchills are there?'

'More than you'd think; what does it say?'

Drabble started to explain when quite suddenly, there was a sound of movement behind him.

A sharp, painful jab in the small of the back sent him

lurching forward – almost onto the body of Wilkinson. He steadied himself and span round. It was a young woman – a rather pretty young woman at that, notwithstanding the fact that she was pointing a shotgun at him. She wore a scarlet-coloured pullover with a pair of green tweed breeches that led down to brown leather riding boots. Light blonde hair framed a pale typically English face, which was inspecting him intently from the vantage point of both barrels.

'Hands up.'

Drabble raised them, the telegram still held in his left, telephone receiver in the right. The gun looked bigger than her, he thought, but it wasn't wobbling a bit.

'Put the telephone down.'

He heard Harris' insistent voice asking him questions over the line – 'Ernest, *Ernest*? What's going on?' – and hung up.

For a moment he held the girl's brown eyes.

'Who are you?' she barked.

He offered his best smile.

'My name is Drabble.' He stepped backwards, looking down to make sure he wasn't going to tread on the outstretched arm. 'I-I was looking for Dr Wilkinson.'

'Well,' the girl frowned, 'it looks like you've found him.'

Her focus flicked from Drabble to the body, and back again. Drabble saw traces of mascara on the girl's cheeks where it had run.

'Who are you?' he asked.

Her eyes narrowed.

'Miss Honeyand. Dr Wilkinson's secretary.'

'I'm sorry,' he said, his voice softening. 'I don't suppose you've any idea about what's happened?'

Her chin rose and she pulled the stock of the gun to her shoulder.

'*You tell me.*'

'What?'

'What's that bit of paper in your hand?'

The side-by-side barrels lifted up an inch or two, so that once again they aimed at his head. He coughed.

'Hey, look, please. Take it.' He held it out to her but she did not approach.

'*Don't move!*'

He froze and took a breath.

'It's a telegram for the doctor. I just found it next to him. I don't know anything about it. It's from someone called Churchill.' The woman was impassive. '*Look,*' he continued, 'I had an appointment - surely you knew that? Didn't Dr Wilkinson mention he had a visitor coming today? I'm here to see the head, of Oliver Cromwell. I've nothing to do with this. I give you my word.'

He gave a gentle, slow nod. The two black dark circles hovered just a couple of feet in front of him.

'Come on,' he said. 'How about lowering the 12-bore?'

'How about you convince me *not* to shoot you?'

'*What*?'

'Why did you murder Dr Wilkinson?'

'I *didn't* murder Dr Wilkinson. I'm not a murderer, I'm an historian.'

He looked down at the rug before him. That *was* true, wasn't it? He restored his gaze to the girl and saw her finger fatten as it pressed against the metal of the trigger. Her jaw muscles hardened. Drabble swallowed.

'Sit,' she said.

She took a step back and swept the barrel of the shotgun towards one of the little wooden chairs by the fireplace. He edged across, not breaking eye contact, and lowered himself into the seat, his hands still held high.

'I've telephoned to Constable George,' she said.

Her forefinger massaged the trigger.

'Miss Honeyand,' he said calmly. 'Where were you when your employer was killed?'

'In the village, at the baker's.' She brought the shotgun to her hip but it still pointed at him. 'You can put your hands down but tie your shoelaces together.'

He bent forward and started on them.

'I assume,' he said, craning his face up towards her, 'you have no idea who *did* kill him?'

'If it's not you,' she shrugged. 'Lord knows.'

'Well, they've ransacked the place. Did they steal anything?'

She glanced around the room.

'I've no idea.'

He finished knotting his laces together. A crow cried in the garden. For a moment he saw the girl look down at the body beyond the desk. Her face darkened, but the hardness, which had been evident when she pointed the gun at him previously, vanished. Drabble saw faint white streaks on her cheek, where she had been crying.

'Can I get you a cup of tea?' he asked gently. 'Or perhaps something stronger - *Scotch*?'

She bit the side of her cheek.

'I'd sooner have some Scotch.'

He reached into his pocket, took out the flask, placed it on the carpet, and shoved it across to her. She stopped it with her raised toe.

'You know you're going to have to put the shotgun down to open it.'

She nodded. 'But those laces will slow you down, and I'm going to keep my eye on you.'

She laid the gun on the desk - it still pointed at him - and picked up the flask. She undid the lid and tipped her head back and drank. Drabble saw the smooth underside of her chin. She then screwed the lid back and tossed it over to Drabble. He caught it.

'I did a slip knot,' said Drabble, separating his feet.

She snatched the gun up and studied him. He watched her finger; it moved in a slow, erratic circle on the length of the trigger. A bead of sweat trickled from Drabble's armpit. He breathed in.

'On my way here, last night, a man tried to kill me. Fortunately, I'm pleased to report, he didn't manage it. Here -' Drabble pulled the collar of his shirt adrift so that she could see the chafed skin on his neck. 'I'd hate you to do what he tried so hard to achieve.'

She inspected him coolly.

Drabble continued, 'I came here to see your employer and to examine the head of Oliver Cromwell as part of my historical research. It's all true, I *promise*. I'm a professor at Cambridge - I know I don't necessarily look like what you imagine a professor of mediaeval and early modern history to look like, but there you go; I am. I don't know what's happening but it strikes me that there just might –

might – be a connection between someone trying to knock me off a few hours ago on the Penzance sleeper, and the death of Dr Wilkinson. If not, it's just a massive, dreadful coincidence. And look, there's this.' He held the telegram. 'I'm positive this is important.'

He reached the telegram out towards her.

'Here – take it!'

She did not approach. Not a bad little speech, he thought. Drabble could tell that beyond her unblinking light brown eyes, she was thinking it over. He was distracted for a second by the line of her bra, trapped in the stretched fabric of her jersey. He cleared his throat. He saw her focus roam to the telegram and then back at him. She grimaced; the gun jumped to her shoulder. Her finger went to the trigger.

'You bastard,' she said. 'You *did* kill Dr Wilkinson. You're one of *them*.'

'Who?'

'THEM!' she shouted. Her top lip twitched. 'You say you're a historian?'

'Yes. *Yes!* I am!'

'Fine,' she wiped away a tear. 'Name the Prussian Johnny who saved Wellington's bacon at Waterloo.'

Drabble frowned.

'*What?*'

'Name him!'

The two round black circles at the end of the shotgun rose and pointed at his nose.

'Um... Err...'

He stared ahead at the end of the barrel. What on earth was the chap's name? His eyes flitted from side to side.

He saw the fireplace, he saw the fountain pen lying by the bin, he saw the muddy streak on her boot. He looked at the window; the branches of a tree bowed in the wind. He stared at his toes. His mind was blank. *Think man, think.* He opened his eyes.

'For God's sake, I've no idea. *It's not my period.*'

'That's it,' she said, lingering over the final 't'. She brought the hammers back.

He gulped.

'I promise you,' he pleaded. '*I didn't kill him. It wasn't me.*'

He heard a noise from outside and leaned forward. Looking left, up the corridor, he saw a car wheel and black bonnet through the open front door.

'And also,' he added, pointing, 'there's a car coming up the drive.'

Keeping the gun trained on him, she stepped forward and peered out through the door. Her face fell.

'Ruddy hell,' she said, and shot her gaze back at him. 'There're three of them.'

'What?' He looked out. Another car pulled up in front. 'Bugger. It's a convoy all right.'

'Who are they?' She dropped the shotgun to her hip and jabbed it at him. '*Come on, talk.*'

'I've no idea, but I'm fairly certain it's not Constable George.'

They heard several car doors being slammed shut.

'Come on,' he said, reaching very slowly out to her. He kept his voice super-calm. 'We've got about thirty seconds to get out of here. Otherwise I've a terrible feeling that we'll end up like Dr Wilkinson.'

Her light brown eyes blinked; once, then twice.

'All right,' she said, 'all right – the window. Here, give me a hand with this –' she passed him the shotgun. He took it, slid back the safety catch and went to the door, keeping watch. He heard scraping metal and looked over. The girl had pulled the filing cabinet away from the wall.

'I think they might have been looking for this,' she said, her voice straining. She stood up, a dark wooden box, topped with a brass handle, in the crook of her arm.

'What is it?'

'It's Cromwell.'

'What?'

'Let's go,' she said. 'Come on.'

They stepped from the window, their feet landing in the soft soil of the flower bed. The girl led, sprinting, bent forward, the box in her right hand. Drabble followed, looking back occasionally to see if they had been detected. They ran along the back of the house, and arrived at the far end: the barn was beyond a narrow track and Drabble saw the glinting grille of the ladybird red Alvis through the open barn doors. The girl threw a glance around the brick corner and sped across; in four strides she was safely at the rear of the garage. Drabble peered around the corner. He saw one black Rover, then a second beyond, and the prow of the third was just in view. A thought struck him: the cars blocked the front of the garage as well as the driveway. He looked back: the field beyond the garden fell away into the trees. There might be a way out there. Mind you, the Alvis wouldn't be much good – especially if it was damp underfoot. He looked down at the thick mud that had already collected on his shoes.

Drabble heard the growl of an engine and a little burgundy and black Austin swooped towards him, stopping with a squeal. It was the girl. Through the windscreen he saw she wore a pair of sleek black spectacles. He hurled himself towards the running board, leapt in, the barrel of the gun poking out the window. She released the clutch and they bounced and jerked about unhappily across the grassy field. She changed down and they picked up speed.

He looked back, just as three men in dark suits tumbled out of the back door. They began pointing and then were lost from view.

'Where are we going?' he said, bracing himself against the dash as the car jolted violently.

'It's a cut-through.'

He looked over the door at the muddy grass below; lumps of earth and grit splattered up onto the car and into the air. If they didn't get stuck in this lot it would be a sodding miracle, he thought. But the car was light and a glance told him the girl knew how to drive. They approached a pair of stone gateposts - too narrow for most modern cars. He looked over at the speedometer: it read 35mph.

'This is going to be tight,' he said, gesturing towards the gateway.

The Austin appeared to accelerate.

He braced himself against the dash and glanced over.

'I said, 'It's going to be a bit tight'.'

The passenger-side wing mirror exploded against the gatepost as the Austin swept through the gap. Now, though, they were on the road. The tyres squealed as they passed through a long left hander.

'Ruddy well done,' said Drabble. 'Tell me you've done that before.'

The girl looked over and smiled at him, revealing a pair of dimples.

'What's your Christian name?'

'Kate.'

'How do you do, Kate?'

'How do you do?'

They snatched a handshake between gear-changes.

'Please call me Ernest.'

Her smile widened, causing her dimples to deepen.

'Your glasses are very fetching,' he remarked.

She blushed and looked away. 'I hate them.'

A loud shot rang out – shattering the rear window. Kate shrieked and ducked; the car veered and the running board kissed the stone wall, sparks flying from the front wing.

A second shot rang out.

'Keep going,' shouted Drabble. He looked back: broken glass covered the back seat. There was the crack of a pistol. He saw the large dark Rover from the driveway moving back and forth in the road behind. They must have come around on the main road, he thought. *Their car was bigger, faster, and getting closer.* 'Stick your foot down,' he cried.

'This is as fast as she goes!'

He looked back: the other car was just a few feet away. He bent down and slid the shotgun from the foot-well. He swivelled around in the seat and took aim. The Rover moved from side to side behind them, sliding in and out of view through the remnants of the oval rear window. He brought back the hammers and watched the black silhouette of the Rover pass to the left. In a second, it would move back into view: this wasn't going to do the back of her car any favours.

'Keep steady,' he said.

The Rover came into the line of sight, the passenger, and... *now the driver*.

He squeezed the first trigger.

Click!

He pulled the second trigger.

Click!

'It's not loaded,' shouted Kate, over the sound of the engine.

'It's not loaded?'

Kate shook her head.

'The cartridges are in the kitchen.'

'You might have told me.'

'Sorry. It's where they're kept –'

A shot whistled past: Kate flinched and the driver side wing-mirror sheared clean away.

'Ruddy hell,' she shouted. '*That was close.*'

He pointed up ahead to the side of the road.

'What's up there?'

Not waiting for an answer Drabble grabbed the steering wheel and pushed it hard around. The Austin swerved through a gap in the hedgerow, snatching branches with it. The car bounced up an incline. He looked back and saw the long nose of the Rover poking through, jammed in the gap.

'We've made it,' he said.

They heard more gunfire.

'You mean we're done for.' Kate strained at the lever to change gear. 'This field doesn't go anywhere.'

'It must go somewhere.'

She shook her head.

'We'll work it out.'

'Got any more of that Scotch?'

He yanked out the flask, unscrewed the lid, and passed it. She tipped it to her lips: the Austin bumped and she missed, pouring against her chin.

'You know it's not advisable to drink and drive,' he said.

Kate tried again: for a split second she closed her eyes and held the silver opening to her pursed lips.

'What is it about historians?' she asked, handing the flask back. 'Every time you ask them a ruddy question, they never know the answer.'

He had a drink.

'One can't be expected to know everything.'

'Yes, but I might have shot you.'

'Not without cartridges you wouldn't.'

He saw ahead that they were fast approaching a high hedge. He strained to look back.

'I don't suppose you happen to know who the Churchill of the telegram is?'

She looked over.

'Of course I do. It's Winston Churchill.'

'As in the MP?'

'Dr Wilkinson wrote to him last week. He thought he'd be interested in it.'

'In *it*?'

She looked over her shoulder at the wooden box on the back seat. His gaze followed her.

'You're kidding?'

'Why should I?'

'I don't suppose you've got the faintest idea what he wants with the cranium of Oliver Cromwell?'

She shook her head.

'I expect he's just curious to see it.'

'Oh really?' he said, as the Austin bounced violently. His head struck the roof. 'I hope he's not dying to see it, too.'

***

Harris replaced the handset and lay back down, the blue and white collar of his pyjamas unfolding behind his head on the pillow. He looked up at the dark canopy of his four-poster bed. Great Scott, he thought. His eyes widened. Some Johnny tries to kill Ernest on the train and then when he arrives at the Cromwell fellow's house, he's a goner, too? Blimey. Harris frowned and reached to the bedside table; his hand patted the polished wooden surface, finding the tumbler with its dregs of whisky, his reading glasses, and then his slender silver cigarette case. He took out a Craven A and slotted it into his mouth, and produced a lighter from the folds of the covers. He lit the cigarette. He was still virtually horizontal and the smoke spiralled above him, obscuring his view of the silk canopy above. What the devil was going on? Why would someone want to kill Ernest? He thought for a moment.

The first port of call had to be Winston Churchill, didn't it?

He took a long drag of the cigarette and then reached over, exhaling smoke from his nostrils, for the wide glass ashtray that sat on the far bedside table. Harris froze and looked down.

'Goodness,' he said quietly. His voice rose, '*Hello!*'

He drew back the covers to reveal a pale profile, a dark bob, and a gamine, white arm.

'And who might you be?'

The girl turned onto her head; her dark-ringed eyes blinking at him. He saw her smile.

'Lady Emily,' he said, at last. He chuckled, 'Of course!' He reached across her and stubbed out the cigarette, 'has it really been six *long* hours?'

CHAPTER FIVE

The Austin crested the brow of a grassy field and then bounced down an incline towards a low brown stream. The gearbox crunched as Kate changed down. She turned to Drabble, the mechanical grinding ceasing as she located second.

'I promise,' she said, 'I used to cycle it. It's really not that deep.'

The little Austin surged into the stream, throwing up a wall of water. Drabble felt its wheels slip on the pebbles beneath. Kate jerked at the steering wheel and the front of the car twitched right as the rear slid out. The Austin turned, juddering uncertainly, but it now pointed straight upstream. They picked up speed.

'Actually,' said Kate, leaning out over the side. 'It's deeper than I thought.'

Drabble patted her arm. 'You're doing just brilliantly.'

Kate brightened.

'Good old Boothroyd.'

'Boothroyd? Oh.' He rubbed the dash. 'Ruddy amazing Boothroyd.'

It was true, he thought, its tiny engine and frame had somehow saved them. Either side of the stream were high banks, thick with undergrowth and trees. I wonder if we'll be able to get out, he thought. He turned to the girl; she was leaning forward over the wheel, her brow knitted in concentration. She glanced over.

'I don't suppose you've any idea who those men

were?'

He shook his head.

'Did they want to kill us?'

'It's certainly a possibility.'

She bit her lip.

The stream was getting deeper and the banks higher, and the Austin's wheels where throwing up a high bow wave. Nonetheless, thought Drabble, they were making good enough progress - for now. He cleared his throat.

'Do you know where this leads?'

'Roughly,' said Kate. She frowned, 'I was wondering: what am I going to do about Dr Wilkinson?'

'How do you mean?'

'He's lying on the study floor. Drat!' She stabbed the brake and car jolted to a halt. 'Mrs Jones will be in at eleven. I can't let her find him like that.' She turned to him. 'It'd kill her.'

Drabble looked behind.

'We really can't go back.'

'We have to!'

Drabble gripped the wheel.

'I'm afraid it's out of the question.'

'But -' Kate's eyes widened. 'W-what happens if they're still there? What will they do to her?'

She frowned and looked down at the centre of the black steering wheel.

'Almost certainly nothing,' said Drabble. He sighed, 'I'm afraid they're either after you or me, or improbable as it might seem, the mummified skull of a 300-year-old dictator – not Mrs Jones. Who is she, anyway? The cook?' He caught a nod from Kate. 'In that case, I think the greatest danger she faces is being forced to make them breakfast.'

Kate pulled at the gear lever and the Austin moved off. She glanced over. 'If they've stomach for it.'

Drabble looked over the side. The water was now almost as high as the running boards.

'What we need is somewhere to get off the stream and back onto terra firma.'

'I've been thinking about that,' said Kate. 'I'm not sure we're going in the right direction.'

Drabble continued looking over the side. The height of the river had probably risen by six inches.

'I'm pretty certain, in fact,' she added, shooting him a grimace. 'And I'm worried if we go very much further Boothroyd'll be done for.'

Drabble considered that a distinct possibility.

'I think we'll just have to go as far as we can and then proceed on foot.'

Two hundred yards later the Austin spluttered to a halt and misfired – Drabble ducked. The engine misfired again.

'Come on, Boothroyd,' appealed Kate. 'You can do it.'

She revved the engine – BANG!

There was silence and he heard only the sluice of the water running past them.

Kate tried the ignition and jammed her foot on the throttle. They heard a couple of 'clicks' from the engine and then nothing. For a moment Drabble saw her stare down at the steering wheel, her eyes flitting up and down – and then tears erupted from them and she bent forward, hugging the wheel and wailing. Hers was a loud, convulsive cry and her body shuddered with each explosion of emotion. Drabble put his arm around her.

'I can't leave Boothroyd,' she said, shaking her head. 'I can't.'

She turned her face to him and he saw the tears were running down her cheeks. He pulled her close to him.

'We'll come back and get her later,' he said softly. 'I promise.'

He felt her press her forehead against his chest.

They drew apart.

'Sorry,' she said, wiping her eyes.

'No need.'

'No,' she said. 'I've got mascara on your shirt.'

He smiled and stroked her face.

'I'll be all right in a second,' she said, bursting into tears again. 'It's been rather a rum morning, that's all, what with one thing and another.' Drabble patted her shoulder – that was one way of putting it. He looked back and saw the river was still clear. She blew her nose loudly on a white handkerchief. He pressed her shoulder.

'Come, we've really got to go,' he said. 'I'm sorry.'

He reached back and pulled out the wooden case.

'Now,' he said, bringing forward the shotgun, 'take this.'

She looked up from the wheel and took hold of the gun.

'Right,' he said, 'come on.'

She nodded dismally, her face streaked with mascara.

'Ready?'

She nodded again, and forced a smile.

'I'll meet you on the far bank.'

He watched her get out. She raised the gun above her head and waded across the stream towards the far bank. He plunged in and took a few hasty steps. The water was up to his knees and chilly. He paused and looked back at the grille of the car. He turned and saw Kate push the gun onto the bank and scramble up the slope after it, pulling with one hand at the root of a tree and clutching a grassy clump with the other. She slipped, leaving a muddy cut in the undergrowth, but recovered her footing and clambered up. When he arrived at the side he stretched his arm and held his hand up to her.

'Take this,' he said.

'What is it?'

He passed her the slanting chrome Austin logo from the front of the car. Slowly, her mouth formed a smile.

'Thank you.'

He climbed up and, taking the shotgun from Kate, they started across the field, their shoes snatching at the damp grass.

'What are we going to do now?' asked Kate.

'I think we should find ourselves a car and take Mr Cromwell here, to see Mr Churchill.'

'It sounds like a plan.'

They hurried on.

'What about Dr Wilkinson?'

He thought for a moment.

'You said you'd called the police? I don't know much about it but I'm sure they'll make the necessary arrangements.' He reconsidered this statement. 'If we could get to London tonight, then we could conceivably be back tomorrow, so you could see him and Mrs Jones then.'

She nodded.

They had reached a stile. He climbed over and offered her his hand as she followed. She took it and jumped down, landing with both feet.

'So why did you want to see it?' she asked, letting go of his hand.

'What, the head?' He thought for a second. 'It's of great historic interest.'

'Is it really?' Her tone softened. 'I've always thought it was just rather ghoulish. The doctor took great pleasure in scaring the children from the village with it. It never occurred to me that it might actually be of historic significance.'

Drabble pointed towards the hedge and they moved in closer to it.

'You probably think it very childish of me to name my motorcar,' she announced. He was going to reply but she continued, 'it's just a silly superstition Dr Wilkinson had. He named all of his cars.'

'Really?'

'Yes, the Alvis is called Lulubelle.' She shrugged. 'No idea why.'

They took a few more brisk paces.

'Who do you think those men are?'

'I really haven't got a clue,' he said. 'The man on the train was an insurance broker; mind you, he was also a member of the British Union of Fascists.'

'A fascist!'

Drabble nodded grimly. 'That's what I thought.'

They continued in silence for a moment.

73

'I'm sorry I called you a bastard,' she said.

'That's all right,' he smiled at her. 'I've been called far worse.'

She thought about that.

'I'm sure you didn't merit it,' she finally pronounced, adding a laugh.

They strode on, following the high hedge until they reached a gate. The hill sloped down gently away from them.

'That's the Dundases,' she said, pointing to a long low stone house in the distance. It lay at the end of an adjacent field. A wisp of smoke was just visible from one of the chimneys.

'Are they friends?'

She nodded. 'They'll be upset about the doctor.'

'Do you think they might lend us a car?'

She shrugged.

'They'd certainly give us a lift.'

'Good,' said Drabble, pulling gently at her hand. 'That's a start.'

He opened the gate and they went through into the next field, following the footpath by the hedge. Drabble broke the shotgun and positioned it into the crook of his right arm, and carried the box containing Cromwell's head over his shoulder. Kate rubbed her hands together and blew on them. He noticed a tinge of blue to her fingers. She was freezing.

'Hang on,' said Drabble, as he laid the gun and box on the ground. 'Try this.' He removed his tweed overcoat and held it up: under protest she slid her arms into the sleeves. It went down to her shins and the sleeves concealed her hands.

'It's perfect,' she said, a pair of dimples forming on her face.

***

The Dundases' place was a low stone building with Georgian sash windows and chimney stacks at either end of its roof. In front was a cobbled courtyard, irregular in shape, formed by stables along the far end adjoining a large black barn opposite. They opened the gate and went in. Drabble saw bantams questing in the flower beds and assorted flower pots. Light was visible from the far window.

'I think they're in the kitchen,' said Kate.

Drabble pulled the doorbell – there was a faint tinkle from inside - and rapped the knocker. A few moments passed.

Drabble looked over at the lane and knocked again. He pushed back his sleeve and looked at his watch.

The door inched open.

'Kate!' The pink, hot-looking face of a plump woman in her fifties came into view. She beamed at Kate and wiped her hands on her apron, 'it's early.'

'Mrs Dundas, how are you?'

'Exceptionally fine, my dear,' she replied. 'And -' Drabble saw her narrowed eyes take in his face, the shotgun, the box, the sodden trousers, dirty shoes – and then Kate's overcoat. She pursed her lips and looked back at Drabble, scanning his face.

'And, begging your pardon, but who are you, sir?'

'This is my friend, Ernest Drabble,' ventured Kate, inclining her hand. 'He's an historian at Cambridge University.'

Drabble smiled.

'Well, we don't stand on ceremony here, Mr Drabble.' She took the end of Kate's damp sleeve in her hand. 'Will you both come in out of the cold? I was just mustering a hearty breakfast. You must have some, there's plenty.'

Drabble and Kate followed her into the parlour – there was a cast-iron fireplace with neat brasses and miniatures, a couple of farmhouse chairs, and whitewashed walls. They heard a man's voice.

'It's Kate Honeyand, my dear,' bellowed Mrs Dundas, 'and a gentleman – an *his*torian from Cambridge University.' They followed her through the open doorway into a large, bright kitchen as she added in her earlier tone, 'Mr Dundas will be down presently, he likes to read in his study before breakfast. It's Trollope this morning.'

Mrs Dundas filled the kettle and set it on the range.

'Why don't you put that down,' she said to Drabble, who stood the twelve-bore in the corner. 'So you're the one who's been shooting.' She tutted. 'You didn't manage to hit anything, then?'

'Unfortunately not,' said Drabble.

'I'm a terrible shot,' continued Mrs Dundas, who went to the door, and sang out: 'George, my dear. Can you be a poppet and fetch some coal?' She went to the Welsh dresser and took down some plates.

'I'll go,' offered Drabble.

'Would you? Oh, that's kind,' then to Kate, 'isn't he kind.' And then back to him, again, 'It's just out in the

76

shed - the little black door, you can't miss it.'

He took the empty coal scuttle and went out of the back door, entering the far end of the yard, with the stone stables to the immediate left and the barn opposite. Straight across, he spotted a small door, the cobbles in front were smudged grey with flakes of coal. He filled the scuttle and on his return wandered over to the gate. He looked up and down the lane.

In the kitchen he found they had been joined by a man, one who looked like he probably belonged to Mrs Dundas. He was talking but fell silent when he noticed Drabble come in.

'Good morning, sir,' he said, taking the bucket and then shaking Drabble's hand firmly. 'George Dundas.'

Dundas had neat grey hair and wore a striped military tie. He immediately knelt and started feeding coal through the small metal door into the furnace at the bottom of the range, while he addressed Drabble: 'I'm very sorry to hear about Dr Wilkinson.'

'I can't believe it,' chipped in Mrs Dundas, shaking her head mournfully, as she prodded a rasher of bacon in the pan.

'What are you going to do?' asked Dundas, looking up from the scuttle.

'We need to go to London as fast as possible.'

'London?' His voice arched and he trowelled another load in.

'We've got to make an important delivery,' added Drabble.

'In that case,' he scraped the last lumps together with the shovel and thrust it into the flames, 'you'll need a car.'

77

'We've got one,' said Kate. 'Boothroyd's in the stream.'

'What in the Lord's name is she doing there, dear?' asked the woman.

'It's how we escaped from the men, Mrs Dundas.' Kate cracked an egg into the pan. It spread out and began to turn white. 'Ernest realised they couldn't drive into the field; unfortunately the only way out was the river.'

Dundas closed the metal door of the furnace with a rag and went over to the square sink. He washed his hands.

'But who are these people?'

'I wish we knew,' replied Drabble, meeting Dundas' hard eyes. Drabble swallowed and lowered his gaze, watching Dundas towel off his hands. He dried each finger in turn and then laid the dishcloth on the slate surface.

'Come,' said Dundas. 'Let's sit down.'

He strolled over to the table and sat at its head, offering a place on the form by the wall to Drabble.

'I see you've got the doctor's shotgun,' he announced.

'Yes, Kate had it out already. Unfortunately we don't have any cartridges.' He looked over at Kate, who was now in conversation with Mrs Dundas.

Dundas stroked his chin.

'Kate says you were visiting Dr Wilkinson,' he stated.

'Yes, I'm an historian and I came down on the sleeper last night to inspect an artefact which is, or rather, *was* in Dr Wilkinson's possession.'

'Not the "secret" head?'

'The very same – obviously it's not such a big secret around here.'

Dundas nodded.

'And I'm right in thinking that that's what's in the wooden box on the floor over there?'

'That's the case.'

Above his host's head Drabble saw a plate on the wall, showing a brightly coloured cockerel. His red-crested head was raised to the heavens, his beak open wide.

'Am I correct,' asked Dundas, 'in supposing that you think that's what these men you speak of were after, too?'

Drabble looked over at Kate; she was unloading a dish from an oven.

'As unlikely as it seems, I think so.'

Dundas contemplated this sternly for a moment. Then his expression softened.

'If you take the Morris,' he said, 'I'll fish the Austin out later with the tractor and see if it can be saved.'

'Thank you. I should have it back by Friday or Saturday morning – if not sooner.'

'Good.' Dundas addressed his wife. 'We'll have some breakfast and then send these young people on their way.'

Mrs Dundas and Kate laid the table with several dishes containing bacon, black pudding, eggs, and a toast rack. They sat and then bowed their heads over Spode plates. Looking down, Drabble saw a long-haired spaniel, glazed in white and pale blue, with a pheasant clutched between its jaws, charging across a field. After the last twelve hours he knew how the pheasant felt.

'For what we are about to receive,' he heard Dundas' deep voice intone, 'may the Lord make us truly thankful.' He paused, 'And may we also thank Him for his mercies and pray for the dear soul of Dr Wilkinson. God bless him. And pray for the continued safety of these two young persons here present.'

They said 'Amen' and after a respectful pause, Mrs Dundas dished up the food in silence.

After a few minutes, Kate broke the sombre mood.

'I hadn't realised how ravenous I was,' she said, offering a cheerful smile.

Drabble finished his first mouthful. It had alerted him to his own hunger – suppressed through hours of anxiety. He hadn't eaten anything since the dining car. He forced himself to slow down, and complimented the cook.

Mrs Dundas smiled and wiped her lips with her napkin. The tip of Kate's knife pierced the plump soft centre of the egg on her plate, its orange fluid melted into the buttered white toast.

The doorbell rang.

Dundas laid down his cutlery with a scrape.

'What is it, George?' asked Mrs Dundas, exchanging a glance with her husband.

They heard an urgent knock at the door, followed by another tinkle of the bell.

Dundas took his wife's hand and addressed the table sternly.

'Stay here.'

CHAPTER SIX

Harris heard a sharp knock at the office door and looked up from his typewriter. A slim brunette in an elegant, fitted dove grey suit stepped into his line of sight. She wore a matching grey pillbox hat – arranged at a jaunty angle – and a mink stole covered her shoulders.

'Valerie!' exclaimed Harris, removing his spectacles, 'How *lovely* to see you.'

He rose from his chair and welcomed her in, taking her grey-gloved hand in both of his and shaking it warmly. 'You must have a story for me.'

Lady Valerie Schleighter's large blue eyes took in the room, and Harris thought he detected the faintest of curls on her full lips.

'Why is it, Percy,' she began, her voice was low, moderated, 'that journalists work in such fetid squalor?'

'What are you talking about?' protested Harris lightly. He looked about the room: his eye dancing from one haphazard pile of paper to another, stacked across the floor, desks, and atop filing cabinets, to the overfilled wastepaper baskets, and then to several of the dozen discarded teacups, wine glasses, and empty champagne bottles of differing brands, that he knew dotted the cramped room.

'You should have seen the place *before* the cleaner came in,' he said with a grin. 'Now have a pew. What will you have to drink?' He pulled out the top drawer of the nearest filing cabinet.

'It's a little early for me,' said Valerie, as she lowered herself into the chair. 'But thank you.' The curl had still not quite disappeared from the lip, he thought, and he spotted her stroke a fingertip along the arm of the chair prior to settling herself in it. 'I have a favour to ask.'

This comment struck Harris as being mildly arresting because Valerie Schleighter was not a woman to ask favours. She was married to a wealthy aristocrat – as opposed to a penniless one – and was armed with great wit and grace, and thus had probably not, in Harris' estimation at least, had to ask very hard for anything since she was fifteen, if not before. In point of fact, Harris counted himself among the men who had at some juncture or other allowed themselves to 'hope'. Fortunately, the associated incident had never been spoken of since, something Harris remained grateful for. He offered her a cigarette from the silver box that he kept at his desk. She took one, which he lit with the bulky glass and silver desk lighter. A second flinty rasp sparked a cigarette into life for himself.

'For some reason I always think of you as a pipe man,' stated Valerie.

'I am,' said Harris, 'but the subeditress kicks up a hell of a fuss about the smell so I stick to Craven A's for the office.' Harris was about to share some further insights about the relative benefits of cigarette smoking when he noticed that he'd already lost Valerie. She was looking at him sweetly enough but the eyes had begun to glaze.

'How may I be of assistance?' he asked.

She smiled.

'Percy,' she began, using his Christian name, which he

82

despised, 'I was wondering; have you seen or heard from your friend Ernest Drabble recently?'

'Ernest?' He broke his gaze away and slowly tapped his cigarette on the side of the ashtray. *Goodness*. His mind flitted to the telephone call that had woken him just a few hours before – to Ernest's wild reports about the attacker on the train, Wilkinson's suspicious death, and Churchill's telegram: something *big* was unfolding. Harris looked up and allowed his eyelids to blink several times. 'Gosh, Valerie. W-why *do you* ask?'

Valerie cleared her throat and then emitted that shy, giggling, laugh of hers.

'It's a chum of mine,' she said slowly. 'He would very much like to meet him.'

'Really? Whatever for?'

Valerie's eyes focused momentarily at the ceiling above Harris' head.

'Well, he's developed this mad, Mr Toad-like obsession with all things Cromwellian. He's started buying things that the fellow owned – a chair, a helmet, and so on. Anyhow, he's positively *raving* about him and he thought that how nice it would be to meet Ernest and so on and I wondered if, between you and me, we couldn't just make it happen for him?'

'I don't see that as being a problem. Ernest is very sociable.' Harris thought for a moment. 'But why doesn't your friend just drop him a line at college? I'm sure you know already that he's written a very well-received biography of Oliver Cromwell.'

'Quite so.' She showed her teeth. 'How long have you known him?'

83

Harris took a drag of his cigarette. He looked down at the floor beneath her chair, and frowned. After a moment, he met her eyes.

'We were at school together.'

She nodded.

'What's he like?'

Harris deliberated.

'Well,' he said, finally. 'What's there to say? He's my best friend. He's a gentleman – you know, in thought, word, and deed, and all that rubbish; he's a first-rate scholar, and of course, he's something of an adventurer.'

'Ah, yes,' she nodded in recollection. 'The "Bouncing Don".'

Valerie frowned in thought for a moment, and then lifted her chin and blew smoke from the corner of her mouth.

'You say he is sociable,' she said, 'I gather he is also a *socialist*?'

The first part of this final word carried a hiss.

Harris laughed.

'Really, Valerie, aren't we *all* socialists these days?'

His laughter met a cold stare. He cleared his throat.

'I mean, aren't we all *a bit* socialist, these days?'

'I am most certainly not!' She extinguished the half-smoked cigarette with punishing stabs into the middle of the ashtray. Harris stared down at the still smoking fag-end. It was a buckled sculpture in a pool of ash. He looked back up. Suddenly Valerie's face did not seem quite so beautiful. She brushed the back of her glove.

'Where does he stand on the Empire?'

Harris peered at her, and wondered if she deserved a

84

straight answer.

'I would say that he's not exactly *for* it,' he said in the end. 'He concedes, though, that there are some unforeseen or extrinsic benefits. For instance, I think he recognises that we look after our colonies rather better than the other lot look after theirs. Thirty thousand miles of railway on the subcontinent can't be all bad.'

'Quite,' she agreed, her mouth forming a wide grimace. 'Who would want to be ruled by the French?'

'Good croissants.'

'Hardly adequate compensation.' She thought for a moment. 'Is he republican?'

'Surely that depends what you mean by republican. Look, I'm sorry, Valerie,' Harris leaned forward, blinking, 'but what are you driving at? Why the interest in Ernest's political views? I thought your friend was more fascinated by the past, not the present?'

Valerie laughed.

'Don't be silly, Percy,' she said, 'I was merely being curious.' She took another cigarette from the box and waited with it held between her teeth as Harris raised the lighter to it. 'He does seem such an interesting, resourceful, and complex individual.' She laboured the word 'complex'. 'The only historians I've ever met are about a thousand years old and wake up humming "Jerusalem". You know the sort.'

She smiled and crossed her legs, allowing the hem of the skirt to ride up, exposing her knee. Harris noticed and swallowed.

'When did you last see him?'

Harris' attention left the slim leg.

85

'Last night,' he said, snatching one last glance before settling on the face. 'At the Granville, as a matter of fact.'

'He's a member, is he?'

'Yes,' said Harris, 'although I'm sure you're aware of that. Valerie, I hate being nosy, but are you going to tell me what this is about or not?'

Her eyes fixed on him. They seemed to widen and become bluer than ever. Harris experienced a rush of doomed hope.

'Percy,' she said meekly, reaching forward and placing a hand on his knee. 'Can't a girl be curious?'

Harris coughed and got up, finding sanctuary at the window. He saw the grocer opposite standing in front of the red and white awnings of his shop. His boy was bringing out another box of produce and arranging it on the pavement. He saw a large black saloon parked below; a chauffeur perched against the door smoking, a tall boot propped up against the wheel arch. He had gold flashes on his black lapel.

'How long have we known each other, Valerie?' he asked, adjusting the Venetian blind. 'I ask, because I just want you to be honest with me.' He turned to her. 'Has Ernest been upsetting somebody important?'

Valerie frowned and stubbed out the cigarette with a slow twist of her hand.

'I have a suggestion, Percy. Would you meet this friend of mine to discuss it further?'

Harris studied her face: it was a cool, impassive mask.

'All right,' he said. 'When? Today?'

'If you don't mind?' She cocked her wrist and slipped her glove forward to view her watch. 'I told you, he's positively raving about Cromwell.' She smiled at him. 'How about two thirty, at your club?'

CHAPTER SEVEN

For a moment everyone was still.

Then the door-bell tinkled a third time. There followed another, keener, report on the door from the knocker. Mrs Dundas glanced at the clock, 'It'll probably be the postman, dear.' She pulled her hand free and laid down her napkin. 'I'll go.'

'No, I'll get it,' said Dundas. 'You two,' his focus shifted to Drabble and Kate, 'eat up.' He put his hand over his wife's, 'Dear, come with me.'

As the Dundases left the kitchen and entered the parlour they heard another tug on the doorbell.

Drabble and Kate looked at each other. He squeezed her hand reassuringly.

In the parlour Dundas and his wife moved cautiously towards the door, craning their heads to see through the small window.

'Look,' said Dundas, his voice rising. 'It's Constable George.'

He hurried to the door and pulled it open. A uniformed officer and a second man in a damp belted mackintosh and hat stood at the door. The constable and Dundas exchanged a nod.

'Mr Dundas?' asked the detective, politely tapping the brim of his grey trilby. He and the householder exchanged nods. 'Madam. Inspector Kennedy out of Plymouth. We're looking for a man from up country, a suspected murderer – his name is Drabble. He's a dangerous man.'

Dundas and his wife looked at one another and then back at the policeman. Dundas glanced over at the uniformed constable.

'Don't suppose you've seen any suspicious characters?' asked the constable. Dundas reviewed him for a moment and then turned back to the inspector.

'Can you describe this fellow, Drabble?' asked Dundas.

The detective referred to his notebook.

'He's about six foot, sir, dark hair, well spoken, dressed in a country suit of green tweed, we think, sir. He caught the sleeper down from London last night and was dropped first thing this morning at Dr Wilkinson's in Stoke Climsland by the dog cart from Plymouth, sir. I'm afraid to say that there are signs of a struggle at Dr Wilkinson's, sir.' Kennedy folded away his notebook, 'And Dr Wilkinson has been killed.'

Mrs Dundas nodded grimly and looked up at her husband. He gave an infinitesimal shake of the head. She looked backwards into the interior of the house, her hand going to her quivering mouth.

The detective pulled a revolver from the pocket of his overcoat.

'Where is he?' he growled.

Mrs Dundas clasped up her mouth.

The detective pushed past, followed by the constable. They bundled into the kitchen.

'Hold it,' said Kennedy, raising his pistol.

Drabble raised his hands; Kate, who was chewing, froze. She lifted her hands: one still held a triangle of buttered toast.

'Come here, you.'

Kate rose from the table, upsetting her chair and went over to stand behind the detective. The Dundases entered the room, and gathered at the range. Drabble's gaze dodged from the end of the barrel of the revolver to the frowning face of the detective, to Kate, who was looking at him searchingly. The Dundases stared on.

'What do you want with me?' he said, returning his attention to the detective.

'Ernest Drabble,' the policeman stepped towards him. 'I am arresting you on suspicion of the murder of Mr Thomas Woolley. Additionally, I'm arresting you on suspicion of the murder of Dr Hugh Wilkinson.'

'*Murder*?' he shouted. 'I didn't murder him. He was dead when I got there. And Woolley – that was self-defence!'

The detective's gaze did not waver from Drabble.

'Constable, the cuffs.'

The officer approached, the pair of handcuffs held out in front of him. Once he was in those, thought Drabble, that was going to be that. The detective took another step towards him. He was now just the other side of the table.

Drabble rose slowly from the form.

'Easy, Drabble,' said the detective, the revolver level. 'I'll shoot, I really will.'

'Kate!' cried Drabble. His eyes darted about the room. 'Dundas, fetch the shotgun. You know as well as I do that policemen aren't armed in this country. Look,' he declared, aware of the falsity of his statement but hoping his conviction could win the crowd, 'the man's clearly an imposter. This is a plot, I tell you!'

The faces around the room looked back at him blankly.

'Kate,' he appealed. 'Kate?'

She broke her gaze away and turned to Mrs Dundas, who offered her the sanctuary of her embrace. The older woman rubbed her shoulders and looked away, shaking her head in apparent shame.

'Come along, sir,' said the constable, with the open cuffs, coming at him. 'There's a good gentleman.'

Drabble gazed down at the half-eaten breakfast, his mouth crooked despondently.

'Very well,' he said in a low voice. His hands fell to the woodwork. 'I'll come quietly.'

The constable stepped forward.

Drabble launched the table into the air - plates, cutlery, sausages, and breakfast remnants hurtled over the policeman. A lone slab of black pudding struck Kennedy in the face. As it hit, so did Drabble, who threw himself at him, knocking the gun from the inspector's hand. It clattered to the floor and span away. Drabble dashed a blow across his face and tumbled past. Back on his feet, he dived between the scattering Dundases for the doorway and the parlour. He slammed his body back against the closing kitchen door and slid the bolt across. The handle rattled and he heard shouting. Drabble's gaze roved about the room: he saw the stairs, the furniture by the fire, the front door.

The detective and constable spilled into the courtyard, followed by Kate and the Dundases.

'There he goes,' shouted the constable. 'The bugger's on my bike!'

Drabble pumped the pedals, breathing hard. He looked

back and saw the uniformed policeman at the head of the figures running from the courtyard. He shot along the muddy drive and sped out into the road, passing a parked car on the verge. The road was still not much more than a stony track – grasses and dirty weeds protruded from its proud middle. His back wheel slid on the loose pebbles as he rounded the corner.

The bike built up speed. He glanced over his shoulder, seeing no pursuers. It would not be long before they caught up though, he thought. Could Kate be trusted to get the head to Churchill? He slowed up at the pedals. *Was she safe?* He braked and put his foot down, stopping the bike and looking back along the lane. One thing is certain, he thought, I'm no good to Kate or Churchill in a police cell.

He hunched over the handlebars and pedalled away. He saw a stile at the side of the road. Skidding to a halt next to it, he slung the bike into the field, and clambered over the stile after it. He mounted the bike and started to cross the ploughed field.

The wheels gathered soil quickly, and Drabble fought the pedals, pushing them hard. He continued but the wheels seized, the mud-guards clogged, and the bike went over. He cursed and inspected the tyres: a layer of clay running two or three inches thick jammed them solid. *Bugger.* He glanced back at the stile – there was no one there - and picked up the bike, lifting it to his shoulder. He broke into a jog and crossed the open ground, heading towards a tall oak. He was out of breath when he arrived and slumped down behind it, seating himself between two of its great roots. He picked up a stout stick and dug it into the clay that fouled the rear wheel. He pressed harder and the point of the stick entered but stuck rigid. He wiggled it and it snapped off in his hand. *Bugger*. He pushed the bicycle away with his foot and leaned back against the tree. He'd have to run for it. *But to where?* Looking out, he saw he was at the top of a low hill and at the end of the next field, where the land was lower, there was a row of trees and a gate. He heart was pumped hard. He laid back and got his breath back for a moment. He checked the stile and saw it was free of pursuers. His gaze returned to the bike's rear mud-guard. He frowned thoughtfully and pulled the muddy wheel slowly towards him. *There had to be a way to make it work.*

A bullet whistled past, taking a splinter from the trunk above his head. He flung himself flat to the ground and rolled onto his front. Looking back, he saw the detective and the policeman. A small cloud of smoke erupted from the end of the detective's pistol – Drabble ducked and heard another shot. Grit and grassy debris covered his face.

He surveyed the scene and his eyes narrowed. The bastards, he thought. What about the great British tradition of presumed innocence? The detective raised his revolver and another shot rang out. It whistled past. Drabble looked back, to where the open field tapered off out of sight. It was all open land. Another bullet flew by and he pressed himself to the ground. He turned to see the pursuers: they were closing…

He could now make out the inspector's face clearly; he was shouting and gesturing to the other officer. The constable jogged, one hand steadying his helmet, across the field to the far side. The detective was striding straight towards him, reloading his revolver. He had maybe a minute, thought Drabble. *But after that, I'm done for.* He saw the detective raise his pistol and take aim. There was a puff of white smoke. Drabble dropped down and the bullet struck the tree above, cracking twigs. Splinters and debris rained down on him.

He looked back at the mud-guard and his eye ran along its muddy semi-circle, pausing at where it met the frame of the bike. There was a narrow metal arm, joined to a collar, which wrapped around the principal upright. Drabble gritted his teeth and crawled back from the vantage point, snatching the bike towards him. He yanked the mud-guard, pulling it away from the tyre. The metalwork gave and it buckled. He wrenched it back further and then swivelled it back and forth on the fastening. It came adrift. He tossed it to one side and bent forward over the front wheel. The back mud-guard was off in a moment.

Bending low, he gripped the handlebars in front of him and sprinted, launching the bike down the hill. Without the mudguards the wheels turned freely. He jumped into the saddle and pedalled hard. He heard a shout – and then another - and hunkered down. A bullet whistled past his right ear. His heart pounded against his chest. His eyes fixed doggedly ahead: he saw a route in the muddy field and worked the pedals, urging the bike onwards, towards the distant row of trees and the gate.

There was a shot, and his left arm flicked. The bike swerved but his left hand relocated the grip and corrected the handlebars. He was breathing hard but kept his focus on the trees ahead. An intense heat spread through his arm and he looked over, seeing a small tear in the fabric and the green tweed starting to turn brown. He looked forward at the juddering trees ahead, gulping for air.

In a minute he was through the trees and beyond into a grassy field which fell away gently, revealing a wooded verge and a small stream. Standing on the pedals he charged down towards the water, gravity speeding him on. He shot through the trees, down the little bank into the brook and darted across, up the far side and into the next field. He looked back and saw the pursuers in the far distance.

Suddenly his left arm gave way and the bike went over.

'Arggh!'

He cried out as he collided with the ground, still straddling the bike; his left arm taking the weight. He rolled over and lay on his back, breathing hard, staring up at the white sky; his right hand wrapped tight around his left bicep.

'Sod,' he said, sucking the air in. 'Sod!'

The upper arm burned. He looked down and saw the stain spread across the whole of the sleeve above his elbow. He pressed harder on the wound, gritting his teeth. Blood oozed through his fingers.

'Oh, bugger!'

Drabble rolled onto his right side and, sitting up, raised himself onto his feet. He was panting. Still gripping his arm, he dashed towards the next line of trees across the open ground ahead. As he ran his feet splashed through deep puddles of muddy standing water.

He saw that beyond the row of trees there was a river – a much bigger affair than the one he had just passed. The penny dropped: it was the same river where not two hours before, he had fled in the opposite direction with the head - *and* Kate. He sprinted for it and dived feet first – scrambling sideways down the bank and sliding into chilling water. His heels connected with the loose gravel bed and he braced himself by grabbing hold of a low-hanging branch. He rested against the bank and shut his eyes, concentrating on ignoring the pain in his arm. His pulse raced and his head was spinning. For a moment he imagined his book-lined study in Sidney Sussex – his black gown and climbing rope hanging from the hook on the back of the door, the fire full of coal and his feet parked on the stained, sisal mat by the hearth. This business was madness, he thought. Where was it going to lead?

CHAPTER EIGHT

Drabble's eyelids parted slowly – and then, with a jerk, his head went up. He had fallen asleep. He swore and scanned the landscape behind and then ahead, where he saw another, similar, thin row of trees. He saw the black outline of a bird, a crow, fly from the nest silhouetted in the large elm at the centre, and swoop down and up and over to the next tree where it alighted on a branch at the top and cried out. He checked his watch: it was shortly after one p.m. He climbed back down and bent low, cupping some of the river water with his hands, and splashed his face. He wiped his eyes with his dripping fingers. His left arm throbbed. The tawny stain had seeped to below the elbow. He pulled apart the knot of his tie and looped it around his neck and about his left wrist, forming a sling. Clutching the tie beneath his right hand and his teeth, he pulled the knot tight.

Keeping low, he climbed up the bank and lying on his right side had a second look around. He could see no one – *not a soul*. He shook his head. Where were the lines of policemen and Wellington-clad volunteers with shooting sticks and baying dogs? Where were horsemen and rows of pitchfork-toting yokels? Surely if he really *were* a dangerous double killer, it seemed highly unsatisfactory for them to cease their search so abruptly as this, he thought. He was a dangerous man: he must be pursued to the ends of the Earth. He repositioned his sling to raise his left hand. No wonder criminals kept slipping through the fingers of the authorities...

He descended back into the stream. Pressing his left forearm to his chest, he proceeded along its shallow edge at a gentle jog, his shoes splashing against the flow. It couldn't be much more than a mile to Dr Wilkinson's, he thought, but the route that he would require - avoiding open ground - would be longer. He hurdled a tree trunk that lay across the stream. His front foot plunged into the water and slipped on the riverbed, sending him stumbling. He gasped and gripped his left arm tighter.

He drew to a halt and stared up at the white sky. Was he doing the right thing? At Wilkinson's there would be bandages and iodine for treating his wound, which would offer at least a temporary solution, he thought. There might even be the chance that Kate would be there – with the head. He contemplated this eventuality and moved on. Would he be able to convince her of his innocence? He looked down at his feet, surging through the silvery stream, and realised he could no longer feel the uneven ground beneath them: they were numb. He bit the corner of this lip. Another worrying possibility was that the police would still be at the house, too. He would have to keep his distance until they left.

In any event, Wilkinson's Alvis *ought* to be there. With the car he could drive to London - a much safer bet than being trapped on a train. He sighed. Rail travel no longer had quite the same appeal.

Drabble followed the next long bend in the river and saw the Austin. The water was slightly higher now - it was well above the running boards and trickled through the front grille. At the rear he paused to inspect the damage. The bodywork was flecked with splintered tears from the bullets and peppered with tiny holes like it had been eaten at by woodworm. Boothroyd, you've served us well, he thought.

Drabble moved on. After about ten minutes the banks widened and the incline eased and he reached the spot where they had driven the Austin down into the stream. He saw where the tyres had churned up the soft muddy margin and where they had tracked across the field.

He left the stream and entered the field, following the hedgerow at its edge. Away from the cover of trees he saw that the bright, clear morning skies had given way to a ceiling of low white cloud. He heard the distant rumble of a car approach – it grew louder – and then faded as the vehicle passed on the road on the far side of the hedge. He saw a dark shadow pass beyond the dense branches. Then he heard a second car, and another dark shape swept past.

He arrived at the break in the hedge, through which they had escaped earlier. He saw broken, snapped branches hanging limp and askew. He continued along the field.

After a few hundred yards his path was blocked by the hedge, which turned sharply to the right, while the road went off ahead. He followed round and crossed into the next field over the wooden stile. He halted for a moment and wiped the sweat from his brow. Ahead of him lay another large square grassy field, bordered by hedges. His chest was heaving and his feet were heavy. He saw the next stile – and glancing to the left, then right – trotted straight for it, increasing the distance between him and hedge on the left. He cut across the open ground.

At the next stile he rested on the wooden step and leaned against the timber struts, closing his eyes. He was exhausted and his arm ached savagely. He opened his eyes and saw in the distance, the tall thatched roof of Wilkinson's house protruding from the tree-line. It was no more than half an inch in height, and it was smudgy grey against the dark surroundings of the woods.

He looked out into the next field and then clambered over the stile. Ducking down, he marched along the hedge-line, the little copse that lay to the left of the house growing larger in his sight by the minute.

The sky was greyer now and he felt the air chill. He saw the bare branches of the trees bend in the copse. A fat holly tree swayed. The house was in darkness.

He reached a row of five mature horse chestnuts. Underfoot in the half-light, beneath the canopy of their dense branches, were the rotting husks of conkers. He knelt at the foot of one tree and reviewed the land ahead and the buildings. He saw the rear quarter of the barn, which served as the garage, and part of the back and side of the house beyond. There was the white-painted back door with its black handle and either side kitchen windows - dark and lifeless. Behind the house, the grassy parkland of the garden fell away, terminating in the dark prow of a hill.

To the left of the garage, he saw a large black shed, and next to that the copse with its substantial, swaying holly tree.

The wind ruffled his hair and chilled his face. He crouched and took a couple of deep breaths. He glanced left, then right, and dashed for the copse.

He charged, his heart pounding, closing on the copse. As he got in range he flung himself forward, diving into the cover of the trees and grasses. He landed hard and stifled a cry of pain. He lay still, his chest heaving, and counted to ten. With his teeth gritted, he crawled through the undergrowth, the dark outline of the buildings growing clearer through the branches above. A twig cracked: he froze. Nothing.

At the side of the building there was only one tall window in the eaves of the first floor that he could see from this angle. Just like those in the kitchen this was murky, oily and flat. He skirted around under the trees to the rear of the garage and ran along the back of it, until, peering round, he saw the front of the house and the drive. He saw a fox trot into the earthen lane. It paused in the middle, about a hundred yards away, and looked up the track, before nibbling at the ground. After a few seconds, the animal looked over at the house sharply and sprang back into the shrubbery.

The house looked deserted. It did not make sense, he thought. Surely the police would still be there? The pain in his arm was growing. He scanned the front again – the place was in darkness. There was nothing else for it.

Drabble crossed the gap to the house and continued along its rear until he reached the first set of windows. He looked in and saw the end of the kitchen – a broad pine table and a couple of wooden chairs. There was a tall dresser with shelves of enamel containers. He went on and stopped at the next pair of windows. Inside sofas were arranged around a high, broad fireplace with wooden mantel. Paintings decorated the walls, and over the closed door was a set of antlers. He stopped again at the next group of windows and peered in: he recognised the desk and filing cabinet, its drawers still yanked out and abandoned. Wilkinson's body was gone. Still imprinted in the flowerbed he saw his and Kate's footsteps from the escape. The window was shut.

He took off his shoe and beat the heel against the pane next to the fastening. The glass smashed and he cleared the shards from the lead frame with the shoe. He reached in and opened the window.

Drabble unhooked his arm from its makeshift sling, and took a deep breath as he hauled himself over the windowsill. He dropped down into the study and closed the window behind him. He slumped down to the floor, gripping his arms and breathing fast.

He saw that apart from the closed window, the room was as before: late leaves dotted the carpet and the debris of the attack still lay untouched on the floor. He removed his other shoe and, carrying them both, trod silently along the corridor and halted in the darkness. He heard no sound other than the wind buffeting the house.

He proceeded up the stairs to the galleried floor, where he found two principal corridors leading off at either side. He went left, checking each room in turn. Opening the third door, he saw a freestanding enamel bath and a washbasin, with a shelf of perfectly folded towels above the thick, gloss radiator. He eased the door shut behind him and set the shoes down. Next he slid his right arm free from his jacket and slowly pulled the fabric away from his left side. The dried blood had caked his coat to his shirt and arm beneath that. He winced as he drew the sleeve away. Fresh dark blood seeped, glistening into the torn and already stained cotton of his shirt. He unbuttoned it and peeled the shirt off, inch by inch. The cotton tugged at the wound and then broke free. This done he ran the cold tap and hunched over the washbasin, cupping handfuls of water onto his arm. He sucked his teeth and tensed, then put his hand under the gushing water once again. Tiny red rivers spread across the basin, each giving issue to new tributaries and branches. He rinsed the wound again – the sink went red once more - and then a fourth time, before reaching for a towel. He pressed it to the wound and sat on the edge of the bath, his eyes closed.

He counted to sixty and then lifted the bloodied towel away. At the back of his arm he saw the small hole where the bullet had entered. At the side of the front was a larger tear. He saw more blood peep up from the crack in the broken skin, lifting up the wound, and he pressed the towel onto it.

Drabble went to the cabinet. He scanned the contents and saw plasters and a couple of packs of bandages on the bottom shelf. He pulled out a narrow brown glass bottle of iodine and set it down. Next, he found a paper bag containing cotton wool. He laid the reddened towel on the sink and unscrewed the lid of the iodine. He took a deep breath and poured it liberally over the wound, front and back. His arm tensed as the cool fluid mingled into the wound and he saw the flesh part momentarily. He gritted his teeth and felt the iodine run down, leaving an orange streak and dripping to the floor from his fingers. He set the bottle on the corner of the basin, next to the towel, and tore open the cotton wool with his teeth. He packed a handful onto the wound and breathed out.

From the cabinet he removed a bandage. He put the brown packet to his mouth and ripped it open. He blew the paper pack to one side and started to unravel the delicate white gauze.

Behind him, he heard the door creak open.

He turned and his face, for a second, brightened.

'Kate!'

He frowned and raised his right hand, the bandage uncoiling and falling to the floor.

She lowered the shotgun.

'Oh, Ernest,' she cried.

CHAPTER NINE

Harris snatched up an early edition of the *Evening Standard* from the pile as he passed the front desk of the office, and emerged into Fleet Street. He shivered, and pulled his hat down and the lapels of his overcoat closer. Harris hailed a taxi and instructed the driver to take him to the Granville.

The driver performed a piecemeal U-turn, waiting for a tram to pass, and then they went up the hill towards Aldwych. Up ahead Harris saw a group of people leafleting outside the Pen and Wig. One held up a banner which proclaimed: 'Germany is our friend'. Harris grinned: the patrons of the Pen and Wig would give them the welcome they deserved, he thought.

As they passed, the driver pulled over closer to the pavement and slowed right down. He tooted the horn, and leaned over to the passenger side window.

'Stupid sods,' he shouted, before driving away. Harris looked out and saw a row of angry faces and raised fists, but the cries were drowned out by the sound of the engine. The driver looked over, 'Apologies, sir. I lost a leg at Passchendaele.'

Harris raised his hand, 'Feel free to abuse the pedestrians, driver. In the case of the British Union of Fascists I'd say you pretty well took the words right out of my mouth.'

'Very good, sir.'

'Which leg was it?'

The driver gave him a look. 'The right one, sir.'

'But you can still drive all right?'

'Nothing wrong with my driving,' said the cabbie. 'They gave me a new leg.'

'I'm relieved to hear it.'

The taxi stopped at the traffic lights at Aldwych. Harris saw a journalist he knew emerge from the offices of the *News Chronicle* over the road. Outside on the pavement was a newsagent's stand, coated in racks upon racks of folded newspapers. Harris scanned the billboards. One of them read: 'Fog in Channel, Continent cut off'. He smiled and removed a cigarette from his silver case. He lit it and rolled down the window, blowing out some smoke. He noticed a smear of black ink on his hand. Blimey, he thought, his newspaper really *was* fresh from the presses. Harris unfolded it carefully and glanced at the front page. He inhaled sharply:

CONSTITUTIONAL CRISIS: 'MAJOR STATEMENT' - BALDWIN

THE PRIME Minister, Mr Stanley Baldwin, is this evening expected to make an emergency statement to the Commons on the Constitutional Crisis.

Mr Baldwin will update Members of Parliament on the latest developments in the affair - and disclose that plans are being laid for a special Constitutional Summit to be convened tomorrow night at Fort Belvedere, His Majesty's Windsor Residence. The meeting will be attended by senior members of the Cabinet, Opposition and the Archbishop of Canterbury, Dr Cosmo Lang.

Harris took a heavy drag on his cigarette. Ruddy hell, he thought. The Archbishop of Canterbury? That was serious. He frowned and read on:

Overnight it emerged that the Prime Minister of Canada has spoken to His Majesty on the telephone at Buckingham Palace from Ottawa and communicated the concerns of the Canadian people at the prospect of a morganatic union with Mrs Wallis Simpson in the strongest possible terms...

Harris stopped reading and his eye drifted down the page. A second headline caught his attention:

'BOUNCING DON' NAMED IN MURDER HUNT

Harris' eyes bulged. Dear God, he thought.

THE DEVON County Constabulary this morning named the man they are seeking in relation to the death of Lloyd's insurance broker, Mr Thomas Woolley, of Blackheath, south east London.
The wanted man was identified as Professor Ernest Drabble of Cambridge University. Prof. Drabble, 30, is a well-known mountaineer and survived a dramatic 128-feet fall this summer during an attempt on the north face of the Eiger in Switzerland. His climbing team-mate Hubertus Reichman was killed in the ascent.
Police said officers came close to apprehending Prof Drabble this morning
at a farm in Stoke Climsland, near Plymouth in Cornwall.

Mr Woolley's body was discovered this morning by a farmer shortly after six o'clock. The Home Office pathologist was alerted and the Devizes coroner opened and adjourned an inquest into the death this morning.

In a separate development from the south-west of England, the Cornwall County Constabulary announced that the body of Dr Hugh Wilkinson, of Stoke Climsland, had been discovered at his home amid signs of a robbery.

Great Scott, thought Harris. His face went pale and for a moment he sat motionless. He reviewed the headline – *'Bouncing Don' named in murder hunt*. Murder? He gazed from the window, a dew drop glistening on his eyes, and mouthed the word, *MURDER*. Ernest really *was* up to his neck in it.

The taxi pulled over and stopped outside the Granville, where Harris alighted. He paid and passed an extra sixpence back through the open window.

'God bless you sir,' said the driver.

The squeak of the revolving doors announced his arrival in the club, a presence acknowledged by the porter, who touched the peak of his cap. Harris proceeded through the lobby and passed the telephone booths, the alcove leading to the Ladies' Room, and trotted down the stairs to the Long Bar. Unsurprisingly, he thought, given the time of day, the room was empty save for Le Goff, who was tending to his bottles, and the plethora of painted figures above. The room smelt strongly of stale tobacco. He saw another man in a buff shop-coat polishing the mirrors with a pleasing thoroughness. Harris continued through the bar and went out of the leather-inlaid door at the far end.

Entering the windowless billiard room, he was struck by the expanse of darkness. There were perhaps a dozen full-sized snooker tables stretching, one after the other, into the distance. The only illumination came from the rows of lamps suspended directly above each table. They shone an intense, bitter light down on the green baize below, giving it a grainy quality, like an over-exposed photograph. The rest of the room was plunged in blackness, a darkness so complete that it was impossible to tell how far away the ceiling really was.

Harris saw Sir Carmen Kelly, the moustachioed Conservative Member of Parliament for Rochester in Kent, standing in his shirtsleeves and waistcoat bent over a table at the far end, snooker cue primed to take a shot. He struck the white and the ball sank into a mixed pack, emitting a decisive crack as the arrangement of the snooker balls disintegrated. There followed the satisfactory noise of netting – once, then twice.

Kelly looked over.

'Ah,' he barked, laying down the cue, 'Harris.'

Harris knew little of Kelly, except that he was positively *rabid* on the Empire and virtually unprintable on the subject of Mr Gandhi. Mind you, there was nothing all that unusual about that. He noted that Sir Carmen was dressed in a Tory's uniform of navy blue pinstripe - appropriately enough, he thought - and he stretched out his hand to meet the approaching MP.

'Good to see you,' bellowed Kelly, not sounding convinced. 'Pleased you could come at such short notice.'

They shook hands.

'Coffee?' Kelly gestured towards a pair of wing-back armchairs. There was a small table laid with a silver coffee pot and accoutrements. 'Or would you prefer brandy? I quite like a little lift at this time of day.'

'Brandy, please.'

Harris sat down as Kelly poured him a glass, passed it, and then poured another for himself.

Harris noticed that Kelly's teeth were perfectly straight; in fact, he felt, they were *too* straight. He grinned to himself and remembered his brandy.

'That's good stuff,' he said.

'Yes,' said Kelly, he raised his glass. 'It is, isn't it. Cheers.'

'Cheers.'

Kelly sipped his brandy and then placed the glass on the low table in front of him. His fingers lingered on the stem.

'Lady Valerie tells me you're a great admirer of Oliver Cromwell,' said Harris.

'Quite so.' He smiled. 'Rather late in life, I've developed an enormous passion for all matters related to the Lord Protector.'

'She also mentioned that you would be interested in meeting my friend – Professor Drabble of Sidney Sussex, Cambridge?'

Kelly nodded and absent-mindedly picked at one of his fingernails.

'Yes, *yes*, that's right - there're a couple of things I'd very much like to ask him.' He fixed Harris with his cold stare. 'I don't suppose you happen to know where he is?'

'What?' Harris broke into a chuckle, 'Right now?'

Kelly gave a smile. 'Well, there's no time like the present, I always say.'

Harris stroked his lip.

'If you don't mind me asking but what, Sir Carmen, is the great hurry?' He took a drink from his glass.

Kelly turned in his chair to face him and folded his arms. His expression was grave.

'If you must know, Professor Drabble has something that belongs to me.'

Harris leaned forward.

'Ernest? Surely you're mistaken? Ernest is a -'

'No, *Mr* Harris,' a look Harris could not quite fathom swept across Kelly's face, 'I am *not* mistaken.' Kelly's cool grey eyes stared at him, unblinking. 'He has something of mine and I trust that you will help me to recover it.' With his eyes still fixed on Harris, Kelly reached down and collected his brandy glass. He tipped the vessel to his lips and emptied it, setting it back down on the wooden table.

Harris looked over and hastily raised his glass to his mouth.

'So Mr Harris, while I feel sure that your friend has this item on an entirely unimpeachable basis - that is, sir, I impute no criminality on his part, I shall leave that to the appropriate authorities - I wish merely to recover my property as soon as possible.' He brought his stare upon him once again. 'So, I repeat my previous question, have you heard from Professor Drabble?'

Harris gave an uncomfortable smile. Drabble really was in a genuine spot of bother, wasn't he? And now I might be, too. Harris looked over; Kelly was not an exceptionally large man – perhaps six foot, though stoutish, but there was something about him, Harris thought. He's the sort of man who has a psychopathic streak and is not afraid to use it.

'Mr Harris,' said Kelly, topping up his own glass, and proffering the decanter. 'I'm waiting. Please, I ask you once again, where *is* your good friend Professor Drabble?'

Harris shook his head, declining the top-up, and then met Kelly's grey eyes.

'I'm afraid, Sir Carmen, I could not say.'

Kelly's eyes widened.

'*Could not say...*'

'No, I-I don't want to.'

'You don't want to?' He shook his head and gazed up at the ceiling. 'I'm afraid, Mr Harris, you *will*.'

'No I won't,' said Harris. 'I won't - and anyway, I can't. I really have no idea where Ernest is. He could be in Timbuktu, Tipperary, or anywhere else beginning with T for all I know. But furthermore, sir,' he stood the glass on the table and rose from the chair, 'I don't care very much for your impertinent tone or the line of your inquiry. Furthermore, I feel it is my duty to point out to you, *sir*, that if I *did* know of Professor Drabble's whereabouts, I would still not tell you. Indeed, I suggest that if it is true that Professor Drabble has genuinely misappropriated an item of your property then you refer your enquiries to Scotland Yard.' He fastened the top button of his jacket and raised his jaw petulantly. 'You'll find that despite popular opinion, they're rather good at relocating lost property. Good day to you.'

From behind a pair of great hands seized Harris'

112

shoulders. He flew backwards, his arms windmilling, and thumped to the floor, the air knocked from him. The powerful hands now dragged him to his feet. Kelly was up too, his eyes glinting and a snooker cue swishing in his hand. Harris' eyes darted about the room – there was no one, not a soul at any of the dozen tables, and no one at the narrow bar either. He wrestled at the unseen assailant behind, but the man's grip was firm. Kelly approached, cue raised up. My God, Harris thought, this man's for real.

'You won't get away with this, Carmen, you *swine*,' he cried. 'I've got friends in high places.' He looked towards the door, lost in darkness. 'Help! HELP!'

The fat end of the cue swept through the air towards him and slammed into his belly. Harris buckled forward, retching. The unseen man behind drew him up by his hair and as Harris stood, crushed his knee into his back. Harris cried out. The cue struck again.

'Tell me now,' hissed Kelly, through clamped, perfect teeth. 'Where is Professor Drabble? Has he communicated with you?'

Harris, bent double, shook his head.

Kelly motioned with his hand and Harris was hauled upright once more. The MP raised the cue back, as though he was about to take the strike in baseball or rounders. Harris blinked. My good Lord, he thought, he's going to bally well kill me. He really is. Harris saw Kelly's thin lips form a hideous smirk. Oh, no, thought Harris. *Oh no*. He cried out. The cue struck his sternum, causing his insides to explode. Harris' legs gave way and he hit the floor, gulping for air like a landed fish.

113

He was pulled back to his feet. Kelly raised the cue once again; he smiled.

'Come on, Mr Harris. I'm all for knocking the fourth estate but this is too much.'

Harris gasped for air, unable to draw breath. The figure behind held him upright. Harris' head lolled forward, his eyes closed.

'I don't know where he is,' he croaked. 'Except in Cornwall, or Devonshire, *Devonshire* - and if you read the papers you must know that as well as I do. For God's sake man!'

Kelly stood close and inspected him. He lifted Harris head up and pressed the fat end of the cue against his chin.

'Has he made contact with you since boarding the train at Paddington?'

'No,' wailed Harris.

'Look at me.'

Harris' eyelids opened. He saw the pale grey eyes staring into his.

The cue tapped again on his chin – where it rested.

'You'd better not be lying to me, Mr Harris, or I won't give you the opportunity to regret it.'

'I don't know,' gasped Harris, shaking his head, 'I don't know.'

Kelly lowered the cue and turned away.

'Very good,' he said, waving his hand in the air above him. 'I believe you.'

Kelly moved over towards the stand and put the cue away in the rack. The hands released him and Harris fell to the floor, sobbing. He shook his head. You bastard, he thought. *You ruddy bastard.* Harris looked up, a scowl across his red, stained face.

'Believe all you like,' he said. 'But I wouldn't ruddy well tell you anyway, you bastard.' He coughed, saliva drooled from his mouth. 'You *fucking* bastard.'

For a moment Kelly froze. Harris saw the hand return to the cue-stand and select the same implement as before. Kelly turned to face him. Harris swallowed.

'Young man,' said Kelly, 'you are a dreadful fool.' Kelly flicked up his chin and Harris was pulled to his feet. Kelly stepped towards him, the thick end of the cue once again circling in the air.

'Isn't it amazing,' announced Kelly, 'that Mr Harris here has not yet learned the true value of keeping his counsel? Well, Mr Harris, you're about to learn once again that I never, *ever* pull my punches.' With his grip on the narrowest part of the cue, he raised it back and high, as though he were about to strike a golf ball – a very long way.

Harris saw the cue swing down and cried out. He collapsed, his hands pressed to his groin, sobbing. Kelly lifted the cue to his eye and inspected it for a moment. He nodded and slotted it back into the stand.

'Arkwright,' he barked. He pulled on his coat and adjusted his waistcoat. 'Please give Mr Harris a lift home.' The man began to heave Harris up.

'And one more thing Harris,' Kelly shoved the cue ball across the table. 'If your friend makes contact with you – I expect to be the first to know.'

CHAPTER TEN

Kate's hand went to her mouth.

'Ernest!'

She pushed the shotgun against the corner and flung her arms around him. He tensed and she pulled away.

'What is it?' she said, looking up at him. She gasped and she covered her mouth, 'You're hurt.'

She took hold of his arm and pulled back the cotton wool pack. He winced.

'Is it a bullet wound?'

He nodded.

'Ernest,' she laid her hand on his cheek and gazed up at him for a moment. 'Here,' she gently steered him over to the bath and sat him down. She bent forward and inspected the wound. 'It's your lucky day,' she pronounced. 'Looks like the bullet went clean through. Would have been a different story if it had stayed put.'

'Or if it had shattered the bone,' he added. He saw her focus move from the bottle of iodine to the bottom shelf of the cabinet and then to the blood-stained towel. She picked up the bandage from the floor.

'Let me do this,' she said, pushing back the sleeves of her scarlet jumper, revealing her slender forearms.

'Are you Dr Wilkinson's nurse as well?'

'Not exactly.' She looked up and smiled and then returned her attention to the wound. 'I *was* technically only his secretary, but Dr Wilkinson *was* a general practitioner – and this is a farming community, so...' her lips pursed for a moment, 'the role was somewhat more expansive than secretarial college let on.' She rolled the bandage around his arm, keeping it taut and partly overlapping the neat layers of gauze until she had covered the whole area. Holding the dressing in place, she reached over to the cabinet and took out a pair of scissors. 'He once amputated the arm of next door's gamekeeper – on the kitchen table of all places. Mrs Jones never forgave him.' She trimmed the excess bandage and then divided the end of the gauze with a snip. Drabble felt her warm breath against his skin. From this angle, with her face inclined towards his arm, her nose was foreshortened and her long eyelashes were brief, flawless semi-circles. She ripped the bandage to where it met the arm, wrapped it around, and tied a knot, finishing it with a bow.

'Proper job,' he said. 'Thank you.'

'I'll fetch your bag.'

'You've got it?'

'Of course,' she paused at the open door, jumper pressing against the frame, and arched an eyebrow, 'otherwise I would have shot you on sight. You're a double murderer, don't you know?'

'Oh yes, how could I forget?' He flexed his left arm back and forth. 'I'm just delighted that you believe in me.'

She sighed.

'Ernest, killers *don't* pack pyjamas; nor do they inscribe books they've written to their intended victims.'

Kate left and closed the door behind her. He chuckled. *Killers don't pack pyjamas*. Drabble went to the basin and washed his face. He dried himself off and looked into the mirror. There were dark patches beneath his eyes and he had picked up a deep red scratch on his forehead. He tipped some of the iodine onto a lump of cotton wool and pressed it to the cut. He sucked his teeth again. The door creaked open.

'Here,' continued Kate, 'I've brought you a shirt.' She was unbuttoning it. 'Would you like a bath? There's plenty of hot -'

'Kate.'

'What?'

'What are you doing here?'

She looked up from the shirt and frowned; her mouth held open.

'What do you mean? This is my home!'

'But it's not safe. I mean, look what happened this morning.'

'Oh, they won't come back.'

'How can you be so confident?'

She arranged the shirt on the back of the wicker chair by the end of the bath and stroked back her blonde hair from her face. For a moment she inspected the brown carpet at his feet, a tooth visible at the side of her bottom lip. Her eyes travelled up to his face.

'When we came back here,' she said, her voice low, 'I found your bag – I hid it and showed the police the open second safe behind the filing cabinet. I then told them that you must have come back here already after running off - and stolen the head.'

'*You did what*?'

'I'm sorry, but I knew that otherwise, they – whoever *they* are, the fascist people - they'd come back here looking for it again. I thought it was the best thing to do.

You'd given everyone the slip, anyway, so it seemed all right by you – and they were after you anyway, so frankly,' she raised her eyebrows, 'it didn't seem like it would get you into any *more* trouble than you're already in. I didn't know you were going to blimming well come straight back here.' She perched on the side of the bath. 'At least then I knew I'd be able to drive it to London myself - in safety.' She lifted her shoulders and then dropped them. 'I appreciate that it doesn't help your current situation much, but I reckoned it'd all come out in the wash.'

For a moment he stood there, blinking, looking at her. She was staring down at the white gloss-painted skirting board, her full lips parted, just fractionally. His gaze travelled across the floor, to her boots, up the shins, and to the spare tweed plus-fours, where it confronted the figure-hugging red pullover at her slim waist. His eyes then alighted on the shoulder and moved along to the hand that was pressed against the white enamel of the bath. He knelt down beside her and caressed her cheek. She turned to him and offered him a flat smile.

'I've another confession to make,' she said, looking down at her hands. 'I actually read about you in the *Western Morning News* in the summer, when you fell off that mountain.'

'You did?'

She nodded and met his eyes. 'And I saw your photograph. I just didn't recognise you this morning without the beard. Well, not until we were in the car.'

'I only had the beard for the climb.'

She brushed his chin with her fingers and stood up.

'Good.'

***

Harris stirred. It was dark, but he saw the tassels on the standard lamp and the sofa opposite and knew he was in his rooms at the Albany, his address off Piccadilly. He groaned and raised his hand to his forehead: there was a large, hard, egg-shaped lump. Next he felt his chest: he gasped. He half slid, half pulled himself backwards onto the sofa and sat more upright. Blimey, he thought, I ache all over. Those thuggish bastards.

He looked down at his groin, his eyebrows raised. With a groan, he eased his thighs apart and put his hand to his zipper.

'Oooh-*ah-ah.*'

He snatched back his hand, his wide eyes fixed on the front of his trousers. He looked to the window, where some light came in from the courtyard and saw the telephone. There were tears in his eyes. He could call his mother, he thought. *No, that would never do.* He rested his head against the cushions, gasping with pain. He could call his mother's butler, he thought. No, that wouldn't do either – he would, on balance, probably tell her. And then there'd be no end of fussing. He shook his head, leaned back against the sofa and shut his eyes.

'Oh my God,' he wailed, tears tracking down his cheeks. 'Dear Lord, what the ruddy hell have they done? I'm going to be impotent!' He looked down at the fold in the groin of his trousers. 'The bastards.' His teeth chattered uncontrollably. 'THE BASTARDS!'

He shut his eyes and sobbed, 'What am I going to do? Help!'

He raised a hand to his face – a fresh rush of tears spilling from his eyes. 'Oh Lord God, heavens above,' he whimpered. 'I should have had children.'

He sat back blinking tears away, staring into the darkness. He reached into his trouser pocket and tugged out his handkerchief. He wiped his face.

'Get a grip, Harris,' he said, pushing himself up and standing. 'Get a ruddy grip.'

He straightened himself and staggered over to the wall, where he flicked on the light. The room was neat and tidy – just as it should be, he thought. Nothing was missing. Several weeks' newspapers were piled up in heaps on the statuesque marble and gold coffee table. He saw his reflection in the mirror opposite: his cheeks were flushed from the tears but apart from that – and the egg-like lump on his forehead - he looked completely normal. He smiled at the looking glass and wiped the loose strands of his never-quite-blond hair back from his face. Beyond the swelling he noticed the widow's peak on his forehead was more pronounced than normal – and passing his fingers through the hairline at his temples wasn't much better. Cripes, he thought, at this rate I'm going to be bald soon, too.

He lowered himself into the leather armchair and, leaning forward, awkwardly withdrew the glass stopper from the decanter, which stood on the side table. He set it down and brought the decanter to his mouth. He held it, pouring, for several seconds, before lowering the vessel.

God, that was good. Scotch *was* the only solution to a

situation like this. He heard the glass stopper roll on the woodwork and then fall to the floor. It did not smash. What manner of man crunches another fellow's orb and sceptre, he thought? Not a gentleman, that was for certain. He shook his head grimly and brought the decanter back to his lips. The last time someone had done that to him, or at least something similar, was when he was outside the tuck shop at school. *Fullerton, that's right*. And a big chap, too, he was. Harris sighed. No one went to *his* funeral when he got chopped in the desert by tribesmen.

He shifted uneasily in the chair.

He couldn't see his GP about this; oh no. Dr Newman – unsympathetic cove - was suspicious enough already, what with Harris' so-called 'heavy' drinking and those other treatments he needed after that business in The Hague. Harris shuddered at the recollection. Given half the chance, Newman would probably report him to the magistrate for being a homosexual or some sort of moral deviant. He sighed and then began to chuckle. This was the beating that dare not speak its name.

His bruises were hurting. He had another stab at the whisky. Golly, he thought, Scotch really was capital fluid. He stretched down and located the stopper with his fingertips. He slotted it in the decanter and set the lot back down next to the glasses on the silver tray.

He heaved himself out of the chair and inspected himself in the mirror. He looked all right, he supposed. Yes, he really did. Harris straightened his tie, tightened the knot and corrected his collar. He pressed several wayward strands of hair flat. There, he thought. Much more like normal.

He took out the flower, which had snapped above the stem and hung forlornly from his lapel and tossed it onto the coffee table. So where *was* Ernest? What had become of him? Harris shook his head; actually, if he knew Ernest, he would be safely tucked up in a warm railway compartment, having had a sensational high tea, and be about twenty miles from Paddington. He peered at the clock. Look at that, no wonder it was dark, he thought, it was coming up for five. Ernest might even be back by now. For a moment Harris recalled the smirk on Carmen Kelly's face, the split second before he walloped him with the snooker cue. *The bastard.* Harris scowled and went over to the telephone. He lifted the heavy black receiver and started dialling. He stopped and put the handset back down.

The editor would never believe me, he thought. And if he did, he wouldn't dare print it. Gutless cove. He picked up the receiver and dialled. The line rang twice before being answered.

'Houses of Parliament,' said the voice at the other end of the line.

'David Howse's office, please.'

He was put through and the line went quiet.

'Hello?'

'Grubby?' he asked. 'It's me, Harris.'

'Hello, old man. Ah, thanks for the drink the other soir. How the dickens are you?'

'Not bad, can't complain - listen. I wondered, are you free for a drink in a bit at the club?'

There was a momentary pause.

'Does a dead Frenchman reek of garlic?'

123

'Jolly good,' said Harris, offering a pleased snigger. 'Shall we say sevenish?'

'Spot on - see you there. Anything up?'

'Oh, no, just something I'd like to run past you.'

They said their goodbyes.

Harris replaced the handset, smiled, and then lifted it again. He dialled. It rang. He waited, and peered at the ceiling, exhaling audibly. Eventually, he heard the receiver being mishandled.

'Yep. *Express.*'

'It's Harris. Any news?'

'What ho, Harris,' said the speaker brightly, 'about bloody time, the chief's been asking after you all afternoon.'

'I thought he would. How are we set for the morning?'

'Fine, fine,' he pictured Sebastian inspecting the copy before him on the desk, 'two juicy engagements, nice snap of Wallis Simpson and a good little yarn about the Prime Minister of New Zealand.' Sebastian broke into a giggle, 'he was spotted at Simpson's last night loading mint sauce onto his sirloin.'

'Goodness,' said Harris, chuckling. 'Colonials!'

'I know,' said Sebastian, adding a sigh. 'Ridiculous.'

'Well,' remarked Harris, 'well done, sounds like you've got things under control. I had a bit of a heavy working luncheon, so probably won't make it in, all right? But I'll be at the club if anything urgent crops up. You can always get me on the telephone – just ask for the Long Bar.'

He put the handset down and stared once again into the looking glass. I'm buggered if I'm going to let that sadistic cur get away with this, he thought. He did up his jacket button and headed to the door.

Out on Piccadilly, he hailed an approaching taxi from the far side of the street. The car performed a rapid U-turn and squeaked to a halt in front of him. He bent his head to the window.

'The Granville, please.'

CHAPTER ELEVEN

The Long Bar was dotted with a smattering of patrons, mostly seated in the armchairs in pairs and engaged in discreet chatter. Harris stopped at the counter and ordered a large Scotch and soda before taking up one of the seats he liked in the corner. From there you see everyone come in through the door. He had another cigarette and browsed the last edition of the *Evening News*.

'What ho, Harris old man.'

He looked up and smiled.

'What ho, Grubby!' He pushed the newspaper behind him and stood up, extending his hand.

Grubby plonked himself down on the seat next to him and beamed. He wore a lounge suit garnished with a lemon yellow handkerchief in his breast pocket. This coordinated with his tie and socks.

'Bloody hell,' said Grubby, staring at him. 'What the deuce happened to you?'

'Oh? This?' Harris' hand went to the lump on his forehead. 'I had a bit of a binge last night and missed the step at the top of the gents at the Grosvenor House.'

'Oh, bugger – sorry to hear. That's a long way down.' Grubby smiled at him. 'Well, I'm pleased to report that I've had a bloody *great* day today, sold three – THREE - Spirits to the Grand Fakir of Togo.'

'Oh really, Grubby, I didn't know they had Grand Fakirs in Togo. I thought they were in India.'

Grubby shrugged. 'Oh, Lord knows! All I care about is

whether they come up with the loot.'

'How is the Rolls' business these days?'

'Clipping along,' said Grubby. 'Lots of foreigners of course, but I've noticed some movement among the dukes, so there's life in the old dog yet.'

'Rather. Drink? Whisky?'

He nodded and Harris waved to the barman; giving his glass a tap and pointing to Grubby and himself.

'How's everything in the House?'

'Fine, fine, you'll know we've this big announcement due tonight.'

'Yes, I was just reading about that as a matter of fact.'

'Thought you'd probably got wind of it. I fear Baldwin's boxed him into a corner all right. He's got the Dominions onside.'

Harris agreed.

Grubby continued. 'Frankly, as far as I'm concerned the Canadians can jolly well rot. Who cares what some salmon-munching former convicts in the Arctic tundra of Saskatchewan think – most of my constituents haven't even heard of Saskatchewan.'

'Let alone spell it,' added Harris, grinning. He rubbed his chin. 'Actually, I don't think I can.'

'Precisely,' said Grubby wearily. 'It's got "atlas" written all over it.'

The barman set a tray with the drinks down. There was a brief pause as they raised their glasses.

Grubby continued, 'I'm sick to death of this Simpson business. Met her the other night actually – perfectly acceptable creature. Obviously bonkers – and a complete nymphomaniac – but then who cares? So many of them *are*, frankly, and if it's what the top man needs to get him through the day, let him marry the woman, I say.'

Harris watched the bubbles from the soda separate and float away from the clutch of cubes of ice in his glass.

'Baldwin's a cretin of the highest order,' added Grubby, shaking his head. 'We all know where it's going. Tomorrow night he's going to throw the gauntlet down and threaten to resign, unless of course the King drops her.'

'Will the King do that?'

'Will he hell. And why the buggeration should he? He's the bloody King. He should jolly well call Baldwin's bluff and let him resign. That'll show him who's boss.'

Harris was surprised.

'Really? What happens then?'

Grubby sighed. 'In the normal course of events, the King would then ask the leader of the Opposition to form a government. Alas, in his great wisdom, I gather Clement Attlee has decided to side with Baldwin.'

'What? Clem'll refuse to be PM?'

'Correct.' Grubby took a sip from his drink.

'Looks like the King's in a bit of a bind, then?'

'It might do,' said Grubby, looking over to the next table, where two newcomers were arranging themselves. 'But you never know. Anyway, Attlee might have a change of heart – you know, once he sniffs power and all that.'

'He wouldn't be the first.'

'Correct,' added Grubby.

'But Grubs, aren't you, er, a Tory? Surely you'd have to support Baldwin, if it came to it?'

Grubby smiled.

'This is all strictly off the record, isn't it?'

Harris cleared his throat and nodded.

'Of course, old man.'

Grubby edged over.

'There are many of us on the government benches who are not,' he coughed into his hand and dropped his voice, '*particularly* sympathetic to Baldwin's position on this. We think he's out of step with popular opinion – and with a significant proportion of the party for that matter.' He nodded, 'I think I've made my views plain enough.'

'I'll say.' Harris produced his cigarette case, clicked it open, and offered it across. Grubby took one and leaned in to Harris' lighter. Harris added, almost thinking out loud. 'But the King can't really do that can he? Baldwin's the elected prime minister.'

'Really?' Grubby arched an eyebrow and blew smoke contemptuously from the corner of his mouth, 'Elected by whom? I didn't vote for him. Did you?'

'Well... now you're just being pedantic.'

'No,' Grubby's voice died off again, 'in my opinion, the King can do as he likes – within reason – and if it comes down to it, *if I'm ask to vote on the matter,* I know who'll I'll be supporting. Plus, it'll mean we can at least get rid of that useless old sod Baldwin.'

Harris sighed.

'But what happens if Attlee stands firm and he refuses the King as well?'

Grubby took a drag of his cigarette and leaned in closer.

'If that happens, we'll be entering uncharted territory.'

'Uncharted territory!' Harris lowered his voice, 'I'll say.' His eyes narrowed, 'What precisely are you suggesting? Another leader? But who? There *isn't* anyone. It couldn't be done.'

For a moment Grubby held Harris' gaze.

'Couldn't it?'

There was a pause.

'Do you mean a minority government? It's not democratic.'

Grubby put his glass down.

'Oh yes? And what good, precisely, has *democracy* done for us?' He shook his head and scowled. 'Strike after strike, the Americans biting at our heels, being damned soft on the Soviet Union – the Subcontinent up in arms. The City of London being run to ruin by Jewish financiers who are selling the Old Country down the river? No, no, I don't see how so-called rule by the people has helped. *Damn the people*, I say.' His hand formed a fist. 'We've become soft. We need a new path – and this might just be our chance to get back on track.'

Harris gazed down at his drink. Good Lord, he thought. Keep staring at the glass. The ruddy man's unhinged.

He finally looked back up at Grubby. The man was grinning.

'And if it happens,' said Grubby, 'we'll need good trustworthy Englishmen like you in charge of the popular press.'

Harris gave an uncomfortable chuckle and picked up his drink.

'I'm not sure I follow you precisely, old man?'

Grubby raised his eyebrows and placed the cigarette on the silver ashtray. Harris tipped his drink to his mouth, feeling the ice fall against his lips.

The concierge came over.

'Mr Harris?'

'Yes?' he wiped his mouth with the back of his hand.

'There's the telephone for you, sir.'

Harris excused himself and rose from his chair. The club attendant led him back through the bar, along a passageway and to a small corner, where there was a gilt armchair, parked by a marble-topped occasional table stationed with an upright telephone. The concierge moved away and Harris bent forward to the mouthpiece and set the handset to his ear.

'Hello?'

'Harris, it's me,' said Drabble.

'Ernest?' He glanced over his shoulder. 'How *are* you?'

'Very well, old man, but look, I'm in a bit of a pickle.'

'I'll say, you know you're all over the papers?'

'What?'

Harris looked back down the corridor.

'You're wanted for murder, old man. *Murder*. And that's not the half of it. I'm afraid that other people, *prominent people*, have also been asking after you. What the devil's going on?'

He snatched another glance over his shoulder.

'I wish I knew, old man,' said Drabble, 'I've told you: some bloke tried to do me in on the sleeper and when I got to Cornwall, Wilkinson was dead. For whatever reason, it appears that someone is trying to get their hands on the head of Oliver Cromwell.'

Harris looked back.

'Ernest, I know who it is,' he said in a whisper. 'It's a Tory MP. His name's Sir Carmen Kelly. He bloody well beat me up today. But he's after *you*. Was going on about you stealing something from him.'

'Stealing?' said Drabble. 'Stealing what? *The head*? Are you serious? Who is he? Is he a fascist by any chance?'

'A fascist?' Harris rolled his eyes and gave a chuckle. 'That's probably not quite doing him justice – *worse*, I'd say. *Officially* he's a good old Conservative-Unionist but I wouldn't be surprised if he had irons in other fires. But look, what are you going to do?'

'I've got to contact Winston Churchill. Do you know where I'll find him?'

'Have you tried the House of Commons? Give him a call.'

'I can't telephone him, can I?'

'Sure you can. It's what the bally things are for, old boy. Easy-peasy. Dial the operator and ask for Westminster 2300. Got that?' Harris chuckled. 'Of course, he might not speak to you, but that's another matter. Tell me, what are your plans?'

'I'm going to bring the head to London and give it to Churchill – just as he asked Wilkinson to do in the telegram. He'll know what to do with it. He's got connections; he'll help with the police and the charges.'

'If he ruddy well believes you. Otherwise he'll turn you in.'

'That might just be safer than being out here.'

132

Harris saw a shadow fall across the wall in front of him. He looked over and his bottom lip trembled.

'Grubby,' he said brightly, lowering the handset.

Behind Howse he saw two figures in dark suits.

'Oh, bugger.'

Ding -

***

'Harris?' cried Drabble, '*Harris?*'

He hung up.

'What happened?' asked Kate.

'The line just went dead.'

Kate lowered herself into the leather armchair and fastened her wristwatch. On the floor next to her was Drabble's Gladstone bag and a hold-all packed with her belongings.

'Now what?'

'We've one more call to make.'

He picked up the black receiver and dialled 100.

'Trunk call, please: Westminster 2300.'

Drabble heard a click and gentle hiss on the line and then he heard ringing. A telephonist answered.

'May I have the office of Winston Churchill, MP, please.'

'Very good, sir.'

The connection was made and there were several peals of a bell, before it halted abruptly. For a moment Drabble heard nothing but a hollow sound accompanied by a plastic, scratching noise; then breathing.

'Hello?' said a woman's voice.

'I'd like to speak to Mr Churchill, please. It's Professor Drabble.'

'*Professor Drabble*?' The speaker's voice lifted. 'Sir, there's a Professor Drabble on the telephone.'

Drabble heard a deeper voice in the background. The telephonist cleared her throat.

'Sir, Mr Churchill asks if you have "the item"?'

Drabble saw the box in the darkness on the floor, beside their belongings.

'Yes madam I do; tell him, "yes".'

'He says he does, sir,' she reported.

There was a pause and Drabble heard the low voice once again.

'Mr Churchill sends his felicitations, sir, and begs you to bring it to him at the House at once. And, sir, he implores you "*not to spare the horses*".'

CHAPTER TWELVE

Drabble replaced the receiver and pulled on his tweed overcoat. On the floor of the dark hallway were the box containing the head, his Gladstone, and another leather hold-all on which sat a pile of folded blankets and a long chrome torch. Among the items, Drabble saw a Thermos flask and his hat. He went up to the window and looked out. He saw the branches of the trees that lined the drive sway to and fro in the breeze. Beyond them was blackness. The moon had risen and was bright in the clear sky, just, the thought occurred to him, as it had the previous night. He looked over. He could make out the faint outline of Kate's face and hair in the darkness. She stepped towards him and her features suddenly appeared. Her mouth widened, its corners pitched up, and revealed her teeth. He returned her smile. There was a noise of wind from outside and he looked out – peering to the corners of the field of view. He saw no one. He went over to Kate and the pile of bags, and took her hand.

'Right,' he said. 'I'm sure the house isn't being watched but we'll creep out without the headlights on just in case.'

'Sounds like a plan - here.' She pulled on a pair of leather gloves and reached down and handed him his hat. 'Are you sure your arm's up to the drive?'

He nodded. 'It feels a lot better already,' he said, picking up the head and his bag. 'Just a bit sore, that's all. And anyway, I've been dying to get behind the wheel of a

Speed Twenty ever since I read about them in *The Autocar* a year ago.'

She smiled but her eyes looked afraid, he thought. He set his bag down and pressed her hand.

'You don't need to come, you know. I could take this to Churchill on my own.'

'I know,' she said.

He pulled her close and held her.

'We'll be all right,' he said.

She nodded, her soft hair pressing gently against the side of his face. He raised her chin and kissed her cheek. For a moment her eyes shone in the darkness.

'Come on.'

They broke apart and he saw her dark form bend down and gather up her bag and the blankets. They moved along the dark corridor and passed the door to the kitchen. He stopped by the back door.

'Right,' he said, turning back and seeing her silhouette halt at his shoulder. 'Good luck.'

'You too.'

He cracked the door open and looked out, feeling the cold air on his face. The side of the garage was a looming black shape. He saw the front of the house and the drive. There really was no one out there. *Where were they? Surely, the house would be watched?* He glanced back at Kate and nodded.

He darted for the side door of the barn. She arrived a moment later and they were inside. It took a second or two for the monolithic pitch black surroundings to transmute into a live stage with differing depths of field and freestanding objects. The air was pungent with oil, paint, and turpentine and Drabble smiled when the caught the sweet, grassy odour of a lawnmower. He felt the cold of the stone floor through the soles of his shoes as he edged along the side of the Alvis, feeling the cool coachwork of the car next to him. The gritty ground was tacky with grease and hugged greedily at the soles of his shoes. He ran his hand along the smooth running board and arrived at the front of the car, where he nudged the garage doors ajar. A shaft of moonlight fell across the long low bonnet, catching the red and chrome triangular marque at the top of the grille and glinting on the spread-eagle mascot. She's a beauty, he thought. *A real beauty.* With her six-cylinder, 2.8 litre engine, she was reportedly capable of ninety miles per hour, and if she delivered on that, thought Drabble, she'd spurn any of those fascist Rovers.

Drabble heard a low metallic click and looked up: he saw Kate open the passenger door and start laying the travelling gear on the back seats. He went to the boot and loaded the bags and the box containing the head into the shallow recess. They unfolded the black mohair roof and fastened it with stout chrome levers to the narrow rectangular windscreen.

'I'll get the garage doors,' he said, his breath forming clouds.

'Watch out for the bolt,' she replied. 'It catches.'

He edged around to the front of the car and felt his way along the gate: his fingertips found the cast iron lever. Slowly, he pulled it up until it was clear of the gravel and opened the door fully, repeating it on the other side.

He got into the driver's seat. He turned to Kate.

'Ready?'

She nodded. He reached to the mahogany dashboard and turned the black plastic switch from 'off' to 'start'. He then adjusted the choke and pressed the 'start' button. There was a *tick-tick-tick* from beyond the dash, then the engine announced itself with a juicy whisper. *Whut-whut-whut-whut*, it panted, waiting, Drabble knew, for him to introduce the throttle. He depressed the clutch and put the gearbox into first.

The car surged from the barn, and accelerated smoothly along the drive.

'You can't beat an Alvis,' he said in a low voice, changing into second gear. 'She's solid, taut -'

'And,' interrupted Kate, 'cost about the same as a four-bedroom house in Plymouth – at least that's what the doctor always said.'

Pausing at the end of the drive, he flicked on the Lucas P100 headlights: rabbits scattered into the hedgerow, escaping the intense glare of the vast globes. They turned left.

'Ernest, what do you think they want with Cromwell's head?'

Drabble glanced over.

'Honestly?' he asked. 'I haven't the foggiest.'

They slowed as they approached a T-junction. The signpost said, 'Plymouth 7 miles'.

He depressed the clutch and worked the gear stick. The controls were light and put little strain on his arm, which was a blessing. The change completed; the car charged along. The road broadened and Drabble accelerated, till they were pulling a comfortable 50mph.

'You would have thought,' said Drabble, 'that nearly three hundred years after his death, he would have ceased to be such a sought-after item. But…'

The car built up speed as they went down a steep incline.

'Dr Wilkinson used to describe him as a Godly tyrant.'

'And that he was,' said Drabble. 'He wanted to make Britain as close as possible to his vision of a moral, Godly state, where everyone lived a good life.'

She looked over towards the boot.

'How can we certain that *that's* him?'

Drabble shrugged.

'We won't know until we have a proper look at it but I don't particularly doubt it. There will be various marks on the skull that are consistent with the known physiognomy of Cromwell – the wart above the right eye, the trepanning of the frontal lobes of the forehead after his death, et cetera.' He grinned at her, 'They really went to town on you when you died in the seventeenth century.'

The Alvis sped along, accompanied only by the growl of the great engine, rumble of the tyres and hum of the wind. Drabble cleared his throat.

'We can always compare it against the death mask in the British Museum if needs be, but to be honest I don't see why it's not him.'

Kate swallowed.

'You don't think it could be a fake?'

'What?'

'Well,' she said, 'It's got to be a possibility, hasn't it?'

Drabble nodded.

'It is, but to be honest, I'd say it'd be virtually

impossible: or rather, you'd have to be pretty ingenious. For starters, you'd need the corpse of a man of about sixty, who looked a bit like the real deal. Then you'd have to embalm him in the way they did back then; and then you'd have to bury him for a decent period of time, before chopping his head off and ageing it.' Drabble shrugged and shook his head. 'There have to be easier ways of making the rent.'

'Is it valuable?'

'Heavens above, I should imagine so. Lord knows what it's worth though.' He looked over. 'I read that the head was sold in around 1780 for £230. In today's money that's something like £10,000.'

'Ten thousand pounds! I had no idea...'

'It's a real king's ransom all right,' he shook his head. 'I'm sure the irony would not be lost on the Lord Protector. But that can't be why the fascists are bothered with it.' He made an expansive gesture with his hand. 'They'll have plenty of loot – and if they were short, they'd be far better off robbing a bank. No,' he sucked his teeth for a moment, 'there's got to be something else.' He frowned. 'Buggered if I know, though.'

The road twisted and he braked hard, changing into a lower gear.

'I bet you're itching to see it.'

He nodded. 'Rather.'

He dipped the headlights as a car passed by in the other carriageway. He slipped the Alvis into fourth and the throaty growl of the engine subsided.

'Why haven't you, as a matter of fact?'

'What? Looked at it?' He thought for a second. He

looked back at her, the light cast from a passing car cutting across his face, leaving his eyes in shadow. 'Time and place, Kate. Time and place.'

She nodded slowly.

'Also,' he continued, his tone flat and informative, 'it almost doesn't matter *now* if it is him or not.' The face turned towards her, his square jaw caught in another fleeting shaft of yellow light. 'They're after it: they tried and seem to be continuing to try to kill us – so frankly, Cromwell or not, we're in it up to our necks.'

Kate clenched her fist.

'But why?' she cried.

He sighed. 'I suppose the simple fact of the matter is, the head of Oliver Cromwell has never ceased to be a controversial item, simply because he was so controversial himself – he killed a king, he established the world's first republic since Rome, he butchered Catholics in Ireland, he butchered them in Scotland, frankly he butchered them wherever he could find them. He abolished the House of Lords – he even abolished Christmas. Whatever the fascists want with it, Lord alone knows.'

He patted her hand.

She raised the corners of her mouth.

'Hopefully, Mr Churchill will have some idea.'

'I'm sure he will.' They bobbed over a humpback bridge. 'I'm also interested to know what has spurred *his* interest in all this.'

They dashed through a crossroads.

He slowed the Alvis and changed down as they entered a village. They passed a hostelry, the Fox Revived, its interior basking a warm yellow light across the pavement.

'Looks inviting,' said Kate.

'Reminds me of a pub I go to in Cambridge,' said Drabble, studying it for a moment in the rear view mirror. 'The Baron of Beef. Landlord only has one hand, but you never see anyone waiting.'

They left the village and he built up speed.

'Do you know the way to London?'

'Oh, it's just a jolly jaunt through Exeter, Yeovil, on to Salisbury, where if I recall correctly, the road passes Stonehenge, then to Andover, Basingstoke, and then you're there, more or less. I think we should make it by tomorrow lunchtime. We'll need to refuel, of course.'

'I'd like to see Stonehenge.'

'That shouldn't be a problem. We could stop for bit, if you like.'

She opened the door of the narrow glove box and took out a silver hip flask.

'Want some? I've refilled it.'

'Rather.'

She unscrewed the lid and passed it to him. He drank.

'Do you think they'll be looking out for us – the fascists, I mean?'

He glanced at her. 'They'll be looking for me, because they think I've got the head. But they won't be looking for this car – yet.'

He looked over; she frowned.

'Once they've noticed that it's gone – and I've gone – they'll put two and two together pronto.'

The hedgerows thinned and they drove past a row of large Victorian villas, which were set well back with long front gardens. Kate looked over at the windows. They glowed with light from within.

'Who would live on a road like this?' she asked. 'The noise would drive one barmy. Shall we have a cigarette?'

'I won't, thanks.'

Gas streetlights showed telegraph and telephone lines criss-crossing above the road. Pavements replaced the grass verges. She took a cigarette packet from her bag and bent forward to light one. He changed gear, up into fourth.

'I suppose we could always catch the train?' she suggested. 'If we think they'll spot the car.'

'I'd thought about that,' he saw a set of headlights pass in the rear view mirror. 'But I've rather gone off rail travel.'

She rolled down the window and tapped the end of her cigarette into the ashtray that was mounted on the dash. 'How's the arm?'

'It's fine,' he smiled. 'Bit sore, that's all. The steering's exceptionally light.'

He changed the subject.

'What are you smoking?'

'Craven A.'

'Harris smokes those too, from time to time. Usually, he's a pipe man.'

'How do you know him?'

'We were at school together.'

'That's nice,' she said. 'The friends one makes at school are very special.'

He glanced over. 'Harris is very special, trust me.'

She laughed. 'Where were you?'

'Lancing.'

143

'Oh really? I don't suppose you knew my cousin Gregory Hughes?'

He shook his head.

'He was probably a few years above you.'

'Harris and I were in the same house.' Drabble looked over. 'It essentially meant we were forced into friendship.' The road narrowed and they stopped at the traffic lights. The station was over to the right; people were emerging, porters were darting about. A street lamp illuminated a lady in a fur hat and overcoat. She summoned a taxi.

'It looks like the London train has arrived,' said Drabble. He looked over at Kate. 'Harris and I didn't really hit it off at first, but in the end he ground me down.' He shook his head. 'He's very good at grinding people down.'

He smiled but saw that she wasn't listening. He followed her gaze.

Up on the left, parading two-abreast was a gang of men – perhaps twenty of them in all. They wore uniforms of black and their banners announced, 'Stand By The King' and 'Flog Baldwin'. One of them struck a large drum which was strapped to his chest. They approached on the nearside pavement.

'They're chanting,' said Kate, turning her ear to them. She wound the window down. 'Can you hear?'

Two-four-six-eight, the King must not abdi-cate...
Hurrah!
Two-four-six-eight, the King- must not- abdi-cate...
Hurrah!

The traffic light turned green and Drabble dropped the

144

clutch. They pulled off. From the car, he saw that behind the front rows of uniformed fascists, there were others dressed in civilian clothing who had added simple black brassards to their sleeves. He saw women marching, too.

Kate gasped.

'Blackshirts!' she said, looking back as they left the throng behind. 'Loads of them. I had no idea these people existed here. I'd read about them but I thought they were only in the big cities.'

'I'm afraid they're all over the place,' said Drabble.

'But there's so many!'

He saw her face adopt a disbelieving frown and her eyes blink in an expression of mild shock. He looked along the Alvis' long bonnet and up the road ahead.

'People are unhappy,' he said, as though he were thinking out loud. 'And quite justifiably so. They're out of work; they're poor; they're hungry; they can't put shoes on their children's feet, let alone afford oil for their heaters, or such luxuries as books or a Sunday joint. In many cases the economic reason for the existence of their very communities has imploded. And, funnily enough, they're fed up to their hind teeth with the National Government – the Tories, the Liberals, they're all the same...'

He saw she was looking at him and listening.

'But I can't believe there were *women*.'

He looked over. 'Why not? They're angry, too.'

Kate gave a despairing chuckle. 'It just doesn't seem right.'

Drabble glanced over and smiled.

'I'm afraid they come in all shapes and sizes.'

She frowned at him and looked away.

He cleared his throat.

'I don't suppose I could have some more brandy? It's very warming – and there's still a lot of road between us and London.'

She tugged open the door to the glove box and pulled out the flask. She held it out for him. He tipped it to his lips.

'So what should we do if we're stopped?' she asked, as she put the flask away.

He met her gaze, and grinned.

'Why don't we cross that bridge when we come to it, eh?'

The Alvis pitched up over a low stone bridge.

'Oh, sod it,' he said. His heart sank.

'What?'

'You were just saying.'

She looked up from her handbag.

'Oh Lord!'

Up ahead a couple of policemen stood with lanterns in the road.

'Quick,' said Drabble. 'Take the wheel…'

***

Harris' head knocked against the window and he awoke with a start. He exhaled painfully. His hands, he realised, were tied together, and he raised them to his head, where he felt a large new bump on the right side. Blimey, it hurt. His eyes opened slowly and he saw what he felt: he was moving. Before him, in darkness, two heads were silhouetted in the front seats by the headlights of traffic on the other side of the road. He rolled his lips – they felt swollen and cracked. It's where the buggers hit me, he recalled.

'Where are you taking me, you bastards?' he cried, sitting up. An arm came across him from the adjacent seat and thrust him back. 'Who are you, you curs? Where's Grubby? Let go of me,' he shouted, pushing back. 'You dogs. You'll regret this.'

The passenger in the front seat turned back to face them, his face lost in darkness.

'I told you we should have gagged him. Shut him up, Arkwright.'

Harris looked left and saw a black fist loom up.

'Hey –'

CHAPTER THIRTEEN

The Alvis halted before a police officer's raised hand. The sergeant bent down and peered through the driver's side window. A lantern and his face came into view. His moustache looped beneath his nose like an extension from either sideburn, so it resembled the helmet strap of a Grenadier guard. Kate rolled down the window.

'Evening, miss,' he said, placing his hand on the top of the door frame and leaning into the interior. 'Where are you off to tonight?'

She saw his face was white and his cheeks were tinged with blue. 'I'm going to my aunt's in Chagford,' she reported.

'Chagford? I've a sister there.'

'Have you? Lovely, isn't it.'

'Ain't it just,' he agreed, 'and the bank has a thatched roof, which I always think shows an honest streak in the community.'

She raised the corners of her mouth and allowed her eyes to twinkle at him. 'I'd not thought of that.'

The policeman's face softened momentarily. He cleared his throat.

'Right,' he added, surveying the back seat; his eyes narrowed. 'Is this your car, miss?'

'No,' she swallowed. 'It's the property of my employer.'

The policeman looked at her hard.

'Has he given you permission to borrow it?'

'Oh, *yes*,' she insisted. 'He most certainly has.'

She smiled up at him and stroked her blonde hair back behind her ear. A dimple was caught in the lantern light.

The sergeant nodded and studied her face.

'Very good, miss.'

She smiled back and gripped the top of the gearstick.

'So that's his shotgun is it, miss?'

She froze – and then turned to look at the back seat, which was covered in a tartan blanket.

'I can't believe it!' her voice rose and she slapped the top of the steering wheel. 'I'm sorry, officer, he's so forgetful. I've told him about this before. I promise, officer, it won't happen again. I'm only away for a night and I shall telephone him directly I arrive to let him know it's safe.'

The sergeant smiled.

'Safe journey, miss,' he stepped back from the car and waved her through. 'On you go.'

She put the Alvis in gear and the car moved away slowly. She wound the window back up. They continued along for a few seconds. Drabble pulled back the blanket and sat up.

'You were perfect.'

'I was petrified.'

'Do you really have an aunt in Chagford?'

'I do, as a matter of fact.'

He laughed and twisted himself into the passenger seat. 'That's one of Harris' mottos. He says that at the root of every good lie is a grain of truth.'

She referred to the rear view mirror.

'He knows a lot about lying, does he?'

'Well, that's what he does for a living.'

She didn't reply.

'You really were very good, Kate,' he said. He pressed her shoulder and saw her eyes brim with tears. She turned away.

'Hey -'

'The doctor,' she explained, wiping her eyes. 'He really terrorised those rabbits. They'll run amok without him.'

He pressed her hand. They drove along. She changed gear. He took out the flask.

'Here, have another drink.'

She took it.

'Thanks.'

They passed a pair of tall, rectangular granite gatehouses, with crenellated roofs and small low bastions jutting from the corners.

'The doctor was excessively proud of the Alvis,' said Kate. 'He only got it in the summer. The first thing he did was charge round the village blasting the horn at all and sundry.'

'Are you happy driving for a while?'

'It takes my mind off things,' she said, her jaw fighting a yawn. 'Why don't you try and sleep.'

'I will try a little later.'

She checked the rear view mirror.

'What time is it?' she asked.

'It's only just after nine.'

At this rate, he thought, if they didn't stop and drove through the night they could reasonably expect to be in London in the morning. He peered at the instruments.

150

Their problem was fuel; there was only a quarter of a tank left. It didn't do to run down the fuel level, even on a modern car like this.

'Depending on how we go,' he added, 'we might be better off stopping for the night at a garage when we reach one. At least then we can fill up first thing and be on our way. We'd also both be able to have a short sleep.'

'I keep a jerrican in the boot of the Austin,' said Kate.

He gazed out of the window at the trees and fields. The black sky was clear and stars were bright above. It was going to be a cold night. Fortunately the engine was giving off a great deal of heat, which was warming up the cabin nicely.

They went under a brick railway bridge and entered a village. Kate slowed the Alvis to about twenty-five. Drabble saw a small green and a church with a stone tower and a pub. There were half a dozen cars parked in front, including a yellow, two-seater Talbot.

Up on the left was a filling station.

'Pull over,' said Drabble.

'But it's closed,' said Kate. The car slowed and they drove into the forecourt, stopping by the pump. The shop was in complete darkness.

'I'll see if I can raise someone,' he said. 'It's not *that* late.'

They went over to the narrow cottage that abutted the shop. Drabble knocked on the door. It was small, with a rectangular window. A light came on inside. The door was opened by a man, probably in his fifties, dressed in a vest and dungarees. They heard the sound of an orchestra in the background – sighing strings in the main, but with building brass, attended by the low hiss and crackle of a gramophone.

'Good evening, sir,' said Drabble, offering a broad smile and raising his hat. 'Sorry to trouble you – but we wondered if by any chance we could purchase some fuel? I appreciate that it's very late, but it's an emergency.'

The man eyed Drabble and then Kate, who beamed winsomely. He removed his pipe.

'I'm closed.'

He moved back and started to shut the door.

'Please, sir,' Drabble took out his wallet and produced a banknote. 'I will give you five pounds for some fuel - any. We're desperate.'

The large eyes rolled down to the unfolding, white, note. They narrowed and the man nodded slowly.

'You must be.'

***

Drabble looked up from the round fuel gauge, where the indicator pointed to above the 'full' mark, as the Alvis sped along a densely tree-lined road. The bright stars above were obscured by the overhanging branches. Occasionally Kate glimpsed the white glow of the moon through gaps in the foliage. The light sparkled on the spread eagle on the prow of the bonnet.

'I think I might try and sleep,' she said. She yawned. 'It's been a long day.'

'That's a good idea.'

She reached back, pulled up one of the blankets, and arranged it over herself. She stroked his arm.

'Would you like a blanket?'

'Not while I'm driving, thanks.'

'You really don't mind if I sleep?'

'Not at all.'

'Are you sure your arm's all right?'

He looked over and smiled. She turned on her side and curled up in the seat.

'It's odd,' she said, 'but we've only known each other for about twelve hours. To think I might have shot you.'

He glanced over.

'I know, I know,' she murmured. 'Not without cartridges I wouldn't.'

'Good night.'

'Night-night.'

He drove on. His arm *was* sore – very sore, and tired, he thought. Still, it's nothing like the break - then, the thing had been unusable. He slowed as they entered a village, passed a post office, a pub and a brick church, all in darkness. The Alvis drove through barren black fields, then woodland, and through avenues and tunnels of trees that reminded Drabble of the long straight roads of Bordeaux. He saw no other traffic. He kept the speedometer at a level fifty-five miles per hour.

He looked over at Kate. He could see her straight nose, a crescent of eyelashes, and a portion of her cheek emerging from a mass of tartan. He sighed.

Drabble checked his watch. It was eleven o'clock. He stretched his knuckles out on the black steering wheel and took in the rear view mirror. Harris, doubtlessly clad in his finest dinner suit, was probably right now at a table at the Savoy or the Ritz, surrounded by glamorous – and clamorous - society girls, their short bobs rocking back in laughter, with a wide glass of champagne in his hand. Or, Drabble wondered, was he reclining in one of those comfortable leather sofas at the back of the Long Bar at the Granville, feet up, on his second post-prandial pipe, slowly soaking up the best of the Highlands' distilleries? *Lucky sod.*

CHAPTER FOURTEEN

Harris blinked away his tears as he watched Arkwright pull on the thick red rubber glove.

'Very well,' said Sir Carmen Kelly, a lone bright light hanging above his head, 'this is the moment that you should volunteer all the information you have in your possession.'

He grinned, showing his perfectly neat teeth.

Harris' right eye was swollen and had adopted the florid hues of a peacock's tail. He looked at Kelly, his face a harsh jigsaw of white skin or shadow, and then peered at Arkwright, who was attaching metal crocodile clips to Harris' wrists, which were strapped to the arms of the chair. The heavy gloves creaked. Harris looked down and felt the curved steel jaws of the clasps bite into his exposed skin. He tried to move his feet but they were tied to the legs of the chair.

Kelly wore a navy jacket, a white stock, tan jodhpurs, and black leather riding boots. He tapped the silver pommel of his swagger stick against the side of his boot.

'We could, of course,' he announced, 'had we been particularly cruel, have attached the electrodes straight to your genitals.' He smiled. 'But, then, I think we did enough harm to those earlier, what?'

Arkwright got to his feet and moved back to the table at the side.

There was quiet. Harris heard Arkwright flicking metal switches and attaching various leads. He looked down, and his eyes followed the wires along the floor, to the tall, metal and glass device. It was crowned with a large chrome globe and stood about six feet tall. A fabric belt hung limply beneath the dome. His eyes widened. Great Scott, he thought, it's some sort of electricity generator – *a bloody huge one.* He looked over at Kelly. The man was sitting in a chair some yards away, his head and shoulders slightly blurred in the gloom, at the very limits of the single bulb's field of illumination. Harris saw the crossed legs, and the silver knob of the stick move back and forth against the side of the boot, like a cat swishing its tail.

'What are you doing?' cried Harris. 'Are you going to electrocute me?'

Kelly tutted and rose to his feet, stepping into the light.

'You should choose your words more carefully, Mr Harris.' He chuckled. 'To electrocute, my dear sir, is to cause death by electricity. For your sake I hope we don't go that far.' He nodded to Arkwright. Harris looked over. The man wheeled the generator towards him.

'You no doubt recognise this device to be a Van de Graaff electrostatic generator. It is of course somewhat different from ones you may have read about in the newspaper: it is very much larger. This device is capable of generating one million volts. Of course,' Kelly smiled, 'we shouldn't need *all* of those.'

Harris looked at the floor; a cable ran from the machine to a small red metal lever which stood on top of the box on Arkwright's table. From the red lever, a twist of wires ran across the table, onto the floor and over to him, culminating in his wrists.

'You can't do this,' he cried, 'what are you?'

Sir Carmen Kelly gave a small nod. Harris looked over. The small noisy engine kicked into life and the loose belt on the Van de Graaff started to move. First it was floppy, but it got faster and tauter. Harris looked back over at Kelly and then back at the device. It's a static electricity generator, he thought. That means the longer the belt goes round, the greater the charge. Oh, Lordy. This means the sooner he shocks me, the better. He started counting. *One thousand...* Ahead, Kelly removed a slim cigar from a silver case and lit it. He returned to the chair.

Six thousand... seven thousand... eight thousand... nine...

Harris closed his eyes. He heard the metallic rasp of the lever. For a moment nothing happened. Harris opened his eyes and they flashed with gladness. He grinned. It was a cruel trick. *Everything was going to be OK!*

'ARH-*R-R-R-R-R-R!*'

His face tightened and his body started juddering in the chair, causing his teeth to chatter. The involuntary shaking worsened and his head and shoulders started moving laterally as well.

'BRH-*R-R-R-R-R-R!*'

Kelly sniggered, and looked away. After a few seconds the charge faded. He gave a flick of his hand and Harris heard the whirr of the belt fade.

'Do forgive my mirth, Mr Harris,' said Kelly, offering an insincere frown. 'But there's something so inherently comical about the administration of an electrostatic charge to a subject. It's the noises people make.'

Harris was breathing hard, his eyes closed. The bastard, he thought. *I can't believe the ruddy bastard's just electrocuted me.* He looked at Kelly.

'Kelly,' he cried, spit flying from his mouth, 'funnily enough, I don't see it quite the same way. I certainly don't share your *mirth.*'

Kelly stood up.

'I'd curb that tongue of yours if I were you.' He approached and tapped Harris' head with the pommel of the swagger stick. 'You only had ten seconds of charge that time and even then it's a small miracle you didn't experience a full, involuntary – dare I say - *spasmodic* colonic evacuation; I promise you this, you *will* next time.' He smiled. 'I suppose we should just hope that you didn't have a heavy lunch.' He turned and walked back to the chair, waving the stick through the air. 'Arkwright!'

The engine started.

'What do you want from me?' cried Harris, seeing the limp belt begin to stir.

'I want information,' said Kelly, turning and raising his stick – the generator fell silent. 'More precisely, I want to know where your friend Drabble is and what he is doing with *my* property; it's as simple as that.'

Harris looked down at this feet. What sort of company was Ernest keeping these days, he wondered? Was this all about a head? He looked up, his face steeled with determination. *It had to be.* The light picked out the billowing cloud of smoke from Kelly's cigar. This was Churchill's fault. Harris looked over at Arkwright; he was a big man, with a cold, hard face. The fellow's eyes watched him with an uncaring, professional candour. Harris looked away. What was Ernest doing right now, he wondered? He looked at the concrete floor, a sense of panic rising in him. Where *was* Ernest? Buggered if he knew. He glanced over at Arkwright, and at the various jars and instruments on the table next to him. Actually, he might *be* buggered in a moment - probably after the colonic discharge. He shook his head. It was no good. Ernest, the bastard, was probably enjoying a comfortable dinner courtesy of Great Western Railways, tucking into a glass or two of port in the restaurant car, and gently plotting a return to his cabin.

He looked at Sir Carmen Kelly.

'I have no idea where Drabble is. And that's the truth.'

Kelly shook his head.

'In which case, Mr Harris, you will discover that the truth hurts.'

'Kelly,' he shouted. 'I can't tell you what I don't know.'

Sir Carmen nodded sharply at Arkwright.

'Let's see if another shock to the system will help release some of those lost memories.'

The motor started up. The flop of the rubber belt gave way to an efficient hum.

'Oh, Lord!' Harris looked up to the ceiling. *One thousand...*

He saw Kelly get up from the chair and move it back several feet before sitting down again. Harris looked over at the belt. It was turning so fast. Now the dome was vibrating. The belt now resembled a fixed, metal loop.

Fifteen thousand... sixteen thousand...

He looked back at Kelly, his blinking eyes wide and fearful. This was going to hurt.

Eighteen thousand... nineteen thousand...

He heard the rasp of the lever and clenched his -

Harris and the chair shook vertically; his shoulders sprang up and down, his head snapped back and forth, and his hands flicked up and down, his wrists secured with rope ties.

'Enough,' said Kelly, at last. He was grinning broadly. 'We want Harris to talk, not to toast.' He chuckled.

Arkwright laughed too. 'We've already given him a hair-do, sir.'

Harris coughed and gulped at the air. His heart raced: it felt like every blood vessel in his body was pumping, his forehead throbbed, his fingertips tingled, his eyes bulged... Oh, Lord, he thought. He looked down to his groin and saw a dark stain overtake the grey fabric. The shadow spread along the thigh, and then to the lower leg, before appearing as droplets running down the back of his brogue onto the stone floor. Oh, God, he thought, *and* I'm drooling. Strands of the stuff hung from his mouth to his knees.

Sir Carmen approached and stood next to the machine. Harris looked up at him through bloodshot eyes.

'I'm impressed, Mr Harris,' said Kelly, as he tapped the great chrome dome with the end of his stick. 'You just endured a full twenty seconds – the mongrel we tested the device on positively *exploded* at 20 seconds.'

He grinned. Harris thought there was something demonic about the white teeth flashing so cheerfully at him. You grinning bastard – you'll get it.

'Now, Mr Harris, I don't like to see you in this distressing condition, *really*,' Sir Carmen pulled his chair closer and sat, 'I do hope that isn't one of your best suits.'

He took a drag of his cigar. 'Tell me what you know. First of all, has Professor Drabble got the head?'

Harris saw that his hands were shaking. Kelly caught his eye and repeated the question. 'Come on, Mr Harris. I wouldn't like to put you up to thirty seconds.' He glanced at Arkwright. 'That's enough to run the District Line.'

Harris' gaze left the flashing white teeth and moved down to the leather riding swagger stick which played against the side of the black boot. He looked down at the cold dusty stone floor. Where in the name of God am I, he thought. Where? And what in the Lord's name could he say about Drabble that might satisfy them, without betraying Drabble, to save his own skin?

He looked up and met Kelly's eyes. They were solemn, hard and staring. He looked back down at the floor, his teeth playing along this bottom lip.

'Come on, sir. I'm not interested in your half truths. Didn't your mother ever tell you that to tell a half a truth was worse than telling a lie?'

Slowly, he looked up at Kelly.

'What do you want it for?' he said, breathing hard.

'Want it for?' Kelly looked over at his man. 'Listen to this, Arkwright. This is the trouble with extorting information from journalists. It's their professional reflex to *ask* questions, not answer them.'

Harris snarled. 'For goodness' sake, Kelly. I might as well know what I'm being electrocuted for.'

Kelly's face flashed angrily and he lashed the stick across Harris' face.

'I've told you,' he snapped, flecks of saliva flying through the air, 'you have not been electrocuted *yet*. You

161

have *merely* been administered with electric shocks. Now, before you *are* electrocuted, tell me: where is Drabble? What is he doing with the head? Where is he taking it?'

Kelly raised the stick, as if to strike him again. Harris lifted his head, rolling his jaw. He hawked and spat at Kelly's foot. Kelly looked down just as a large globule of phlegm struck the toe of his right boot. Kelly's eyes widened and a scowl formed on his mouth. He clicked his fingers and moved away, dragging the wooden chair with him into the darkness. The engine started.

'Kelly, this is ridiculous,' cried Harris.

One thousand...

'You won't get away with this...'

Two thousand...

'Halt!' Sir Carmen raised his hand and stepped into the light. The growl of the motor died away.

Harris, breathing hard, looked up. The corners of his mouth lifted and he began to blink back tears. Perhaps this beast had discovered mercy. Maybe this was over.

'Arkwright.'

'Yes, sir.'

'Be so kind as to transfer the electrodes to Mr Harris' earlobes.'

'What?' Harris' eyes darted between Arkwright, the Van de Graaff generator and back to Kelly. 'You can't do this,' he cried. 'I'm not an animal.'

'Quite right, Mr Harris,' said Kelly. 'Although you might be a vegetable by the time we've finished.'

Harris wrestled against the ties that gripped him at the ankle, waist, and wrist.

'Damn you, Kelly.' He felt the pressure release on his

162

wrist as Arkwright removed the first clip. 'And damn you, Arkwright.'

He inhaled sharply as the metal jaws compressed the soft flesh of his ears. Arkwright sponged water onto his ear.

'You bastards!' Harris felt his bowels loosen. 'You're going to damn well be held to account for this. You know that. My uncle's a lord, for Christ's sake. That's right. A full baron. Ermine and everything. Whatever you do to me, there will be a day of reckoning – and you,' he swallowed and met Kelly's gaze, '*you* will be accountable. Even if you zap me to death like some worthless stray and leave my body, charred,' he sobbed and blinked away more tears, 'cauterised in my own faeces and extinguished of life, you will be held to account. Mark my words.'

Arkwright attached the second clip. There was a trickle of water from the sponge. Kelly began to walk away, into the darkness.

'Kelly,' he pleaded, his toes playing against the floor. 'How can I tell you what I don't know?'

A cloud of tobacco smoke appeared, swirling in the light.

'Mr Harris,' said Kelly. 'Lying to your readers is all very well, but you will not lie to me. We know you spoke to Drabble on the telephone. What did he tell you?'

Harris swallowed and broke away from Kelly's intense gaze.

'Of course, I appreciate your dilemma. It's only natural for you not to want to betray your friend, nor betray your honour as a gentleman, but you ought to remember that

163

there is no dishonour in bartering your life for some harmless information. The dilemma is unequal. We're not going to *kill* your friend – I'll simply take back my property – but we *will* kill you if you don't tell us what you know.' Kelly drew on the cigar and then dropped it to the floor. Harris saw a leather boot enter the pool of light and extinguish it. 'And trust me, if you do insist on our electrocuting you, Professor Drabble will never know how grateful he should be to you. You understand?'

Tears ran down Harris face.

'I understand you well enough, you loathsome cur.'

Sir Carmen waved the stick and the engine started. Harris closed his eyes and prayed. *Dear Lord. Dear, dear merciful Lord... please forgive me my sins, oh, my many, many sins...* He bent his head back and showed his tear-stained face to the heavens. *Dear Lord...*

He glanced at the generator; its belt was turning at full speed. *God preserve my dear mother, my father, and please have blessings on my terrible, sinful soul, Oh, I should have gone to church more...*

These bastards. If Kelly killed him, who would be there to look after his parents in their old age? He gritted his teeth. *Ruddy bastards.* But I can't betray Ernest. I can't. He bit his lip and closed his eyes. But then what harm would it do to tell them what he did know? So what that Drabble was taking the head to Churchill – there was little they could actually *do* practically speaking with that information, was there? Was there? The belt of the generator pounded in his ear and seemed to accelerate, becoming histrionic, extreme, overblown. He glanced at it: the whole machine started to wobble because of its own insatiable inertia. *Dear Lord,* he'd lost count. But I won't give in. He shook his head, his lips pursed stubbornly. Kipling, he thought. Kipling is what I need...

If you can force your heart and nerve and sinew
To serve your turn long after they are gone...

Harris opened his eyes and looked over at the generator. Ahead he saw light fall upon the lower part of Kelly's legs, as he stood there watching him. Harris looked back at the spinning belt: once again it looked like a circular band of metal, not a piece of loose fabric. His lower lip started to wobble. More tears traced down his face and dripped from his chin. Get a grip, man, get a grip!

And so hold on when there is nothing in you
Except the Will which says to them: 'Hold on!'

'Hold on!' he cried. 'STOP!'

Kelly stepped into the light.

'Please,' begged Harris, '*Please.* He's taking it to London, to Churchill...'

CHAPTER FIFTEEN

The tart, white light of the Alvis' full beam headlights captured a constantly moving haze of glistening rain, beyond which stood two great standing stones, mottled and dark. Drabble applied the handbrake and turned off the engine. He looked over at Kate and yawned. She was still asleep. He inspected his wristwatch. It was just after two a.m. He shuffled around in the seat, easing his back. *Bugger.* Out there it was cold, wet, and damned miserable. He shook his head and grimaced. *And* he had a headache. The last twenty-four hours were even more exhausting than the Eiger, he thought, if that were possible. At least there, it was only the elements you were fighting – and not fascists. He pulled another blanket from the back seat and stretched it out over Kate. He then took the last one and laid it as well as he could over himself. He lay back and looked across at her face and smiled.

Kate stirred and her eyes half-opened.

'Are we there?' she said. Her tone sounded almost childish, defenceless.

'Go back to sleep,' he whispered. He stroked her hair and ran his fingers over her cheek. She slowly shook her head.

'No, I want to know where we are.'

'Stonehenge,' he said softly.

She lifted her head but her eyelids were still mostly closed.

'Oh, wonderful. I can't wait till morning.'

She laid her head back down and he stroked the top of her forehead.

'We'll be awake to see the sun rise over the stones in a few hours.'

'That sounds wonderful,' she said, yawning into the jumper that she had rigged up as a pillow. She moved towards him and leaned her head against his shoulder; he put his arm around her. 'I'm not worried, now.'

***

It was still dark when Drabble woke, chilled to the bone. Condensation clung to the inside of the misted windscreen and dew coated the dash. He shivered. Outside, Drabble saw a steady drizzle fall on the grassland and mossy stones. His teeth chattered and he quickly started the engine. Kate stirred.

'Are we leaving?'

'Rest,' he said, his breath forming clouds and fogging the windscreen. 'I'm just getting some heat.'

She stretched her arm over to him and pulled him towards her.

'I'm hot under the blanket.'

Drabble put his arm down to her waist; beneath the tartan blanket, it was surprisingly oven-like. They huddled together. She moved her hands up to locate his face and, finding it, came towards him and kissed him on the cheek.

'Thank you for taking care of me.'

He smiled and stroked her hair.

'Are you joking? I thought you were taking care of me?'

***

It was half dark; the proud menhirs of Stonehenge that encircled the Alvis were outlines against a gun-metal sky. The glaucous grasses that sprouted up at the foot of the stones were wet and tinged with white. In front, Drabble saw two tall uprights supporting a lateral stone that lay across them. Close by the car was another large boulder. It was squat and leaned off to a sharp angle. Kate sat up.

'Goodness,' she said, rubbing the windscreen. 'I hadn't noticed the stones.' She turned to him. 'It's a small miracle you didn't hit one of them last night.'

'Charming,' he said, looking over. 'Want to investigate?'

'Rather!'

They got out of the car and stepped into the fresh air.

'Ruddy hell,' Kate rubbed her arms, 'it's freezing.'

'Come on,' he wrapped one of the blankets around her shoulders and led her between the standing stones and into the heart of the henge. She gazed up at the proud, ancient stones and performed a 360-degree turn.

'Goodness me,' she said, her eyes wide. 'Look at that.'

'They say it's three thousand years old,' said Drabble. 'If not more.'

'What a place.' She turned to him. 'I can honestly understand what the druids see in it.'

It was quiet for a moment; the only sound was the patter of rain against the stones and grass. Drabble felt the wind blow against him and saw it ruffle her hair; the loose wet blonde strands were dark and fidgeted against her

168

face. Her attention was completely absorbed by the henge.

He went over to her and pulled her to him. Raindrops peppered his face. We're still in terrible danger, he thought. He looked down at her and then over at the large gap between the stones, seeing the sweeping landscape beyond. Kate was still in danger. I've been foolish.

'We've got to get to London,' he said softly.

'I know,' she said, looking up. Her hair was matted to her forehead and cheek. He stroked her face. 'Now?'

'Before we catch cold, I reckon.'

'I did so want to see Stonehenge at dawn,' she said.

He moved towards the car.

'I'll bring you back once this is all over,' he squeezed her hand. 'Promise. Besides, I don't think this dawn will be much to write home about.'

They parted and went to either side of the Alvis.

'Do you think we'll be introduced to Mr Churchill?' she asked, shutting the door after her.

'After this lot,' said Drabble as he alerted the engine. 'I should ruddy well hope so.'

He reached forward and cleared the steamed-up windscreen with a rag. Kate leaned over the back of the seat and brought out the Thermos. 'I wonder if he'll offer us a cup of tea.'

Drabble looked over and put the Alvis into reverse.

'I think we deserve something a lot stronger.'

***

The Alvis' powerful headlights forged a tunnel of light along the dark London road, tarmac vanishing beneath the end of the bonnet. They left the cover of the trees and drove out between open fields. Above the horizon the pale yellow winter sun glinted on the bonnet from below the thick, low cloud.

'Actually, it's going to be a beautiful day,' remarked Kate.

They swept past a white painted roadside sign which read, *Basingstoke 20 miles*.

She looked over and saw Drabble's face – lost in concentration on the road. For a second, she bit the side of her mouth and stared down into the dark footwell.

'You know,' said Drabble, after a few moments. 'It's a funny thing but I've always wanted to see it. Ever since I was a boy and I learned of its existence. But then, of course, it was thought to be lost, so I never thought I actually would.'

'The head?'

She tilted her head to one side, her eyebrows raised quizzically.

'I mean to say,' he continued, 'I've seen the death mask that was made of him; but there's something perversely exciting about actually seeing – or if you like, actually making contact with - the genuine article. It's just so much more tangible. I assume you've looked at it?'

'Oh, no,' she said, looking over his shoulder towards the boot. 'Well, *not properly*. Dr Wilkinson used to have it out on occasion, but I never took a close look. I didn't really want to.'

Drabble was driving faster.

'Do you know how he came by it?'

He looked over again; she was thinking.

'I think he inherited it from his father, though quite what he was doing with it, I've no idea.'

They drove along in silence. She reached down to her bag and took out a cigarette.

'And I don't know why I'm saying 'it'. He's a *he*, really, isn't he?'

CHAPTER SIXTEEN

Harris awoke. The room was still and light came in from a skylight overhead. He saw iron bars through the grimy glass. It's early, he reckoned. He moved stiffly in the chair, his wrists, ankles and waist were still affixed to it.

'Bastards,' he muttered, tugging at the bonds. He turned his face to the skylight and experienced a rush of rage. 'YOU BASTARDS!'

He recoiled painfully, his eyes tightly closed and a frown across his forehead. His head ached. Lord God, he thought. This was worse than any hangover. How it hurt. He sobbed. *The pain of it.* I must have internal bleeding. Maybe I've had a stroke? He imagined the blood oozing out and filling up in the spaces around his brain; he imagined it congealing. Oh God, he probably only had a few hours to live – *minutes!* He wailed. And he couldn't die sober; not in this life. *And what was that dreadful smell? Oh, Lord.* He rolled his weight onto his right buttock – feeling a tackiness beneath. Oh, Lord. The bastards…

His temples throbbed; his ears were numb – were they bleeding too? There was a stab of pain across his temples. Oh Lord. It must be a brain haemorrhage. He sobbed. This is worse, he thought, than when he went on the Eiger trip with Ernest and got thoroughly souped in the chalet. What was that vile, dark, syrupy liqueur they were all drinking that night? It had nearly killed him. Bugger… The name was gone. Christ alive. It must be the electric shocks…

172

what else had he forgotten?

He looked about the room. It was square, and smaller than he'd thought, probably about fifteen feet by fifteen. The ceiling was low, too, and the only window was that rectangular skylight. The walls were blackened bricks, and over by the far wall there was a table with a pair of wooden chairs. On the floor in front of him he saw the spent end of Kelly's cigar. The Van de Graaff generator was still next to him and beyond it he saw the desk and the controls, including the red painted lever.

He inhaled audibly – and his gaze darted back to the machine. He gasped. It all came flooding back. *Good Lord*, he thought. *What have I done?* His mouth fell open. I've spilled the beans about Ernest. He looked up at the sky. 'Oh, Lord,' he wailed. 'I've betrayed Ernest!'

He yanked against the ropes with his wrists. They were well tied down.

Ernest would know what to do. He always did. Oh no, no, *no*! And anyway, Ernest wasn't the sort to get caught in the first place – the clever bugger. He certainly wouldn't have been stupid enough to incur additional torture by shouting abuse at the torturer. Harris nodded forcefully. His swollen, purple eye glistened.

He frowned. He had to think. More than that, he had to think like Ernest. I've got to work out how to get out of here, he decided. Ernest wouldn't take this lying down – and nor will I. He twisted his right wrist at the rope fastening. After all, Harrises were brave and resourceful, too. Absolutely. We've been smiting Frenchmen, Spaniards, and Germans for King and Country for generations – it was positively a rite of passage for a

Harris. And as far as he was concerned, a fascist, even a half-British one like Kelly, was on a par with a Frog, Dago, or Jerry. Perhaps this was his turn to continue the family tradition?

He worked his right wrist. The cord cut into the skin and grazed the chafed, raw flesh. Harris sucked his teeth. He pulled his hand towards him and bent forward, straining to get his mouth to the rope. He bit into it and gnawed. The rope was rock hard. He bit it again, and squeezed as hard as he could.

'Ahh!' He winced and sat up, running his tongue over his smarting front teeth. I don't know what this rope's made of, he thought, but it bloody well hurts.

His gazed roamed around the room. I've got to get out and help Ernest. They'll be looking for him now. And they might find him – *because of what I said*. He blinked, his eyes becoming moist. This was no time for namby-pamby cissiness, he thought. *I've got to stand up and be counted*. Think of Crecy, he told himself. Think of Agincourt.

He worked up some saliva in his mouth, bent forward to his right wrist and licked the rope. He bit the cord – and then kept chewing and sucking. After a few minutes the rope began to soften... or was that his imagination? He worked up more moisture in his mouth and licked it on. He kept chewing...

***

Streaks of cool, tepid sunshine cut across the cobbled square. One shaft of light ran like a strip of golden ribbon

174

up the red brick tower of a Victorian church. The golden hands of its clock glinted towards eight and one on the dial. Drabble referred to his watch: 8.09. The Speed Twenty paused at a junction: Drabble looked either way and they moved on.

'How charming,' announced Kate, as they passed the church. 'Really lovely. I *just* knew Basingstoke would be delightful.'

Drabble glanced over and raised an eyebrow. They stopped at a red light.

'Have we got time to go inside the church?' asked Kate.

He hesitated.

'If you like,' he said.

She looked over.

'I'd quite like to offer a prayer for the doctor.' She smiled. 'We do have time, don't we?'

He reached over and squeezed her hand.

'We could probably do with stopping for breakfast anyway,' he said.

He pulled over and slowly mounted the kerb, parking in front of the baker's, where a man in a cream shop coat was pulling down a white and green striped sunshade with a rod. Drabble pulled the blanket over the shotgun on the backseat. Their pursuers would hardly be looking for them in Basingstoke, he thought. And certainly not at eight o'clock in the morning. Whatever else you could say about them, fascists didn't strike him as early birds.

They got out of the car and Drabble locked the doors. He then waited, hands in his trouser pockets, as Kate adjusted her beret in the reflection of a darkened shop window. On the far side of the square he saw a wide stone building with a portico and clock tower. 'Town Hall', said the sign. Next to it was a row of shops. A boy pushed a bicycle along the parade and stopped outside the newsagents. The billboard leaning by the door proclaimed, 'Baldwin dines with King'. He saw Kate was finishing.

'Ready?' he said. She smiled brightly, but there was a sadness to her eyes.

'Let's go,' she said.

They walked past more gloomy shop-fronts. There was a gentlemen's outfitter; the window full of suits, plus fanned displays of shirts, pullovers, trousers, pitched shoes, hats, and gloves. He saw his dishevelled reflection and gave it a sour smile.

They reached the end of the square and passed the corner, arriving at the church.

'It's perishing,' said Kate with a shudder. Drabble shut the door behind them and removed his hat. His eyes adjusted to the interior: there was a stone font, a central aisle and rows of chairs either side leading up to an altar rail, a plane wooden lectern, and stone and brick pulpit. Kate knelt at the wooden handrail and bent her head forward. Drabble lowered himself onto his knees beside her and bowed his head. He looked up at the window: Christ crucified, with Mary and the Apostles kneeling in prayer below. Drabble frowned. Were they Apostles at this point or Disciples? He looked down at the black and white tiles ahead. Apostles or Disciples? He couldn't remember. He peered over at Kate: her face was buried in her fretting fingers. A tear ran down her cheek. His

176

expression darkened and he looked up at the high window. He placed his flattened hands together and swallowed, awkwardly inclining his face towards his penitent digits. He heard Kate sob and looked over. He saw her wipe away a tear. *Dear Lord...*

She sobbed again. He placed his hand on her shoulder and pressed it gently. She turned to him.

'I'm all right,' she said.

He took his hand away. 'I'll see you outside. Take as long as you need.'

Drabble went to the rear of the church and looked back. His gaze lingered on her. She was a small, unmoving dark object at the centre of the rail. He stopped momentarily at the war memorial by the door and scanned the list of names. He frowned and put his hat on.

Outside, the chilling breeze smarted against his eyes, prompting them to stream. He pulled up the lapel of his tweed overcoat and, snatching a glance over his shoulder, turned the corner onto the square. He stopped. Ahead, he saw a policeman in front of the car. He stepped back, and concealed himself behind the corner. He removed his hat and peered out; the constable was bending forward to look into the interior of the Alvis. He shielded his eyes.

'Good morning, constable!' said Drabble, striding towards the man purposefully. His trilby was pitched forward. 'May I be of assistance at all?'

The policeman stood up with a jolt.

'Oh no, sir, *no, sir,*' he said, turning to Drabble. He beamed, 'An Alvis Speed Twenty, sir. We don't see many of these around here. What a cracker.' Drabble gazed down at the car, his eyes drawn in to the expanse of chrome and red, shining paintwork. The policeman sighed, 'And of course, there's that four-speed synchromesh gearbox - no more doubling-declutching. Is it as good as they say?'

'Better,' declared Drabble. 'I can see you know your cars.'

The policeman nodded. 'Bet she's a fine turn of speed, too, sir?'

'Of course,' Drabble allowed his eyes to widen, 'though always within the appropriate limits.'

'Quite right, sir,' said the policeman with a grin. Drabble saw the policeman give him the once-over, concluding at his face. The man's eyebrows suddenly arched – lost from view by the peak of the helmet.

'Should I recognise you, sir?'

'I don't think so,' said Drabble. 'I'm not from the area.'

The constable stroked his chin. A faint flicker of recognition flashed across the policeman's concentrating eyes – but then it vanished.

'Apologies sir,' he said, genially. 'A good day to you.'

He moved off.

Drabble checked his watch. 8.20. He watched the dark shape of the constable shrink as he strolled away, his hands clutched behind his back, crossing the square and passing in front of the town hall. Drabble looked in the direction of the church, and started to walk towards it. The constable could not be depended upon *not* to have a sudden moment of clarity, he thought. He glanced at the gent's outfitters' window again and shook his head. He turned the corner and hurried towards the door of the

178

church. It opened and Kate stepped out. She saw him.

'Everything all right?' he asked.

She straightened her beret.

'I'm all right now,' she said, and wiped beneath her eyes.

'We should really go,' he said. 'We just had a policeman checking out the car.'

'What?'

'It's fine, he couldn't place me. But he might.'

They rounded the corner of the square. Drabble threw out his arm.

'Get back.'

He pressed his back against the wall.

'It's the two black Rovers that chased us yesterday,' he said. 'I'm sure of it.' He pressed his face to the corner. Looking out, he saw a pair of black saloons parked in a V-formation in front of the Alvis. They were blocked in.

'Bugger.' He glanced back at Kate. 'They're *definitely* the lot that chased us from Dr Wilkinson's.'

'Let me see.' She pushed past him and looked out. 'But there's no one there.'

They swapped back, and he scanned the square.

'They're probably looking for us, or are in one of the shops – the baker's even. I expect they're getting breakfast. Even fascists need to eat.'

'We shouldn't have stopped.'

'It's OK,' he replied. The cars were dusty and the windscreens were grimy save for a pair of interlocking arcs described by the wipers. He felt a tap on his shoulder.

'Shall we run for it?' she asked.

'I wouldn't like to risk it. They'll be watching the car.'

'This is ridiculous,' she said, staring down at the cobbled ground.

'Look – ' he found her hand. 'Why don't you go back to the church? Wait for me there. I'll see if I can get to the car - somehow. Don't come out till you hear me sound the horn twice. All right?'

She stroked the side of his face.

'What are you actually going to do?'

'I don't know yet,' he shot her a reassuring smile, 'but give me ten minutes – if only to make a hash of it, then I'll come and ask for your help.'

'All right,' she said. 'The clock's running.'

He took off his trilby and gave it to her.

'Ten minutes,' she repeated firmly, before striding towards the tall doorway of the church. He waited for her to enter and then edged back to the corner, keeping himself as close as possible to the stonework. He peered around: the shortest, exposed, route to the Alvis lay from the entrance of the baker's. He felt the hard metal of the car keys in his pocket. However, there was of course, the distinct chance that the fascists were in that very shop. His stomach turned. It would be logical, he thought. Pursuers needed to eat, too – and they didn't look like they'd stopped. There was also the small matter of the third car: when they had come to Dr Wilkinson's there was another Rover. *Where was it now?*

He braced himself as he saw the door of the newsagents open. Two men emerged and walked slowly towards the Alvis. The first one was big - the top of the second man's head barely reached his chin. Jumbo, thought Drabble. Just what I need. They both wore three-quarter-length dark overcoats and charcoal grey trilbies. The shorter man was stouter, and a thick moustache spanned the top of his mouth. They crossed the square towards the parked cars. The door of the newsagents opened again and a third man, dressed similarly, exited. He jogged towards the others, catching up after several rapid strides, and fell in with their conversation. They paused by the cars and Drabble saw Jumbo take out a packet of cigarettes and offer them around. The man with the moustache took one - and Jumbo lit them both with a chrome Zippo lighter. Drabble glanced up at the clock tower: 8.25. He looked back over at the three men, now smoking, and then scanned the empty square. Where was a ruddy policeman when you wanted one?

He saw a skinny black and white dog, a Border Collie, scamper across the far side of the square and pause outside the newspaper shop. It barked. The fascists looked over.

Drabble checked over his shoulder and sprang from the corner, darting to the far side of the road. He slid into the recessed entrance of an empty shop-front, just a few doors along from the gent's outfitter. From the corner, he saw the fascists turn their attention back to the Alvis and begin to converse. Jumbo removed his hat and inspected its lining, showing it to the other two. They leaned their heads back in laughter. Drabble saw that Jumbo's face was young and fresh. One of the other fascists removed his hat and they all had a look inside too. This provoked more mirth. Jumbo shook his head gleefully. He couldn't have been more than twenty-one, thought Drabble. Ruddy kid.

Drabble edged along the shop-front in the direction of the baker's, his back flat to the metal shutters. The dog barked.

'Ahrr-uff!'

The Border Collie stood in the middle of the square and looked at the fascists. The piercing, shrill bark echoed off the buildings.

'Ahrr-uff!'

The trio turned towards the dog in time for it to issue a third insistent report. Drabble broke into a jog and passed the next shop. He dodged the shopkeeper who was just coming out of his door and saw the smallest fascist reach down and pick up a stone from the gutter.

'Ahrr-uff!'

The man brought his right hand back and aimed.

Drabble ducked into the alley just as he heard the distant whine of the dog. He pressed himself against the wooden door. There was the faint sound of cheering, followed by a defiant bark. The door was soft, green, and damp to the touch. He shouldered it – the door bowed – and then rammed it again. The timbers split and he spilled into the narrow alley.

He snatched a look over his shoulder and then sprinted along the passage, his shoes sliding on muddy bricks that lined the ground. Tall weeds grew at the sides and got thicker as he reached the end. Here a lane ran along the rear of the parade: muddy grasses protruded from between the cobbles and house-bricks, and it was strewn with litter and the detritus of commerce. There were spent packets, packing boxes, carpet edges, and off-cuts from last season's lines. Over on the left, several shops down, he saw steep piles of empty hessian sacks marked 'flour', and the muddy lane gave way to a hard-standing of stained white concrete.

Drabble glanced up the lane in the opposite direction and hurried over, approaching the back door of the shop with caution. It was open and he looked in. He saw a small dark room. On the right, several dozen sacks of flour and oversized silver tins lined long, wooden shelves. Entering, he heard a metallic rasp and looked over to see a vast mixing machine in the corner, its paddle turning methodically in the high metal bowl. The air was heavy with yeast, dust, and the hot smell of baking bread. The uneven floor was covered in blackened reddy-brown tiles, which were pitted and rutted, and covered in patches of white flour. Ahead was a low doorway. He went over and peered into the next room; it was dark and he felt the heat on his face from the wide iron ovens that stood against the side wall. Beneath them he saw dancing flames reflected on the tiles. On the far side of this room a curtain of green and white streamers hung in the doorway, separating the shop from the bakery. The streamers swayed and rustled gently in the draught. Drabble wiped a bead of sweat from his forehead and crept over to the doorway. He flattened himself against the warm wall and peered past a red conical fire extinguisher that was fixed to the wall by a bracket. Beyond the counter he saw the three fascists in the shop. The chubby one was eating an éclair; white cream caught on the edge of his dark, narrow moustache. Jumbo was next to him. From his vantage point Drabble could tell he was well, *well* over six foot, and heavy with it. Drabble saw several trails of sweat on the side of his

183

pallid face and thick neck. He wore a black pin-striped suit, which pinched at the button beneath the heavy overcoat, and a black felt Homburg. In contrast the third man – the stone-thrower - was older, slighter, and had military-short, grey hair.

Drabble heard the ring of the till over the low chatter. His heart beat fast. He saw the baker's hands clasp together behind him as he shifted his weight between his feet, making polite conversation. The fascists moved to the door and he heard the tinkle of the bell. The baker turned and Drabble dodged to the corner beside the oven, kneeling down in its hot, dark shadow. He watched the baker's brown leather shoes pass and move purposefully into the storeroom. After a moment, Drabble heard the sound of machinery being worked in the back. He crept out to the doorway and parted the green and white ribbons. Keeping low, and with his hands out either side to support him, he moved out into the shop. He reached the door. Beyond the shop sign and rows of loaves, he saw the fascists, smoking again, and lounging against the bonnet of the Rover that was parked furthest away. The éclair-eater was laughing at something said by the stone-thrower. He saw the red running boards of the Alvis. The car was barely ten feet away. The path to it was clear. He removed the car-key from his pocket and silently pulled open the door, taking care not to allow the woodwork to make contact with the bell...

'Hey! YOU!'

He span round. It was the baker.

There were shouts from outside; he looked back, the fascists were coming. He slammed the door shut and put the bolt across. He turned to confront the baker – who had a bludgeon raised above his head. He was slight and as Drabble stood, a flicker of doubt flashed across the man's face. Drabble heard another shout from outside and dived for the baker, seizing his wrist. They tumbled over and Drabble wrestled the weapon free. He heard a smash of glass and looked over: the window in the door exploded, showering the entrance of the shop in glittering shards. A fascist's boot followed, kicking away any remnants of the pane. An arm snaked in, roaming for the lock. The baker looked over at them – his face fearful and confused. Drabble sprang past, pushing him into the attackers' bundling path. The moustachioed fascist collided full-square with the baker; knocking his hat off and messing up the neat parting in his greasy black hair. Drabble snatched up a dense brown loaf and hurled it at the éclair-eater. It thudded against the man's forehead. He recoiled, blinking, and Drabble saw the loaf fall away, leaving a square white mark.

Drabble darted through the back door and into the lane, breathing hard. His shoes skated on the smooth, muddy bricks and he crashed down into the middle of the lane. Cursing, he hauled himself up.

His eyes widened. Up ahead he saw the third Rover. It was parked sideways, about thirty yards off. He saw the window roll down. The barrel and circular magazine of a Tommy gun came into view. *Oh, bugger!*

He dived towards the baker's yard as the sound of gunfire filled the lane. *Rat-a-tat-rat-a-tat…* Sparks flashed around him on the concrete standing.

He burst through the doorway and bowled straight into

the older, grey-haired fascist. They somersaulted onto the dusty floor of the back room. Drabble jumped up first and snatched one of the wooden paddles from the wall. He charged into the bakery proper, the paddle gripped aloft like a baseball bat. There was Jumbo. Drabble swung the paddle; it swept through the air and thudded into his chest. Jumbo stumbled back like a drunkard, and Drabble struck him again. Jumbo arched over backwards, his arms flailing, but kept to his feet. He shook his head and his small dark eyes glared down at him.

'You piggy-eyed bastard!' howled Drabble and he raised the paddle.

The fascist bobbed to one side and caught the paddle mid-air, wrenching it free. He tossed it to the wall and it clattered to the floor. Jumbo chuckled.

Drabble launched at him but the man was solid and pushed his attack away with his hand. Drabble lost his footing and staggered back – his gaze darting either side of the man. Could he dodge around him, he wondered? He saw the metal fire extinguisher on the wall. *That would do nicely*. He looked up: his focus met the piggy eyes.

They narrowed and Drabble saw Jumbo's mouth open and the blackened, gappy teeth within. There was a guttural roar and Jumbo lunged, his grasping hands outstretched. They found Drabble's throat and, laughing, the man drove him against the cast-iron ovens. Drabble cried out as the hot metal levers and handles burned into his back. The fascist pressed him harder against the ironwork.

'*Arggh!*'

Drabble saw the éclair eater enter, the baker's

bludgeon patting back and forth in his hand. The white smudge left by the loaf of bread was still visible on his forehead.

'You know what we want,' he growled, his jowly face and double chin illuminated by the dancing flames of the oven. 'We know you got it. Give us the car keys.'

The hair on the back of Drabble's head started to singe. He strained his neck away but the fascist's strength was greater. Jumbo pressed the palm of his hand against Drabble's forehead. His nostrils flared as he smelt his hair burn. It must be mine, he thought, but why can't I feel it? The sound of the furnace behind him intensified. Jumbo leaned in harder: Drabble felt the heat press against his scalp. His focus travelled from the toothy grin to the éclair-eater waiting with the bludgeon. He swallowed. This was a distinctly sub-optimal situation, he thought. *Distinctly sub-optimal.* He patted his hand along the front of the oven, feeling the levers and handles. His fingers found a loose metal object – it fell away and he grabbed it. He looked up and saw beads of sweat roll down Jumbo's face. The man grinned; he no longer looked quite so young or innocent.

'Go on, Tiny,' cooed the éclair-eater from beyond the bulk of Jumbo. 'Check his pockets for the keys. And no funny business, Drabble. If you won't cooperate, there's always the girl.'

A leer spread across the chubby fascist's wet lips. 'She'll give us what we want – and maybe more.'

With his right hand still gripping Drabble's throat, Tiny released his forehead, and moved his other hand towards the right-side trouser pocket. Drabble felt the

187

fingers locate the keys.

He stabbed with the iron poker, driving into Tiny's groin. At first the pain did not register but then the fascist's eyes narrowed and darted to him; his forehead creased with confusion. He whimpered, let go and sank back. Drabble punched him squarely on the mouth, and he collapsed.

The éclair-eater swung at him and Drabble dodged back, the bludgeon swishing past his face. Drabble lunged with the poker – the man danced out of the way, and shot the iron rod from Drabble's grip with the truncheon. *Clang!* It struck the brick wall and fell to the ground. Tiny stirred.

'Keep down, Jumbo,' shouted Drabble as he swerved to the right, the truncheon tearing through the air inches just from his ear. Drabble dived for the éclair-eater, forcing the weapon to one side. They pirouetted as Drabble chased the bludgeon away and the man retreated. He span back, knocked into the oven, and cried out. Drabble brought his fist back and jabbed the fascist's chin crisply. The man staggered back, blood oozing from the corner of his mouth, just as the older fascist arrived from the storeroom, now armed with one of the wooden paddles. Drabble saw Jumbo rise to his knees.

Drabble sprang for the ribbons and crashed into the shop, breaking his fall on a display of loaves and a pyramid of bags of flour. He grabbed one from the floor and hurled it through the ribbons. It struck the frontrunner and burst, scattering white powder. Drabble snatched up another bag and threw it at Tiny's head as he emerged through the ribbons. It struck hard and sent him staggering back, clutching his face. Drabble dived beyond the counter and rolled to the door, finding his feet just as he reached the broken glass. He seized a broom which leaned against the wall and yanked open the front door. Pulling it shut behind him, he slid the wooden shaft through the handle, locking it shut.

He ran to the car and unlocked the driver's side door. He climbed in and flicked the start switch and start button. *Whut-whut-whut*... the Alvis fired up – just as he saw the black sleeve of a fascist arm crab through the broken shop window and wrestle with the broom-handle.

He found reverse and sped away; the fascist - dishevelled and dusted in flour - burst through the doorway.

Drabble pumped the horn twice as the Alvis squealed to a halt outside the church, the passenger door lined up with the entrance. His gaze fixed on the circular cast iron hoop that hung from the latch. He pressed the horn again and shot a glance back at the corner of the square. In any second the fascists would be round it.

He held the horn down again, looking over at the church door. *Come on, come on.* He knew they would start shooting soon. He looked back at the corner of the marketplace. Come on, Kate. *Come on. Come on.* He turned to the church door. Dear Lord, he prayed. *Please make the handle turn. Please turn.*

He put the Alvis into first and revved the engine. *Come on Kate.* He pressed the horn: once, twice – he looked back at the corner. A black foot came into view; then a leg, then the éclair-eater...

'COME ON, KATE!'

He pumped the horn.

Next came Jumbo, his face and shoulders white from flour. Then, running and armed with a pistol, was the smaller, grey-haired fascist – he raised the gun.

Drabble heard the door.

'Get in,' he barked, as he dropped the clutch – and yanked Kate in by her collar.

The Alvis sped away.

CHAPTER SEVENTEEN

The Alvis cleared the rear of the church, smoke pouring from its rear wheels. Its tyres squealed and Drabble jerked the wheel, correcting the over-steer. He shifted the gear-stick into third and accelerated hard. The needle on the speedometer pointed due north: fifty-five miles per hour. Drabble glanced at the rear view mirror.

'Hold on to your hat,' he said. 'We're not out of the woods yet.'

He pressed the throttle. The speed jerked up to sixty.

Kate gripped the side of the door and turned back. She glimpsed the sloping brow of a black Rover, about a hundred yards off. They turned a corner.

'What's the plan?' she asked, peering down at the instrument panel and spying the speedometer: sixty-five .

Drabble tightened his grip on the wheel.

'Brace yourself.'

'What?'

Straight ahead, at the bottom of the hill, was a set of traffic lights. They approached fast. The light showed green and their carriageway was clear. Kate looked back and saw the Rover behind, the outlines of the fascists visible through the windscreen. She faced forward and referred to the traffic signal.

Amber.

She glanced at the speedometer: seventy. She looked back at the light.

Red.

'HOLD ON!' cried Drabble as he jammed the horn and pinned his foot to the accelerator pedal. *Meeeeeep!*

The Alvis streaked through the junction, snaking through the cross-flow of traffic. There was a blare of horns as a pair of cars slid to a halt behind. In the mirror Drabble saw the two vehicles lying askew. The Rover was caught on the far side. Drabble looked over at Kate. Her knuckles were white on the dashboard. He slowed the car to fifty.

'I tell you something,' he said, his gaze dropping momentarily to the wheel and the instrument panel. 'This beauty's got *pace*.'

'The doctor always said she was a dream come true.'

'He wasn't wrong,' he looked over. 'Unfortunately she's about as discreet as the Household ruddy Cavalry.'

Kate sighed. 'He did admit she was a bit,' she raised her eyebrows, '*flash*.'

'Fortunately she's as quick as a flash, too.'

The Alvis raced along a country road, its 2.8 -litre engine developing a stately sixty miles per hour. The road ahead straightened up and ran ahead for about a mile, gently rising up through fields. The hedgerows thinned and vanished and the broad flat fields spread far off either side, dotted here and there with mature trees. On the straight, Drabble took the car up to seventy-five. The asphalt vanished beneath them. At this rate they'd make Westminster in two and a half hours. He noted the time on his watch: 8.45 a.m. He looked ahead at the straight, undulated road, and pressed the accelerator. Come on, he thought, let's hit the magic hundred.

His foot was still pressed firmly to the floor panel and

the needle of the speedometer crept up to the nine o'clock position: eighty miles per hour. The car juddered on the road but held well, he thought. He saw Kate's hand return to the dash. She swallowed.

Drabble lifted his foot and the car began to slow. The engine became quieter.

'Better?'

She nodded.

'Thank you.' She looked over and smiled, suddenly registering his appearance. 'You've got flour all over you – what's happened to your hair?' She felt the back of his neck where the hairs were short and grizzled. 'It's been... *burned*.'

He leaned away, and shot her a reassuring smile.

'It's nothing - really. Mind you, if I'd hung about any longer I would have been brown bread, as they say.'

He smiled and she returned it, but only half-heartedly. They both knew it wasn't really a laughing matter, he sensed. She looked out of the passenger window and sighed. They drove on in silence. She bent down and took out a cigarette. He heard the rasp of the lighter.

'I don't know, Ernest,' she said wearily. She wound the window down. 'I really don't. The last twenty-four hours have been madness.' She turned to him, tears in her caramel eyes. 'Utter madness. I really -'

There was an earth-trembling, guttural roar - the car shook and everything went dark. There was a gust of wind and Drabble snatched the wheel as the Alvis veered violently across the road. A vast shadow overtook them, sweeping along the bonnet and over the road ahead. Drabble leaned towards the windscreen and looked up. He saw the wide, webbed wings of a plane and the underside of its tapered fuselage shot over. It couldn't have been more than twenty feet above them.

'Bloody hell,' cried Kate, appealing to him. 'It's a ruddy plane!'

He caught her eye as he wrestled to master the erratic movement of the car.

'Is it one of *them*?' she asked, pressing the side of her face to the windscreen and peering up into the sky. She saw the rear of the black outline low and dead ahead. 'Surely they haven't got an aeroplane?' She looked at him. 'Tell me these people don't have an aeroplane!'

Drabble frowned: a plane meant an airfield, it meant a chain of command, it meant resources, it meant organisation – it meant they were in it even more deeply than he had thought.

'Don't worry,' he said, shooting her a reassuring glance. 'All they can do is frighten us. It's a plane: we're on the ground, they're in the air. There's nothing they can do to us.'

The aircraft pulled up and began to climb high and bank. Drabble braked hard as the Alvis approached a sharp right bend.

'It's coming round again, Ernest.' Kate was close to the passenger window, looking back.

'OK, OK - I'm speeding up.'

She jumped round in the passenger seat and looked out through the rear window.

'IT'S COMING!'

The drill of the engine suddenly magnified and pounded in their ears. There was a rush of air. Drabble pushed Kate down into her seat and saw the undercarriage of the plane zoom just overhead. The thick black wheels passed barely a foot above them – before the plane soared away from view.

'Get the shotgun,' said Drabble. 'Quick!'

Kate leaned over to the back seat and pulled out the twelve-bore. She reached back for the cartridges.

'Can you see it?' asked Drabble, craning his head to the driver's side window. 'Where's the plane?'

She shook her head.

'No! No!'

Up ahead he saw a farmer's lane veering off from the side of the road; it crossed the field and led to some woods, grey and low in the distance.

'We'll make for those trees over there,' he pointed ahead. 'Brace yourself.' The Alvis swerved onto the rough track. He saw that she had found the cartridges. 'Right, load her up – *quickly*.'

He accelerated hard and the Alvis bumped along the farm path. He saw Kate's hands were shaking. She fumbled one of the cartridges; it slipped from her fingers and bounced down to the floor. She snatched another from the box. Beside the woods he saw a stone farm building. He pressed the throttle pedal to the floor and referred to the rear view mirror – spotting the black outline of the plane. The woods were too far away, he thought. They weren't going to make it in time.

Kate snapped the breach of the gun shut and pulled the hammers back.

'Well done,' he said, looking back to see if he could spy the plane. 'Aim for the engine, it's our best hope.'

'I thought you said it couldn't hurt us?'

He smiled.

Kate turned in her seat and half kneeled, the shotgun at the ready, its barrel protruding from the passenger window. Oh God, he thought. The trees were greener now, having lost the grey cloak of distance, but still too far – barely an inch and a half tall.

'He's coming,' cried Kate, leaning out of the side. She pulled the gun into her shoulder, the wind throwing her hair across her face. The drone of the plane grew louder. Drabble felt the rush of air as his senses were consumed by the intense drum of the engine. He looked over his shoulder and saw the darkness overtake the window.

Kate fired.

He didn't hear the second shot.

'Get down.'

He pulled her back as the plane swept in. Its black wheel bobbed down and struck the bonnet, jarring the Alvis violently. The car skidded from the gravelled track, throwing up a cloud of dirt, and spinning into the field. Drabble struggled with the wheel – and accelerated.

The Alvis broke free from the spin and they sped towards the woods, the car's wheels juddering on the grassy field. Drabble looked over: Kate had opened the breach of the shotgun and was reloading with difficulty as the Alvis bumped and jerked. Good girl, he thought. He looked back and then strained his neck to see from the side of the car. He couldn't see the plane.

'Kate – can you…'

She turned back – and her scream filled the air. He pulled her towards him…

The throaty grind of the aeroplane engine shook the car and a veil of darkness descended. Suddenly there was a loud bang above them – and an explosion - as the wheel of the plane crashed through the roof and caught the steel top of the windscreen, blasting it to smithereens.

Drabble covered his eyes and then snatched at the steering wheel, pumping the accelerator.

'Bloody hell,' he roared, his chest heaving. He could see the white sky through the tattered remains of the mohair roof. 'Right, we're going to get to those trees in about a minute, I'd say. Have you reloaded?'

Kate, dazed, shook her head.

'Reload, come on. *Now*.'

'Oh, bugger, it's coming back, Ernest – it's coming…'

He looked over and pressed her hand.

'It's going to be all right,' he said, eyeing the approaching plane through the fluttering hole above. 'I'm going to brake really hard: and you're going to shoot it as it goes over. Go for the engine. OK?'

He saw her nod.

'Come on,' he said, 'we'll show them.'

He swerved the car to the left and to the right as the plane approached. Up ahead the trees were close now – perhaps only a couple of hundred yards. The dirge of the engine grew. He looked back and stamped on the brake. The aircraft overshot and dipped in front.

'FIRE!'

She pulled the trigger and there was a flash from the muzzle of the shotgun - and a cloud of smoke – but the sound of the shot was lost in the din. She pulled the second trigger – her shoulder recoiled and there was another plume of smoke. The plane climbed away, soaring high into the sky.

'Good shooting!'

'I've no idea if I hit the bugger.'

'You did, all right.'

BANG!

The Alvis lurched left – Drabble corrected the steering but the wheel span loosely in his hands.

'She's not responding!' He looked over at her. 'Hold tight!'

Drabble yanked the handbrake and jammed his foot to the pedal. The Alvis performed a long, juddering, arc, before coming to a jarring halt. For a moment they were both dazed. Drabble stirred.

'Where's that plane gone?'

She strained her head back and cried out.

'It's behind us!'

'Quick!' Drabble thrust open her passenger door and then went for his own. 'Shelter by the side of the car – if you have to, lie flat on the ground.' He grabbed the shotgun, and the box of cartridges. 'I'll draw him away.'

He broke into a run.

'*What*? Ernest!'

Drabble stopped and looked back: Kate was staring at him from the passenger seat. In the distance he saw the plane approach, *fast*.

'There's no time to explain,' he said, his voice straining. 'Get out, but stay there. He'll follow me – he'll *have* to. I'm going to be shooting at him.'

He turned away and jogged towards the middle of the broad, grassy field. He broke the shotgun open and slotted a pair of rounds into the side-by-side breaches. Still on the move, he snapped the gun shut and looked up, scouring the sky. Come on, you bastard, he thought. *Come on.* Sweat poured from his face.

He looked up and his eyes narrowed. There he is, he thought. A thin white trail of smoke came from the front by the propeller. Maybe she'd hit him after all. Thank God. He continued to sprint towards the middle of the field.

He looked up again. The aircraft completed its slow turn and was now a skinny black outline against the sky directly behind him. The silhouette got bigger – and quickly so. Suddenly the faint chatter of the engine intensified and then became a roar. Drabble dived for the ground and, rolling onto his back, pulled back the hammers of the shotgun. He saw the wheels coming straight at him and the earth trembled. He fired from the hip.

Through the dust and dirt he saw the plane jerk; rather like a fly bumping into a pane of glass. Then there was silence. The plane's wings dipped sharply to one side, then the other. The plane banked and turned towards him, pale smoke pouring freely from the engine. The prop had stopped and it was descending – fast – but plunging straight at him. Leaving the gun, Drabble scampered to his feet, breaking into a run. He felt the whistling draught against the back of his head become a rush of air as the plane approached. He hurled himself forward, arms outstretched, and hit the ground. The plane shot over him.

Immediately, Drabble heard an ear-splitting metallic crunch and was thrown into the air. He landed hard on his back as he saw the plane flipping and crashing upside-down before him, throwing up a huge wave of soil, dirt, and smoke.

Drabble came to his senses and coughed on a mouthful of soil. Wiping lumps of grime from his face, he looked up and saw a fog drifting across the field. Through the smoke he discerned the inverted undercarriage. He coughed and covered his face. He bent down and, fanning the smoke, approached. He glimpsed the leather-lined curve of the open cockpit and saw it disappear into the churned-up heap of soil. He saw the pilot's arm dangling over the side. He then saw the man's head, lying at an impossible angle to his torso. The right lens of his flying goggles was stoved in, bloody and caked in grime. Drabble moved back from the cockpit and looked at the engine, a bent prop folded down its side. He heard hissing and the rapid glug and splash of escaping liquid. He looked down and saw pools of fluid gathering at his feet. He turned away from the wreckage, and broke into a run -

The explosion swept Drabble off his feet and he crashed forward, tumbling head over heels. There was a second explosion as he came to a stop. He looked up and saw a gigantic, black-capped ball of flame rise from the wreckage. The air was thick with burnt oil and rubber. He coughed.

'Ernest?'

Kate.

'ERNEST!'

He turned and saw her legs, the smoke from the plane obscuring the rest of her figure.

'Kate -'

He saw the feet stop and turn. He called out her name. The boots started to run towards him. Suddenly he saw her face, not quite smiling, break through the fog. His throat filled and he gulped for air.

'Oh, Lord,' she cried, rushing towards him. 'You're safe!'

She flung her arms around him and pressed herself to him.

'Thank God,' she said. 'You're safe.'

They embraced and then Kate leaned back. She pushed Drabble's dirty hair off his face. He put his arms around her waist and pulled her close.

'Your hair's covered in mud,' she said, with a smile. She picked a clod of soil from his side parting and flicked it away.

'Yours would be, too, if you'd just fought an arm wrestle with an aeroplane.'

She grinned.

'Ernest Drabble, one, evil fascist biplane, nil…'

His eyes softened and looked into hers. They were golden brown and biddable. I'll kiss her, he thought. She wrapped her arms around his waist and presented her mouth, the lips, curved and full and – Drabble exhaled – she was so utterly, eminently kissable.

'Excuse me,' called a man's plaintive voice through the smoke. They broke apart. 'But could you explain what this *aero*plane is doing in my field?'

CHAPTER EIGHTEEN

There was a loud, grating rasp, followed by a clank and clang from the door. Harris braced himself in his chair and swallowed hard. The small room was now bathed in weak white daylight. He shivered. The door creaked open slowly, revealing a slight figure silhouetted by a bright yellow electric light. The newcomer wore a black fascist uniform of high-topped riding boots, breeches, a military jacket, a holster, a leather Sam Brown, and a tall peaked cap of, Harris thought, Continental persuasion.

'Who are you?' he barked.

The fascist stepped forward and Harris got proper sight of the face. It was smooth, hairless and feminine – a long straight nose led towards a pointed chin. It's a woman, thought Harris. *A ruddy woman!*

She pulled off her hat and tossed it onto the wooden table. He saw her dark hair was cut short in boyish fashion, slicked back from a sharp parting down one side. He noticed a slight bulge across the chest - but nothing, he thought, to write home about. There was more than just a hint of Weimar about her, he thought. A uniformed guard followed her in, carrying a tray – Harris saw a covered plate and bottle on it. His eyes widened and he licked his dry lips. The guard went out and stood in the corridor. He received a nod from the woman and he closed the door.

'My name is Captain Smith,' said the woman, her voice husky and low. 'But the prisoner may call me Charles.'

He looked up and met her gaze.

'Ch-Charles?'

'Yes,' she stepped forward so that her knees pressed against his chair. He saw that her eyes were very, *very* blue indeed, like copper sulphate crystals. 'I'm Sir Carmen's aide-de-camp; cigarette?'

'All right,' he said, looking her up and down.

He noticed the military flashes on her lapels: the motif was a rectangular silver cross with a jagged silver bolt of lightning in each of the quarters. So, he thought, this was it. Kelly was a fascist after all – and not just any old common or garden one at that. Harris swallowed. This bugger meant business. The conversations with Valerie, Grubby Howse, and the earlier interview with Kelly all made sense. *Good God.* He saw her black gloved hand undo her outside breast pocket and the fingers roam inside. They drew out a soft packet of Camel cigarettes. She tapped the packet and then knocked two from it, taking one for herself and pressing the second into Harris' mouth. For a moment her leather glove strayed to the top of his lip. She struck a match, lit his, then hers. Smith tossed the spent matchstick to the floor and Harris met her gaze as he took a long, first drag on the cigarette. His head fell back and he emitted a moan of pleasure.

She smiled at him and turned away, strutting over to the table. She dragged out the chair, its legs scraping on the stone floor, and planted a boot on it. The cigarette went to her narrow mouth: and she then blew smoke from her bowed lips to one side.

'Sir Carmen sends his compliments. He is, regrettably, detained.' She looked at him and raised the corners of her

203

mouth. Harris saw that she had a short white scar under her left eye.

Her blue eyes softened and seemed to relax. His focus ran down her torso – the slim waist, her hip and the pleasing outline of her bottom - and then down her slender leg, to the boot and her narrow ankle and the floor.

'I think you'll find that I'm the one who's been regrettably detained,' he said. He exhaled, smoke pouring from his nostrils.

Smith smiled.

'Sir Carmen told me of your humorous facility with words.' She took a drag of her Camel and shook her head. 'It's a pity that you find it so hard to give the correct answers.'

He scoffed.

'I'm afraid that Sir Carmen and I are unlikely to agree on what constitutes a correct answer.'

She looked at him and nodded. He saw the sheen of black piping half an inch wide on the jacket and followed it south to where its flaps parted below her narrow waist, by her raised leg. The material within was in darkness. He leaned back and regarded her. A cloud of his own smoke filled his view. Was she a lesbian? Probably, he thought. He frowned.

'I have brought the prisoner's food,' she announced.

'I'm not hungry.'

'I find that hard to believe.'

He raised an eyebrow.

'Why don't you call me Harris? This third person prisoner business is a bit *stiff*.'

Smith tossed her cigarette on the floor and watched the

smouldering butt. She emitted a thoughtful groan and brought her foot off the stool and stamped on it. Smith turned her attention to Harris. He puffed at the cigarette, clouds of smoke filling the space between them. Smith came towards him and snagged the burning cigarette from his mouth. She flicked it to the floor.

The skylight caught her face and Harris saw that the copper sulphate was streaked with radiating lines of navy blue. The expression on her unlined face was impassive. Slowly, almost seductively, she tugged off her right glove. She tossed the garment onto the table and bent forward, placing her hand on his cheek. Her skin was cool and soft. She turned her hand and ran the back of her fingers and nails softly down his cheek. Her face – her mouth – was just a couple of inches from his. He felt her warm breath against his face. Her nose creased.

'You stink.'

Harris pecked his mouth forward and pressed his lips to hers. For a moment her eyes widened in mild shock, but then she returned the pressure. She gripped his head powerfully between her hands and they kissed, her tongue pushing deeply into his mouth. Then she pulled away, wiping her mouth with the back of her hand.

'W-What?' said Harris. 'What is it?'

'Silence!' She pulled on her glove and made a fist of her right hand.

'Hang on!' He laughed nervously. 'I'm not into rough stuff-'

Her eyes flashed angrily and there was a momentary blur before his eyes. There was a stinging blow to his face. He cried out.

'What makes you think I might be interested in you?' she barked, as Harris rolled his jaw again. He saw her eyes soften and she smiled. She stroked the side of his face and leaned forward...

CHAPTER NINETEEN

Drabble pulled Kate to him and turned towards the direction of the voice. On the other side of the wreckage – beyond a single twist of smoke that rose from the charred engine section of the biplane – he saw a man in a long green military greatcoat and brown top hat approach. He wore a silvery handlebar moustache and carried a shotgun broken in the crook of his right arm. He removed a clay pipe from his mouth.

'This ain't your aeroplane, is it?'

Drabble glanced back over at the crash and shook his head.

'Not guilty.' He returned his gaze to the man.

'Ah, so you brought the motorcar,' he said.

'That's right.' Drabble waited for the man to reply. 'Who are you?' he said.

'Scobell,' replied the man, stopping in front of them. He made a small circular movement with the stem of the pipe. 'I'm the farmer hereabouts.' He sighed and looked over at the wreckage, shaking his head. 'This is some business, ain't it?' He sighed again, and met Drabble's gaze.

'And you are?'

They shook hands.

'Bristow,' said Drabble. 'I'm Ernest Bristow.' He moved to one side. 'And this,' he cleared his throat, 'is Mrs Bristow.'

'Good to make thou acquaintance, Mr Bristow.' The

farmer grinned, showing yellowed teeth flecked with brown patches. 'Madam,' he raised his hat and bowed.

'How long have you been here?'

Scobell tilted his head to one side. 'I wandered over after the explosion. So the motorcar's busted?'

'I think so.'

The man nodded.

Drabble continued, 'Something's up with the steering - and we've lost the windscreen. I'll need to take a look at it. I don't think she's going anywhere in a hurry.'

Scobell's gaze shifted back to the remains of the plane. The man blinked and pursed his lips. The heavy lids of the eyes lowered thoughtfully and inspected Drabble.

'Nor's he,' said the man with a sigh. 'I suppose,' said Scobell, 'I shall have to get word to the station and have them make a report – and take this contraption away.'

The farmer pushed his hat back and shook his head, revealing a thatch of curly white hair. 'I wonder what he was doing out here?'

Drabble looked at him and raised his eyebrows. I've no *real* idea what the plane was doing here either, he thought. This was true in a very real sense, too. Drabble turned and looked back over at the wreckage. It was still giving off a thick twist of smoke. What was certain was that he was a long way from Sidney Sussex; far from the clatter of a typewriter drifting in from the corridor; far from the tranquil green quad that had long been known as Chapel Court and which his rooms overlooked; far from the cool shade of the great wisteria that was trained against the length of the college wall and was invariably thick with mauve blooms in his mind's eye.

'You know,' resumed Scobell, drawing Drabble's attention. 'I reckon that thing very nearly destroyed one of my favourite trees. That one,' he pointed with his walking stick to a mighty elm. 'It was planted by my great-grandfather.'

Drabble saw it.

'He put those four in,' said Scobell, 'but the one at the end is my favourite. You see the way it's shaped; the way the branches separate. And she's the biggest of the lot by some margin.'

Drabble studied the tree – its infinite lattice of branches was black against the white sky. He turned to the farmer.

'She really is a beauty all right, Mr Scobell.'

The man sighed and looked at the wreckage.

'What a mess,' he said, shaking his head. He turned to Kate. 'Would you and your husband care for a cup of tea, Mrs Bristow?' He moved away, 'I'll then work out what in Lord's creation I'm to do with this lot.'

***

Captain Smith drew back from Harris' face and took a deep breath, her nostrils flaring. The skin around her lips was reddened and her blue eyes were wide and hungry. She stood up and flattened her hair with the palm of her hand.

'You kiss surprisingly well,' she said, half smiling and going over to the desk. She put her cap on and picked up the riding crop. Harris restrained an excited grin.

'You kiss awfully well, too,' he said. 'The question is,

what *else* do you do?'

She turned to him, the smile gone, and picked up her gloves.

'That, Harris, is the question.' She yanked the black leather gloves on, pressing down between the knuckles to ensure a close fit. 'I obtain collaboration from individuals,' she continued, as she gently slid out the drawer from beneath the table. Harris strained to one side to see, and saw her remove something. He heard a low wooden scrape as the drawer closed. Concealing the item behind her back, Smith turned towards him.

'In your case,' she said, as she approached, 'Sir Carmen would like you to collaborate on a special message for your friend Professor Drabble.'

She stopped in front him and stroked a gloved finger along his lips. Harris wriggled in the chair.

'Message?' he snorted. 'Oh, you are terribly naughty. What sort of message?'

Behind her back, Smith flexed a pair of pliers…

***

Scobell's farmhouse was large and from the parlour window they saw the yard and green fields beyond. Flames flickered from a log in the shallow fireplace next to the table. Above it was a gold framed oval mirror, and a mantelpiece on which stood family photographs including two of young men in uniforms of the Great War. They looked like boys, thought Drabble. He dipped a lump of cotton wool into the blue-and-white enamel bowl and dabbed the graze on Kate's forehead. He caught her smile and laid his hand on hers. Drabble heard the tinkle of crockery and saw Scobell enter, carrying a tea-tray. He brought his hand away. The farmer placed the tray down on the oak table and unfolded a newspaper. He put it on the table. There was a photograph of Drabble on the cover.

DON WANTED ON MURDER HUNT:
FIRST PICTURE

Drabble swallowed and looked over at Kate; she stared at it. The photograph was from the summer, he realised, following his accident on the North Face of the Eiger, and showed him with his left arm in a sling and wearing that full beard. Drabble rubbed his cheek, feeling his stubble. Scobell, his hat removed, glanced at the image and then placed a teacup and saucer in front of Kate. 'There you go, Mrs Bristow. I brought the paper; I thought you'd be interested to know what was going on in the outside world.' There was the jingle of china as he put a cup in front of Drabble. He grinned. 'I keep buying the paper but the news doesn't get no better.'

Drabble stroked the ball of cotton wool across the surface of the water and pressed it to Kate's forehead.

'Nasty business,' continued the farmer, turning the newspaper towards himself and taking in the front page. 'Likely as not, I dare say he was defending himself.'

Drabble and Scobell exchanged a glance.

'Milk?'

'Yes, please,' said Kate. Drabble nodded.

'It's from my own herd,' announced Scobell, as he

tilted the jug. 'They're fine animals.' He sighed, 'It strikes me as unusual behaviour for a historian. You tend to think of these fellows as having weak eyesight, pallid skin - limp handshakes.' He chuckled. 'But this one tried to climb a mountain in Switzerland this summer.' The farmer tutted and picked up the pot, for a moment he scanned the crowded tray for the strainer. 'Bloody fool,' he poured the tea into their three cups. 'Pardon my French, but you've got to admire his courage. Wouldn't you agree, Mr Bristow?'

Drabble left Kate's gaze. He looked over at the farmer and grinned.

'I wouldn't say you're wrong.'

Scobell nodded gently, pondering the comment. He drew out a chair and groaned as he seated himself.

'What's your line of work, Mr Bristow?'

Drabble raised his eyebrows in an expression indicating mild confusion. He heard the fire crackle and spit.

'I'm a schoolmaster,' he said.

'Are you now?' Scobell looked over at Kate and raised a sugar cube, gripped between the arms of a silver pincer. She shook her head and so did Drabble. He dropped it into his own cup. 'And where do you do that?'

'Little place in Sussex. Lancing. It's a minor public school.'

'Ah, is it now? And do ye find it rewarding work?'

'I should say so.'

Scobell nodded and tasted his tea. His face pinched - he set down the cup and stirred it.

'Very good tea, Mr Scobell,' said Kate. Drabble

referred to his watch.

'I wonder, sir, do you have a telephone?'

'Telephone? No, 'fraid not.' He shrugged. 'Nor electric, neither.' He chuckled. 'I'm rather stuck in the dark ages – least, I will be after the sun goes down.'

Through the window behind Scobell, Drabble saw a vast flock of starlings surge through the white sky. They passed from view and then shot back across – half their number peeling away to form a different wing. They were beautiful, nimble – a graceful mass, thought Drabble. And free. There was a scrape as he set down his cup in its saucer.

'Mr Scobell,' he said. 'I don't suppose you could possibly give us a lift?'

The man looked up from the newspaper.

'A lift?'

Drabble bit his lip and looked up at Scobell. 'Yes, we very urgently need to get to London.'

The farmer picked up his pipe and struck a match on the underside of the table.

'I might be able to go one better than that,' he said, smoke dancing from the bowl of the pipe. 'It all depends on your point of view.'

He rose from the chair and gestured to Drabble. He followed the farmer out of the front door and into a cobbled yard and over to high wooden doors. Scobell reached up, his hand shaking as he pulled down the cast iron bar. He released it.

'Here,' he said, as the door creaked open. Inside, Drabble saw a car and, beyond it, an old motorcycle. The slender green bike was covered in dust and even the letters and numerals on the curved razor-blade licence plate on the front mud-guard were hidden from view by deep dirt. Scobell tugged a red handkerchief free from his trouser pocket and stood by the machine. He wiped the dust from the top of the cream-coloured petrol tank and then across the leather saddle. 'It's an old Triumph H – belonged to Douglas, my youngest.' Scobell smiled at Drabble and then gazed down at the machine, his yellowed eyes taking in all the details: the engine's bending pipes, cylinder, the cables, wires and the smooth exterior of the tank. He rested his hand on the leather helmet that hung by a leather chin strap from the handlebars. He looked over at Drabble from the corners of his eyes. 'I'd be pleased for you to have it. She still runs nicely, though she's a bit of an old lady now.'

For a moment Drabble was lost for words. He looked into the old man's face.

'Thank you,' he said, softly.

Scobell shook his head, his eyes closed.

'It's nothing.'

He started to moved away, towards the house.

Drabble called out. 'Mr Scobell –' He waited for the old man to pause and turn. 'Why would you be so kind to us? Surely you know who I am?'

The old man removed his pipe.

'My dear Mr Bristow,' he said. 'I might do, and I might not.' He showed the top row of his yellow teeth, 'But that's for me to know, ain't it?'

***

214

The Triumph's 550cc single-cylinder engine hammered uncertainly as the bike sped along the London road, achieving an even fifty miles per hour. Drabble was hunched forward over the chrome handlebars, wearing stout leather gauntlets and driving goggles. His face was set in grim determination against the wind and cold. His hair was swept back and the brown locks fidgeted in the airstream. From a strap, the wooden box hung to his side. On the other side hung his Gladstone-bag. Kate perched behind on the parcel shelf over the rear wheel, her feet on the stand mountings. She wore the leather helmet and goggles and had her hands firmly around Drabble's waist. Her scarf flew out behind. They overtook a lorry and passed a sign: 'London 23 miles'.

CHAPTER TWENTY

It was dusk when they drew to a halt outside the St Stephen's entrance of the Houses of Parliament and the sky was a dense milky shade of brown and purple. A policeman waved them through towards the car park and Drabble stopped the Triumph in a narrow gap between a grand stone portico and a yellow Rolls-Royce. He cut the engine.

'Thank goodness that's over,' said Kate, climbing off. She rolled her shoulders and pulled off her helmet. Running her fingers through her hair, she looked down at the red cushion, which was strapped to the rear parcel rack. The metal frame of the parcel shelf showed through. She rubbed her backside.

'You did well,' said Drabble, as he hauled the bike onto its stand. He raised his goggles onto his forehead. 'That can't have been very comfortable, even with Scobell's best parlour cushion.' He looked at Kate, at her upturned honey-coloured face, at her straw coloured hair that was now tinged with grey from the road. He smiled – and a thought occurred to him. *Now...*

'Shall we go and find Mr Churchill,' she said.

Her eyes moved across his face and she smiled.

'What is it?'

'The goggles,' she giggled. 'You've got panda eyes.'

'You can talk.'

He pressed her chin with his thumb and looked down at her lips: they fell fractionally apart. Movement in the

216

background distracted him and he looked up: a policeman strolled past. He coughed into his fist. Their moment of intimacy had been observed.

'Come on,' said Drabble. 'Once we've given this to him we're free.'

She looked over.

'That sounds nice.'

They passed another constable, who stood beneath the high stone archway, and went inside, ascending the stone stairs. They went up another short flight and then along the wide marble-floored corridor and through the tall double doors at the end. In the main lobby Drabble led them over to a high wooden desk, where an attendant in white tie worked by the glow of an amber light.

Drabble saw a policeman pacing slowly along the adjoining chamber. The attendant looked up and took in the goggles which were still planted to Drabble's forehead. He regarded them severely before meeting Drabble's waiting gaze.

'We're here to see Mr Winston Churchill.'

The man's lip curled; he laid down his pen.

Drabble cleared his throat.

'He's expecting us.'

'Name?'

'Mr Cromwell.'

'*Mr* Cromwell?' The man arched an eyebrow. 'Very good. Please wait over there.' He inclined his head towards a long leather bench seat that lined the edge of the lobby. He picked up the telephone receiver and spoke quietly into it.

The circular chamber had a high, ornate, domed ceiling

217

of clerical design, punctuated at equal distances by tall windows and gothic wooden reliefs. Vast passageways led off in four directions; the byways flanked by four grand, earthy-white marble statues. The figure on the right stood atop a heavy plinth and wore a long Victorian coat and trousers and held a scroll, or speech, in his left hand. Drabble recognised the heavy, angular nose, thick, imperious eyebrows and general look of mild disapproval: William Gladstone. Benjamin Disraeli stood opposite, in the robes of the Garter. Drabble did not know the other two and the angle of the plinths meant the engraved names could not be read from where he sat. On the far side of the lobby was an anteroom, at the end of which was a pair of tall wooden doors. Immediately in front was a free-standing brass sign that said, 'Private: Members only'. A pair of elderly gentlemen passed, both in tailcoats, one of them holding a smoking cigar in his right hand. He suddenly burst into laughter and clapped the other on the shoulder. Drabble looked over at Kate. She leaned back, her eyes closed. She must be exhausted, he thought. He yawned and shut his eyes, resting his head against the back of the bench. And so am I, he thought. Absolutely done in. Just like Pheidippides after Marathon, he thought. *We have won...*

He awoke with a tap to his shoulder.

'Mr Cromwell?' inquired a voice. Drabble opened his eyes and placed his hand protectively over the box. The figure before him adjusted his round gold-rimmed spectacles and made a small bow. Drabble glanced either side and then gave a small nod of acquiescence.

'Mr Churchill sends his compliments, sir.' The man

offered a smile, revealing a top row of narrow teeth. 'My name is Jenkins,' he presented a card. 'Mr Churchill sends his apologies but he is at lunch,' he looked over at the clock – it said 4.50 – and raised his shoulders apologetically. 'I gather you have something which you wish to leave for him?' The man looked down at the box. Drabble placed his second hand over it.

'I'll only give it to Churchill in person.'

The man rolled his eyes theatrically and smiled.

'Mr Churchill said you'd say that. If you prefer to wait, I quite understand.' He leaned in, 'Although I feel it's only fair to advise you that the Foreign Secretary has just ordered *more* port.'

'Port?'

'Yes, sir.'

Jenkins regarded him importantly over the top of his glasses.

'That's all right,' said Drabble. 'We can wait.'

Jenkins' face hardened.

'I'm not sure how advisable that is, sir, given the extenuating circumstances,' he gave a nod to Kate, who was sitting up, 'Madam.' He restored his focus to Drabble. 'Your identity may be detected, if you don't mind me saying so – not to mention your unusual appearance, which will inevitably draw some interest if you wait here too long. Mr Churchill advises most strongly that you pass the item to him as agreed and await his contact in due course. He pledges to do what he can in regard to the *not insignificant* official allegations levelled currently against you, which I hardly need to remind you are of a capital nature.'

Jenkins smiled kindly. Drabble saw a constable over at the far doors. The Portcullis crest on his dark, tall helmet glinted. The officer was opening the door for an elderly gentleman. Drabble looked back to Jenkins. He saw he was waiting for an answer.

'All right,' said Drabble rising. 'Take me to *him*.'

'I-I'm afraid, sir, that that's out of the question.' A note of panic entered his tone. 'As I'm not a member of either House I'm not permitted to take non-members in without the proper authorisation,' he indicated towards to the doors beyond the sign marked 'private'. 'Plus in any event, Mr Churchill is *not* to be disturbed.'

'This is ridiculous,' said Drabble, his voice rising. He glanced over at Kate. 'Do you think this man has any idea what we've been through in the last twenty-four hours?' He rose from the bench and took her hand, 'Come on, darling, we're leaving.'

Jenkins' expression became taut. He placed his hand on Drabble's chest.

'Mr Cromwell!' Jenkins' tone was a firm stage whisper. 'Mr Churchill insists that you give him the item, for its own safety, and – if you had permitted me to explain.' He glanced over at the policeman by the doors. 'I was going to say, that you could alternatively return here at 10.15pm for drinks and to talk the matter over with Mr Churchill in person. But first of all, sir, you must hand over the item. Mr Churchill is most insistent, sir, *for its own safety*.' He smiled kindly and offered his hand. 'I pray, sir, that you will realise that it is vital that we ensure the security of the item rather than permitting the continuing possibility of its interception by those seeking it. Mr Cromwell, you must appreciate that there is more going on than you know.'

Drabble looked down at the upturned hand. He bit his bottom lip and then looked back up at the patient but stern face.

'OK,' he said. 'Just make sure that it's kept safe.'

'I shall, sir.' The man gripped the brass handle, as Drabble unhooked the sling.

'Tell Churchill we'll be back at ten.'

Jenkins said goodbye and walked across the lobby to the far set of double doors, the mahogany box in his left hand, next to the black fluttering tails of his coat. The sound of his feet striking the patterned beige and cream tiles died away. The policeman nodded and opened the door as Jenkins approached. Drabble saw Jenkins enter the adjoining chamber and watched the case grow smaller and then disappear from view as the gap narrowed in the closing door. Drabble sighed and suddenly felt a wave of relief, coupled with exhaustion. He sank back into the leather bench, stretching out his feet and resting his head against the soft hide. Kate sat down next to him. He looked at her.

'I don't feel like a winner now,' he said. She smiled.

'Rest a moment. Then let's have a late lunch.'

'Good idea: or an early dinner.' He closed his eyes. *Darkness*. He imagined a dimly lit restaurant, its walls covered in prints and paintings, candles at each of the tables. He saw a waiter in black, diving between the white-clothed tables, his salver held to his shoulder…

'Mr Cromwell,' said a soft, low voice.

Drabble's eyes creased open. He saw several inches of

a cigarette protrude between the slim first and second fingers of a hand. His gaze travelled up and he saw a young man's face; his fair hair was curly and unruly, but he had effected a side parting. He offered a genial smile. It emphasised his weak chin.

'My name is Hodgekiss, sir. I'm Mr Churchill's assistant. He sends his regards.' He parked the cigarette between his lips and presented his hand.

Drabble looked over to the tall doorway at the end of the lobby. He saw the 'Private: Members only' sign and then the constable manning the door. He and Kate turned to one another.

'Good Lord,' said Hodgekiss. 'What is it?'

***

Hodgekiss poured three large whiskies from the square-bottomed, cut glass decanter and sprayed a dash of soda-water on top of each. He handed one each to Drabble and Kate, who sat beside the fire in matching tan leather armchairs. Hodgekiss raised his eyebrows, crinkling his forehead. 'Cheers.'

He bent forward and they clinked their glasses and had a drink. Drabble set his tumbler on the corner of the desk.

'I'm just so angry with myself,' he exclaimed, placing his head in his hands. 'After everything we've been through, to fall for that was ridiculous.'

Hodgekiss stared down at the rug for a moment. He cleared his throat.

'Now Professor,' he said. 'You really mustn't blame yourself, how -'

222

'Oh come off it, Hodgekiss. In hindsight it was bloody obvious!'

Hodgekiss sighed.

'It really is a most sinister business,' he said, as he moved over to the studded, dark brown leather chesterfield. He put his drink down and began prodding the grate with a poker. 'Mr Churchill was most distressed when he learned that you'd become involved,' he looked up at Drabble. 'He's a marked admirer of your work.'

Drabble stifled a smile.

'Really?'

'Oh, yes.'

Drabble sighed wearily.

'Well, I'm afraid recent events are rather stifling my pleasure of that discovery.' He exhaled and reached for his glass. 'In the last thirty-six hours, Dr Wilkinson has been murdered,' he stared gloomily at the surface of his drink. 'I've been damn' near strangled to death; we've been beaten, shot at, and chased, and nearly run off the road. And we're still completely in the dark as to *why* – not to mention the fact that we've now lost the ruddy head as well.'

Hodgekiss' forehead compressed sympathetically. His mouth opened and he met Drabble's gaze.

A loud peal of bells emanated from the black telephone on the desk. Hodgekiss jumped up and put the receiver to his ear.

'Hodgekiss.'

He listened.

'Yes, sir.' His voice became sombre. 'Very good, sir.' He looked at Drabble. 'Yes, sir. I'll tell him. No time to lose; quite. Very good, sir. I will, sir.'

He replaced the telephone and ran his fingers through his hair. Drabble saw him remove a cigarette from the large silver box on the desk. He offered the case to Drabble, who shook his head. Kate took one. Hodgekiss lit hers and then his own. He picked up his glass and moved over to the window, clearly framing his words carefully. He blew some smoke ostentatiously from his mouth and began.

'Mr Churchill has had a quiet word with the Home Secretary on your behalf. He reckons that the police should lay off you, though you'd be wise to keep a low profile for a few days.'

'So that means I'm still a wanted man?'

'It's a grey area.'

Hodgekiss snatched at his whisky. It didn't seem like a grey area from where Drabble was sitting, but he held his tongue. 'I'm afraid Mr Churchill is quite adamant,' Hodgekiss added. 'About the fascists, I mean.' He looked down at the end of his cigarette and took a drag. 'Winston says it's imperative that they must *not* be allowed to keep the head. It's absolutely critical that we get it back –'

'*We*?'

'Yes, we – I mean,' Hodgekiss stared, his eyes pinched in bewilderment. 'Look. What did you expect?'

'Not as much as you, obviously,' said Drabble, his voice rising. 'I'm sorry – it's out of the question.' He referred to Kate, and added, his tone emollient, 'I don't think Mr Churchill appreciates that we've done quite enough.'

'B-but you don't underst-stand,' stammered

Hodgekiss, appealing to them both. 'You're not connected to Churchill – or anyone, really. You understand – *you're not involved*?'

Hodgekiss glanced down at the surface of his drink and Drabble saw him swallow. The man looked uncomfortable.

'You *mean* we're disposable.'

Hodgekiss shook his head.

'No one said that,' he said quickly. 'No. But,' he took a breath, 'but you are… *unencumbered* by political affiliation.'

He took a drag of his cigarette.

Drabble plonked his glass on the corner of the desk and got up.

'I'm sorry, Hodgekiss, I'm not interested in fighting Mr Churchill's battles for him. I don't care for the fascists, don't get me wrong, but I'm a historian by trade and sometimes stupid enough to climb mountains for fun – but that's where I draw the line. What you need for this job is a bloody Richard Hannay, or a professional – a military man at least.' He met Kate's gaze. 'Come on, Kate.' He picked up his hat and extended his hand. 'Hodgekiss,' The man looked down at it, his jaw lowered, 'it's been a pleasure to make your acquaintance,' continued Drabble, 'but I'm afraid that this is where Miss Honeyand and I get off. I've had enough of Oliver Cromwell for a while.'

Hodgekiss accepted his hand limply.

'B-but-but…' Hodgekiss' mouth opened and closed, 'what the devil will I tell Mr Churchill?'

Drabble picked up his bag and held the door open as

Kate went out into the corridor; Drabble paused at the door.

'Tell him it's not my period.'

***

Drabble and Kate stepped out into the dark evening. The waiting cabbie saw them through his windscreen and stirred his vehicle into life. Drabble leaned into the window.

'The Savoy, please.'

They climbed in and Drabble pulled the door shut. The taxi drew away and nosed into the stream of traffic queuing along Millbank into Parliament Square.

'I'm whacked,' said Drabble, pushing back his cuff to see to his watch. He squinted at it for a moment in the darkness and then gave up. He turned to the window and peered up, sighting Big Ben. 'Goodness, it's only half past six.'

Kate looked over.

'It's been a long day – a long two days.'

He reached over and patted her hand. They exchanged a smile; he cleared his throat and disengaged. The car nudged into Parliament Square behind a double-decker bus. Passengers stood on the curved open rear stairwell leading to the top floor. Drabble sighed.

'I'm really *whacked*,' he said. He looked at her. She stared out of the window up at the Houses of Parliament. 'Sorry,' he added. 'I can't abide people who complain – and that's precisely what I'm doing.'

'No, me, too.' She shook her head and looked over at

226

him. 'I suppose it's just the tremendous relief of it all being over.'

He nodded. She referred back to her window.

'Yes,' he said, resting his head back on the top of the seat, 'thank God it's all over.'

They exited the square and the traffic eased: the taxi drove along Whitehall, passing the black-streaked stone facades of the Treasury and Foreign Office on the left, then Downing Street. Kate sat back and turned towards him.

'Do you think the police will ever catch the people who killed the doctor?'

'I hope so,' he said, but immediately sensed that it wasn't quite right. 'Somehow I doubt it.'

She bit the corner of her lip and gazed out of the window. He looked over at her.

'What will happen to the head now, do you think?'

He shrugged.

'Lord knows. With any luck it'll be lost for another 200 years.'

Kate contemplated this for a moment.

'Look,' said Drabble, 'Can you see? There's Nelson's Column.' She shifted close to the window and looked out. The taxi passed the portico of the National Gallery, then St Martin's-in-the-Fields, and then queued again on the Strand by Charing Cross Station.

'I think the traffic would drive me mad if I actually lived in London,' said Kate, addressing the window. Drabble saw the glass begin to fog. 'All these people. All this noise. It's terribly agitating.'

'It's amazing how quickly you become accustomed to

it. Really.'

She looked over at him, her eyebrows raised.

'You really think so?'

She lay back against the seat. 'I don't think I'd ever get used to it.'

'Is everything all right?' he asked.

'It's fine.'

Drabble looked out of the window as the taxi swept into the forecourt of the Savoy and paused by the door. He saw a man in livery and top hat step towards the door and his hand disappear towards the handle. Kate edged forward in her seat – the door opened – and she stepped out. She paused and leaned back inside the cab.

'Bye-bye,' she said. 'I'll see you tomorrow?'

'Unless you want to go for dinner tonight?'

'No, I'll sleep.'

He smiled but suddenly felt rather deflated.

'I'll be over at ten thirty. We'll go to the National and have a walk by the river, and then some lunch. The room is booked under your name but I'll take care of the details in the morning. If there's anything, contact me at the Granville. And promise me you won't worry about anything. Let's worry about the future, in the future.'

She stood back and closed the door. He watched the man in the hotel uniform escort her to the entrance. Goodnight, he thought. Sleep well.

'Where to, guv?'

He looked over at the shadowy figure in front.

'The Granville, please, driver,' he sighed and picked up his hat. 'And then that's it.'

He watched the taxi edge out from the pavement and
swerve across Pall Mall, turning back the way it had come
with plenty of road to spare, off in the direction of
Trafalgar Square. Drabble slung his bag over his shoulder
and headed up the steps. He was weary now, he realised.
Oh, bugger. He stopped dead as if meeting an invisible
wall: the Triumph. They'd left it parked at the Houses of
Parliament. He yawned and shook his head. He was tired.
Well, it could wait. He put his hand to the woodwork and
heard a low squeak as he went through the rotating doors
of the Granville – catching the familiar smell of oil - and
entered the bright lobby. He paused at the porter's lodge.
The man laid down his newspaper and bobbed up from his
chair.

'Any post?'

For a split second the grey-haired porter tilted his head
fractionally: then his eyes opened wide – and he looked
back down at his newspaper.

'Professor Drabble!' he said. 'Goodness.'

Drabble saw the man eye the telephone.

'That's all right, Bob,' he said. 'It's all been a dreadful
misunderstanding. The police have dropped the charges –
it'll be in all the morning papers.' Drabble shook his head,
'I hope!' He saw the porter nod, and added, 'You
wouldn't believe me if I told you what the last forty-eight
hours have been like. It's not fun being a wanted man.'

Bob, his brow knitted with kindness, leaned forward
across the counter. 'If it's any consolation, sir,' he said. 'I
didn't believe a word of it. Murderers don't join the

Granville.'

The porter cleared his throat.

'Ah, and while I remember it, sir, *this* came for you first thing this morning – delivered by hand, I was told.'

Bob bent down and produced a letter - a small envelope of thick cream paper with a broad bulge in the middle. Drabble regarded the slanted, blue handwriting and set down his bag. For a moment he weighed the little package in his hand, frowning. It was strangely dense.

'Hmmm.'

'I did wondered myself,' remarked Bob, stroking his chin.

Drabble cleared his throat and slid his finger into the corner of the seal. Inside was a neatly folded white handkerchief. He laid the letter on the counter and tugged it out. The handkerchief was soiled. Drabble unwrapped the fabric parcel slowly, taking back each fold, one by one. As he removed the last fold, he pulled away.

'Lord God,' said the porter, covering his mouth.

Drabble lifted a severed finger – its flesh a faint grey-white colour and hard, the stump a dark, ruddy brown, and lumpy - and inspected the signet ring that still adorned it. It showed a bird, a snipe with long beak, in profile above an oak leaf cluster. Only one person he knew wore a ring like that, and had done for almost as long as he'd known him: Percival Harris.

He pushed the cold finger carefully back into its cotton coffin, and prized out a note slotted in the space beside it:

Give us the head: or we'll give YOU a head.

Well, he thought, that didn't leave a great deal to the imagination. Poor bugger. The fool was always getting himself mixed up in things – and now it appeared he had out-Harrised even himself. Poor, *poor* Harris. Drabble pushed the letter into his pocket and picked up his bag. He nodded towards the porter and made for the stairs. The irony, of course, was that their warning was now unnecessary as they'd already got the bloody thing, though they wouldn't have known that was going to be the case when they gave him the chop. He shook his head. Harris' finger had been overtaken by events. Drabble went up the stairs and saw the telephone booths. He halted outside them; his jaw set in determination.

He went in to the first booth and lifted the receiver. He dialled and looked out into the carpeted foyer and watched the members pass as each number purred in his ear. Poor Harris, he thought. The stupid fool. After a few seconds he heard ticking and then the line rang. It was answered. He fed a coin into the slot.

'Hello, operator?' He listened. 'Winston Churchill's office, please.'

He heard a hiss on the line and then it rang.

'Hello?'

'Hodgekiss?'

'Yes...'

'It's Drabble. Listen - I've changed my mind. I'm back on board. I'll be with you in a quarter of an hour.'

He hung up and grabbed his bag and slid the glass door of the booth ajar. His expression changed and he glanced back down at the black plastic receiver. Its surface was dull, with just the faintest of sheens on the curve. He pushed the door closed and picked up the handset. Drabble dialled, heard the pips and then the voice of the

231

operator. He pushed a coin into the slot.

'Hello, operator? The Savoy please... thank you.'

The line went quiet and then there was a click; a man's voice announced the name of the hotel. Drabble saw the lobby of the club was clear.

'Put me through to Miss Kate Honeyand's room, please.'

Drabble heard the sound of rustling paper – then there was a breath at the receiver.

'Putting you through, sir.'

He heard ringing and looked out, scanning the bright lobby. His face softened.

'*Kate*. It's Ernest...' he listened for a moment. 'Look, I've got to go back to see Churchill. Tonight. They've got Harris,' he explained. 'I'm going to have to go and get him – or at least *try* to help him.' He listened again. 'What? No, *no* – absolutely not – no, I forbid it - *please*; it could be dangerous.' He shook his head. 'Of course, I never said that – no, it's nothing to do with that, it's just... *it's just* that he's my friend and he's only in this mess because of me - and his own damned curiosity, I dare say, but it's a job for me. And anyway, it doesn't make sense for us both to be in danger. You know as well as me that these people don't play with a straight bat.' There was a pause, for a moment his mind drifted off to his father's service revolver that he kept in his study. If only I had the Webley, he thought. 'What? *No*... Please, Kate – stay put at the hotel, I'll be back tomorrow night at the latest – we'll have dinner? Kate? *Kate*?'

She was gone. He pulled the phone away from his ear, frowned at it, then hung up. For a second he stood there in silence. He clenched his fist. Bugger, he thought. *Women!*

He dashed down the steps to the door: spinning out into the night. He put his hand up and a passing taxi halted smartly outside.

'The Palace of Westminster, please, driver,' he said. 'And don't spare the horses.'

CHAPTER TWENTY ONE

'Is it fair to assume that Oswald Mosley is behind all this?' asked Kate. She tapped the end of her cigarette on the rising curve of a broad, green glass ashtray. Hodgekiss moved past and lowered himself into the second of the tan leather armchairs. He stretched out his lanky legs, and rested one foot on the other.

'Now, *there's* a question,' he said, bringing his lips together thoughtfully. 'Personally, I think not – and certainly that is Mr Churchill's opinion. He knows Mosley, too – served with him in the Cabinet. These people – the ones who have done all this,' he waved his hand towards the unfolded handkerchief and Harris' severed little finger, 'are a species of Blackshirt all right, but,' he shook his head a touch forlornly, 'they're of an altogether darker hue.'

Drabble sighed.

'And who thought that was possible?'

Hodgekiss leaned forward and shovelled some more coal onto the fire. He cleared his throat, the bright, fresh flames reflected on his face, 'As I'm sure you both are aware, there are lots of fascists out there – not just Mosley's BUF. They're an array of discrete, diverse, obscure groupings of bigots, jingoists and extremists possessed of bewilderingly extremist opinions. For the most part they're frankly harmless – I mean, obviously it would be better for all concerned if they didn't exist in the first place, but actually, usually they confine themselves to venting their spleen in letters to the *Times* or the *Telegraph* or holding furtive quarterly meetings with people of a similar persuasion in darkened beer cellars and exchanging ridiculous passwords. So long as they keep it that way then they're pretty much harmless. The big joke is that there are those on the Left who regard Mr Churchill as something of a fascist,' he looked at Drabble pointedly and smirked, 'I'm afraid they haven't got a leg to stand on.'

On the large map of the world that hung from the far wall Drabble saw the Franco-German border running to the west of Strasbourg and the region of Alsace, respecting the borders of 1870, not 1918. He looked over at Hodgekiss.

'So who *is* behind this?'

Hodgekiss picked up his glass. 'They're an outfit called the Fascist League of Great Britain, the FLGB.' He raised an eyebrow, 'Rolls off the tongue, doesn't it?' He took a drink and continued, his voice low, 'we have information that they're holed up at an old fort on the Kent coast – situated conveniently for the Continent. Their leader is known to us also. He is called Sir Carmen Kelly; ninth baronet, Old Harrovian, Member of Parliament for Rochester in Kent; a Tory of course, and,' he smiled, 'just like Winston, he has an American mother.'

Kate extinguished her cigarette.

'And do we have any idea,' she asked, 'why this man wants the head of Oliver Cromwell so much?'

Hodgekiss contracted his mouth, his bulging cheeks causing lines to crease down the sides of his face. There

235

was a pause and he shook his head.

'Not even the faintest ruddy *inkling*?' protested Drabble.

Hodgekiss looked back blankly.

On the wall behind the desk, Drabble saw a painting. In a pseudo-Impressionist style, the brushwork was controlled and the palette restrained to essentially naturalistic hues and showed an English country view, with the long shadows of evening being cast by a woodland of deciduous and evergreen trees. Situated on the right of the composition was a double-gabled red brick house with red tiled roof and stout Elizabethan chimneys. Below it, the luscious parkland fell away to a series of lakes and ponds. Drabble smiled.

'It's Chartwell,' called Hodgekiss from the sofa. 'Winston's place in Kent.'

Drabble saw the outline of the trees and imagined Churchill standing in one of the tiny black windows. His face hardened.

'Is it now?'

Hodgekiss grinned. 'And the painting's one of his, too.'

Drabble turned, his face a frown.

'That's right,' explained Hodgekiss, his gaze darted to Kate, who was sharing the conversation. 'Winston's a painter.'

Drabble returned to his chair and picked up his glass.

'If Mr Churchill knows *who* has the head and who is doing this, why can't he simply go to the Prime Minister?'

Hodgekiss looked at him sharply.

'I'm afraid that's out of the question. Mr Baldwin and

Mr Churchill don't see eye to eye personally – and they agree on even less professionally. Besides,' he raised his hands, 'what could we tell him?'

Drabble drained his glass.

***

At the foot of the stairs, a motorboat bobbed in the choppy black water of the Thames. Next to it Hodgekiss conferred with its skipper. Their breath left clouds as they talked. Above loomed the dark mass of the Houses of Parliament. Beyond, Drabble saw the glow of the light of the clock from Big Ben. It read 10.45. A double-decker bus travelled south over Westminster Bridge, its passengers tiny silhouettes.

'Right,' said Hodgekiss, the leather soles of his shoes grinding against the wet stone of the jetty. 'This is where I leave you.'

The boatman was coming up the stairs and touched the peak of his cap as he passed them.

'Goodbye, Hodgekiss,' said Drabble.

'Good luck, Professor. Everything you need is on board.'

They shook hands.

'Thank you.'

'Goodbye Miss Honeyand,' he smiled bashfully and offered his hand. She took it.

'Goodbye, Mr Hodgekiss.'

Drabble gave him a parting look and they went down the stone stairs. At the boat's side he offered Kate his hand as she climbed aboard. From behind he heard someone clear their throat.

'Professor Drabble.'

He turned and saw a figure in the shadows. For a moment there was an orange glow – a dot – at about shoulder or head height. A man stepped forward and the spotlight caught the scoop in the crown of his black homburg, but the brim left the face in darkness. He gestured with his stick towards the Thames. His voice was thick.

'The tide is with you, Professor.'

Drabble looked down at the pitch black water. He saw a branch float past at a good pace in the direction of Westminster Bridge. He looked back to the figure.

'At a rate of knots.'

'I should say so.'

The man came forward and shook his hand.

'The very best of British to you, sir. And to you, Miss Honeyand.' He doffed his hat. The light fell on his thin, wispy grey hair and reflected off the gold rims of his small round spectacles. He returned his attention to Drabble.

'Goodbye.'

'Goodbye.'

He put his cigar back to his lips and moved towards the steps. Drabble boarded the boat. He took Kate's hand and looked back up, seeing the figure ascend the steps slowly, his hand gripping the iron handrail. Hodgekiss waited at the top and as Churchill arrived, he opened the door, and then followed him inside. The spotlight went out, leaving them in darkness, save for the light coming from the building above, the flashes and glints thrown off the water and the amber glow from within the cabin.

Their boat was a teak-decked Thames cruiser of, Drabble guessed, some twenty-five to thirty feet in length. Painted white, she had a sharp bow, a low deckhouse and a higher duck-under, affording shelter to the person at the wheel. A red ensign fluttered black and grey from the stern, where a dinghy was suspended from a pair of davits.

Drabble looked down the companionway and in the low glow of an oil lamp, saw a revolver lying black on a rag on the galley table. Next to it was a small cardboard box of ammunition. On the seat were a navy blue rubberized overcoat and a peaked cap. They went below. 'You should try and get some sleep,' he said, scanning the cabin and noting the charts of the Kent coastline on the navigator's table. On the seat was a leather satchel; he opened it and saw it contained provisions. He dimmed the oil lamp. 'I can handle the boat. There are some blankets up forward in the sea berth on the right.'

He saw Kate stand still for a moment, her face soft and pensive in the gaslight.

'Are you OK?'

'Yes,' she said, 'just done in, that's all.' She yawned. 'Wake me up when you want to have a rest.'

Back at the wheel, he felt below the helm and found the key waiting in the ignition. He turned the key, waking the engine. It coughed and then began a gentle rhythmic thump beneath his feet, enjoined by the sluice of water from the side. He went to the bow and cast off the loose fore-line.

He released the creaking aft line and set the launch

adrift. At the controls, he pushed the lever forward, engaging the engine. Quietly, the little boat moved off. As they edged further out into the channel he noticed the wind pick up and spray fly up over the bow. Within a minute they passed under Westminster Bridge. As they emerged from the far side of the bridge, he heard drunken laughter peel through the air. A girl shrieked playfully. He heard a low reply and then more laughter. The boat was a dark, almost invisible mass, passing along the blackness of the Thames and above he saw stars. He nudged the throttle forward, settling it where the engine and boat seemed comfortable. He looked back at the black hands and glowing, yellow clock face of Big Ben: eleven o'clock.

Up ahead he saw several large black shapes in the darkness. Barges moored up for the night, he thought. The tide was going out and he knew he would make good progress for the next three or four hours before it turned foul. There was no other traffic on the Thames, just the occasional burst of light as the headlamps of a bus or motorcar swept over one of the bridges.

CHAPTER TWENTY TWO

It was a little after four o'clock and it felt to Drabble like the darkest hour. The hatch to the cabin slid open, and a cosy glow emanated into the pilot house.

'Morning!' said Kate, cheerfully. 'You didn't wake me.'

He didn't reply, but kept looking out.

'I've brought you a cup of cocoa,' she continued. 'Here.' A steaming enamel mug came into view, a hand outstretched beneath it. He reached forward and took it, seeing her upturned face. 'Hodgekiss has done us proud,' she said, climbing up the companionway steps.

Drabble put his arm around her and they both looked ahead into the darkness. He felt her shiver. 'Here.' He unbuttoned his coat and laid it across her shoulders. She wrapped her arms around him, inside his overcoat.

'It's nice and warm down below,' she said. 'The stove is still belting it out.'

Kate looked about.

'Goodness. What happened to London?'

'Long gone. That's Kent over there. Holland straight ahead.'

'Is it much further?'

'Only about ten miles. I should go below and check – there's a nasty bit of sand off Ramsgate we could do with missing.'

The bows of the boat pitched down into a wave and water sprayed against the glass windows of the deckhouse. Kate braced herself.

'It's getting rougher.'

'The tide's turned against us. It's slowing us down quite a lot, too. Mind you, I reckon we're still making four or five knots.'

He looked down at her: he could just make out the lines of her face in the weak light cast by the binnacle. He felt her arms tighten around him. He pulled her tight.

'It's ruddy cold up here,' he said.

'Not as cold as the Eiger, I expect?'

'A different sort of cold,' he replied.

'I've been wanting to ask you, actually,' she said, her warm breath stroking his face. 'What happened?'

'What do you mean?'

'Up on the Eiger. After your second night on the mountain: the paper said you were making good progress – they were getting jolly excited about it. They said you weren't far from the summit.'

Drabble shook his head.

'We still had at least three thousand feet to go – and some of the hardest feet at that...'

'I know, but the newspapers said you had passed various obstacles – the ice fields, crevasses, and God knows what – that others had failed to pass; you'd gone further than anyone else had, so what made you turn back?'

Drabble saw a ship off the port bow, heading their way. He adjusted course. They moved towards the shore.

'The answer, I think, is that we'd both had enough. We had spent two nights soaked to our skins, bivouacked twice on the side of the mountain, and were knackered.

We were constantly being rained upon by rocks, ice, and avalanches – it was freezing. The North Face of the Eiger is hell on Earth, like a refrigerated version of Dante's *Inferno*.'

She frowned.

'And the truth of the matter is that neither Hubertus nor I were at all sure how we'd feel after another day and night on the mountain. We'd both expected to have it cracked in two nights – but it was harder, *much* harder, than either of us thought it would be. The thing is, you don't really sleep properly up there, or eat for that matter. You more or less have to carry everything, so you basically live on coffee, which you can make with snow, Kendal Mint Cake, and a few sandwiches, which we prepared in advance.'

'Sandwiches?' She frowned kindly, her cheeks dimpling, and stroked his face, 'What did you have in them?'

He smirked.

'Gentlemen's Relish.' He saw her smile and continued, 'Of course the climbing takes its toll. And really, it comes down to basic things like the rock face: it's flat – people who've tried it before, the ones that survived that is, said as much - but really, you know how it is, one tends to take it with a pinch of salt. But they weren't exaggerating. It really *is* smooth. Other climbs are just as vertiginous, but they're made of this lovely rock that has a horizontal grain to it, so you've something to get purchase on. But the North Face is smooth – smoother than a marble floor. And if it's not rock then it's a vertical ice field several hundred yards long - and I wasn't wearing crampons.' He sighed.

'Stupid bugger.'

Drabble stared gloomily ahead. 'No, the Eiger's a right sod all right.' He brightened, 'A sod of the highest order - but I will say this, it *is* climbable. Not that it'll be me who'll do it.'

He saw the oncoming ship had passed safely to their port side and steered back out into the centre of the channel. She squeezed her arms around him.

'So what actually happened?'

'On the fateful day itself?' The bows of the boat pitched forward into a deeper wave, rocking them both gently, and more spray flecked the windows of the deckhouse. 'We'd spent about four hours cold and wet in our bivouac and then woke up on the morning of day three. I say "woke up", but as I said, you don't really sleep, you only really doze when you're on a climb – pinned to the mountain by ropes secured with iron pins, pitons, they're called. It's a beautiful spot and you really do think that you're on top of the world.' He smiled at her. 'Hubertus was keen to go on but I wasn't so sure. I confess my lack of crampons meant I was having to work a good deal harder to move through the ice fields and they were really taking it out of me. I knew I was slowing him down, too, and that we both needed more than Kendal Mint Cake and sandwiches to keep us going.'

Kate smiled.

'Even with Gentlemen's Relish?'

He sipped the cocoa. For a second all they heard was the rhythmic drum of the engine.

'We talked it over and turned back. Huby was disappointed but knew it was the safest course of action.

We still had the dreaded White Spider, as it's known, and that last vast ice field to climb before reaching the summit and neither of us really felt up to it. Huby used a,' he cleared his throat, 'Viennese expression that translates roughly as "Sod this for a game of soldiers".'

He took another sip of cocoa.

'We spent the whole day descending, making very good progress, getting as far as the first ice field - and then Huby was hit. I had belayed down...' he saw her frown and incline her head. His tone relaxed and he explained, 'I'd climbed down first and was handling the safety rope while he followed. The ropes were long – so we could descend about a hundred feet in a single section.' He cleared his throat and the urgency returned to his voice, 'Then suddenly I heard the dreadful roar of ice and I knew an avalanche was coming. I braced myself and looked up: I couldn't see him. Everything was white and grey. I pushed myself against the rock-face to stop myself being swept away. For a moment the rope nearly took me over, and I prayed that it wouldn't break. Then I went. When I came to I was dangling from the rope – the piton had come free from the ice – and was looking down at Grindelwald. Later, we worked out that I'd fallen a hundred and twenty-eight feet. They found Huby's body two days later. His harness had torn.'

He drained the mug and placed it on the dash. For a moment he watched it judder in time to the vibrations of the engine. He edged the throttle and increased the revs.

'If I'd taken some crampons,' he said, staring ahead, 'it might have been a different story. The truth is neither of us knew how difficult it would be. It's as simple as that.'

He sighed. 'It's a great lesson in life: never under estimate your opponent.'

'I think you're terribly brave to have tried.'

He shook his head.

'Terribly foolish, you mean.'

He felt her press against him more tightly and she kissed his cheek. She drew back and for a moment her mouth hovered close to his: he felt her breath warm his lips. He leaned forward and kissed her. She pressed her mouth to his. After a moment she pulled away, a smile on her face, the dimples activated, and the corners of her eyes lifted.

'You *really* are the most stupid man in the world.'

He guided her face back towards his and kissed her. Several seconds passed and he felt her finger tap on his chest. He broke off.

'What now?' he asked, opening his eyes. He saw her grin.

'Are you actually looking where we're going?'

He turned her gently so that her back pressed against the console.

'The coast is clear enough,' he said, stroking back her hair and kissing her mouth. She pressed herself to him and he felt her fingertips pull at him. She moved her mouth away and pressed her nose against his cheek.

'This is the only reason you let me come along, isn't it?'

He pulled her mouth back to his, and they kissed urgently. After a moment he opened his right eye and peered ahead.

On the horizon a dot of light came into view. It

disappeared for a few seconds then reappeared. He broke away.

'That'll be the Ramsgate lighthouse. We're nearly there.'

She looked around, and thought for a second.

'You should get some rest. I'll keep heading towards it, if you want?'

He took off his cap and placed it on her head. He lifted the peak of the hat up and kissed her again.

'What are you going to do?' she asked.

'I'm going to see if this thing's got an autopilot.'

***

Drabble awoke and stretched out his arms, yawning. He hauled himself from the bunk and wiped the sleep from his eyes. Looking through the windows of the galley, he saw light was creeping into the eastern sky. The sun itself was not in evidence but there was a silver glimmer on the horizon and the low clouds above it reflected a pale glow. He lit the stove beneath the kettle and then went to the chart table. The coast of Kent curved around and there, just inland, was marked a fort. Before it was a creek where they could anchor – it was marked in brown, which meant it would dry out at low water. He glanced at his watch; the tide was still rising so they would be able to get in there in time. When the tide went out the boat would be marooned for six hours, askew on the mud, but then she would refloat on the following tide. The kettle began to whistle.

He went up on deck and handed Kate a cup of coffee.

He saw the Ramsgate lighthouse, a vertical white cylinder with black hoops, less than a mile away. He could make out the occasional window and a small door at its base. Beyond it were the white chalk cliffs of Kent. He took the wheel.

'I've been thinking,' he said. She looked over. 'Perhaps you should stay with the boat.' He met her eyes. 'I could leave you the gun and you could guard it for our escape.'

She contracted her lips and an eyebrow lifted.

'I've not come with you this far to miss out now.' She smiled. 'Besides, you could probably do with my help.'

Her light brown eyes regarded him patiently. She really was exceptionally pretty, he thought. He leaned forward and, kissing her, pulled her close.

CHAPTER TWENTY THREE

Drabble knelt on the foredeck of the boat and looked back at Kate, who was at the wheel. He gestured forward and called out, 'Give it another blast.'

The engine revved and the boat bobbed forward; Drabble raised his hand and the engine died off. He lobbed the anchor overboard and it plunged into the water, the chain racing out after it. He raised his thumb and Kate put the engine into a slow reverse. The boat responded and began to move backwards on the chain. Drabble made his way to the cockpit. He put the throttle into neutral and took the helm.

'Well done,' he said, checking their position against the shore, 'We're not going anywhere.' He killed the engine. 'Thank God that din's over with.'

He bent down and opened one of the lockers beneath the seats. Inside, there were ropes and fenders. He pulled out the longest line he could see and coiled it neatly on the deck. Kate watched him. He reached into the locker and took out a small dinghy anchor. It was aluminium, lightweight but traditionally shaped, like a seafarer's anchor tattoo or a pub sign except that it had three equally spaced arms with barbed points. 'This might come in handy,' said Drabble, as he tied it to the large coiled rope. 'Can you give me a hand with the dinghy?'

The sky was now a dark grey and white. Drabble knelt at the stern and pulled back the oiled cotton cover from the boat, which was suspended from a pair of painted steel davits off the stern. He pushed the cover into the bows and laid the coiled rope on top. They lowered the tender into the water. He pulled it around the side by the painter and they climbed in.

The dinghy reared and pitched in the choppy waters of the creek. Kate gripped the sides as Drabble rowed, steering them over to the western shore. The wind blew her golden hair across her eyes and she stroked it away from her face. Her dimples showed and she eyed the shore gravely.

He offered her a reassuring smile.

When the boat grounded, he plunged into the shallows and paddled it in. He took her hand and they dragged the boat up the muddy bank, where Drabble tied it to a tree. He pulled the coiled rope over his shoulder and put the gun in his coat pocket.

They climbed the shallow banks of the creek; it was covered in lank yellow and brown grasses and dotted with clusters of small, gnarled trees, bent by the wind and bare. At the top, they saw it.

Goodwin Fort was low, wide, and black against the horizon. A ribbon of trees and a gentle hill obscured some of it from view. From where they were situated the ground undulated and the undergrowth was thicker: the grasses were joined by broken hedgerows and bushes. Drabble looked over at Kate.

'It doesn't look all that frightening, does it?'

Her eyes brightened.

'OK, let's keep low. They might have posted sentries.'

They jogged along the gullies and kept close to the trees until they reached the top of the next hill. They lay on the grass and took in the fort. It stood about a hundred yards ahead and, he thought, showed itself to be taller than it had previously appeared. The black-painted walls were probably forty feet high and were protected by a dry moat. A drawbridge lowered and they heard the rumble of an engine. A green canvas-roofed lorry emerged and drove into the lane. There was a pair of black-uniformed guards at the gate.

'Blackshirts,' said Drabble, looking at Kate. 'We're in the right place all right.'

'How are we going to get in?' she whispered.

'Let's have a look around.'

They crawled back from the vantage point. Crouching low, Drabble led them downhill, away from the castle and towards the coast. They hurried down the muddy incline, their feet sinking in the deep, soft soil. Low trees and unruly hedgerows snatched and grasped at their clothing and faces. They ascended and the fort came into view but now from the sea aspect. From here, Drabble saw that the structure was circular, with the tall walls curving away in either direction. They saw a series of large, squared-off archways set in the thick stone walls. Within each was a red wooden hatch or cover which Drabble guessed must have been twelve feet across. At the centre of each cover was a small window, probably, thought Drabble, to allow light into a gun chamber. At the nearest point to the sea, Drabble saw a bulge at the foot of the dry moat. It would have been put there for strength. It could also be climbed. He turned to Kate.

'The fort's guns are behind the red hatches – I think they're our best bet on a way in.' He smiled, 'Unless you

251

fancy scaling those walls... Get down!'

He snatched her elbow as he fell to his knees, diving for shelter behind a tree. 'Look,' he whispered. 'Sentries. We'd better be careful.'

Just above the parapet, they saw a couple of figures silhouetted against the flat white sky. Drabble saw the outline of rifles at their shoulders. He looked over at Kate.

'Promise me that you won't do anything foolish,' he said, taking her hand, 'You *do* promise, don't you?'

She nodded. 'The same goes for you.'

'OK, wait here. I'll come back and get you– take this,' he kissed her and pressed the gun into her hands. 'Keep out of sight until I signal for you to follow. If anything happens to me or if I don't return by midday on the dot, I want you to go back to the boat and wait for the tide.' He gripped her elbow, 'You hear me? Then I want you to get the hell out of here. Once you're in open water, turn left and don't stop till you see Big Ben.'

Her expression remained unmoved. He saw her eyebrows were fixed a little higher than their normal position, almost, he thought, in a pose of resolute doubt.

'Have you got that?' he whispered.

She nodded.

'Do you promise?'

'Yes.' She lowered her eyes.

'Good.' He took her in his arms and kissed her. He felt the soft pressure and warmth of her mouth against his. What was she doing here, he thought? How had he allowed her to be here? To be so close to danger. He cupped her face with his hands. They drew apart and she hugged him, pressing her face to his shoulder.

252

'I'm going,' he said. 'Keep safe.'

He gave her a parting look and, ducking down, crawled nimbly towards the fort; the ground was damp and grasses cold and wet. He moved quickly. Soon he was about twenty yards from the edge of the dry moat. Already the stone walls of the fort towered above him, and seemed to cast a shadow in the gloom of the morning. Drabble saw bars protecting the windows of the wooden gun covers.

He adjusted the anchor on the rope at his shoulder and advanced on all fours. Craning his head up, he saw that the sentries were gone – either that or the angle of the parapet meant he could not see them. *But that cut both ways.* Touch wood. He got to his feet, ducked down and sprinted towards the fort.

Drabble reached the top of the concrete rampart and he slid down into the dry moat. He slipped and rolled down to the dirty foot of the moat, crashing into the gutter at its base. He stifled a cry, and gripped his leg. A barb from the anchor bit into his thigh, but it had not pierced the skin or the fabric of his trousers. He opened his eyes and looked up at the walls and cloudy sky above. Ruddy hell, he thought, gasping for air. That was almost it. I've got to do better than that.

He rolled onto his side and massaged his leg. *Buggeration.* He took a deep breath and got onto his knees. He scrambled up the stone bulge at the apex of the circle and crouched beneath one of the red wooden gun shutters. He stopped and listened. Drawing breath, he heard his heart thump against his chest. He looked back and looked for where he and Kate had hidden – he could not see her. Good. He reached up and touched the corner of the stone ledge at the base of the gun hatch above. He jumped and got both hands to the ledge. He hauled himself up, his wounded left arm smarting and the toes of his boots scrambling against the stone wall below. His toes got some useful purchase and he raised himself until, when he was just high enough, he got a leg up on the ledge. He pulled himself onto his chest, and with his left foot levered his body onto the ledge. Breathing fast, he stood up on the ledge, his back to the wooden hatch. *Nicely done, Herr Professor Drabble.* He smiled in spite of the pain in his arm and looked down. The foot of the moat already looked a long way down– but it could only be about twenty feet. He pressed his face against the iron bars and peered in through the small window. Immediately in front was the round black muzzle of a gun– a large cannon made to fire a ball about twelve inches across. To the left of the mouth of the gun he saw a room lit by a gas lamp mounted on the wall by a door. He saw an archway leading, he guessed, to the next gun chamber along. On the stone floor beneath the gun he saw a wide, semi-circular cast-iron cog, like a toothed component of a vast clock. Its teeth intersected with those of a smaller cog, which in turn was connected to several additional cogs which linked to the base of the gun. Drabble tugged at the rusty iron bars – they didn't move. He saw that the red paint was flaking from the splintered timber at the base of the windowsill. He looked inside the chamber, checking either side of the great barrel, and threw his shoulder against the shutter. He tried it again. It was solid.

He sighed and leaned the side of his head against the timber. He breathed hard. His ears adjusted to the silence and he heard the light call of a bird. Then, in the background, he heard a sound from inside. It was a regular beat, but more lingering. It almost sounded like the thud of a train, he thought. There it was again; a definite beat of some sort. He crept forward, and glanced to either side. He lowered himself from the step and landed with both feet on the bulge beneath. He checked up, left, and right. There were no sentries. With short quick steps he dashed into the moat and unhooked the coiled rope from his shoulder.

Drabble scanned the top of the parapet and swung the anchor back. He counted. *One* – the arc of the swing got bigger, *two* - he raised his hand to give greater clearance for the swing, *three* – the light anchor flew up, high into the air, and disappeared over the wall. He clawed at the hemp rope, taking the slack, and jerked the line: it was good.

He ran up the stone bulge and got to the foot of the wall. He threaded the rope over his left shoulder, around his side, then down between his legs and under his left thigh. Drabble gave the rope one more yank – it was fast - and then started to climb, fist over fist, digging his toes into the cracks between the stone blocks. His forearms swelled as he ascended the rope; trembling hand reaching over trembling hand. He gripped hard and felt his arms begin to tingle and grow numb. The power would be gone from them in minutes, and his injured arm felt alarmingly weak. He found a toehold on the edge of a stone block and raised himself up, resting momentarily all his weight on his right leg. He exhaled with relief. The muscles in his arms were in agony. He took a breath and looked up, half expecting to see Hubertus up there, wielding his ice axe as a dense shadow of white dusty snow poured down from the mountain above. The top of the parapet still looked a good distance off. He noticed that there was a lip on the edge too, which would make the final ascent harder. Ruddy Victorians. He grinned, braced the ball of his left foot against the wall, and reached his right arm forward, seizing the rope, followed quickly with the left.

At the top, he dragged himself over the stone parapet and slumped onto the roof, gasping for air and clutching his left arm where it seared in agony from the bullet wound. I'm out of shape, he thought. *So out of shape*. His eye followed the rope and he saw what the anchor had snagged: one of the hooks had caught a metal railing on the inside edge of the walkway. He shook his head, still breathing hard, but became conscious of a noise around him: it was the same thumping, train-like sound that he had heard at the window below – but much louder.

He approached the handrail: his eyes widening. The colour drained from his face.

CHAPTER TWENTY FOUR

Drrum-drrum-drrum! Crack-crack-crack! Up and down the boots went, hundreds of black heels, rising and snapping down in unison to the drumbeat. *Drrum-drrum-drrum... crack-crack-crack...* Drabble looked down and saw rows upon rows of Blackshirts in columns, their rifles to their shoulders, marching past a low podium at the side of the vast circular courtyard. On the dais he saw a black-clad figure, his right fist held up high, his left hand placed on his hip. As each row of Blackshirts passed, their heads swivelled towards the podium as one and their arms went up. *Drrum-drrum-drrum... crack-crack-crack.* The salute then fell and they continued to the end, where they peeled around and joined the massed columns waiting on the left. The marching columns were refreshed by more uniformed fascists arriving through a stone arch at the far end. Behind the leader on the podium was a trio of standard bearers; adorning each black banner was a silver cross of St George with lightning flashes in the quarters. The same design appeared on the brassards on the swinging arms of the marching men. Around the perimeter of the courtyard there were men holding up torches which gave off darting, flickering yellow flames, intensified in the wintry morning light. Drabble swallowed hard. Good God, he thought, his eyes staring ahead. Holy buggeration.

He went over to the wall and threw the anchor far through the air. He saw it arc away and pitch down into the short trees, the hemp rope snaking after it. He knelt

257

down and checked for sentries. The parapet was empty in either direction.

Groups of Blackshirts looked down upon the courtyard from a gangway just below him. He saw now that there were more groups of banner-carriers. He heard a command and the columns in front of the podium halted and turned towards it. The courtyard fell silent.

The man on the podium stepped forward to a microphone. For a moment he surveyed the parade: the silence was marred only by the occasional hiss and whine from the speakers.

'This is not merely a good morning,' the man said, his voice deep, confident, and magnified to an almost uncomfortable level. 'It is a great morning.' He paused and looked about the parade, 'for we are at the dawn of an important day in the history of our great Island Nation – certainly the most important day for a generation. For on the morrow we eradicate a petty, effete government of mediocrities, of old men – *yesterday*'s men - who have piece by piece sought to undo our country and everything it stands for.'

A cheer went up. Drabble saw countless hats and helmets rise into the air.

'Today,' continued the speaker, his voice rising, 'today we will set about sweeping aside a government that dubbed itself a Ministry of all the Talents. Hah! Talents! *What talents*? A talent for error; a talent for giving away our national advantage, a talent for always letting Britain down and being on the wrong side of the argument? A talent for presiding over fifteen years of failure, of steady, inexorable economic decline? Oh, no,' said the speaker, jabbing the air with his fist, 'like a dripping tap, Britain's wealth and jobs have been siphoned off by our foreign rivals. Today, I say to each of you – no more drip, drip, drip away from Britain; no more hunger marches, no more inexorable decline. No,' he wagged his finger ostentatiously at the audience, as though, Drabble thought, he was chastising each of them in turn. 'Today we will fix the rotted washer, mend the broken tap. We will revive the British economy; we will reclaim the British mines of Yorkshire, County Durham, Northumberland and South Wales; Lancashire will once again resound to the sound of textile mills, Sheffield's steel mills will burst back into life; the great shipyards – Harland and Woolf, Swan Hunter, Jarrow - these will once again fabricate the ships that will be the envy of the world.' His hand formed a fist and he thumped his chest. 'Britannia has for too long been idle. But she will wield her trident once more. The old guard have had their day. We *will* create a Britain worthy of its workers!'

A cry went up and a blizzard of hats filled the air, like a flock of Starlings swarming into the sky.

Kelly! Kelly! Kelly!

The figure stepped back from the microphone and raised his right fist, turning to face different sections of the parade. The speaker stepped forward and the din receded. He cleared his throat.

'But first, my friends, my followers, we have a job to do.' He raised his fist, 'Today, we must reclaim our government; we must save our King.' He paused. 'God save the King!' He stepped back from the microphone and a roar went up.

259

God save the King! God save the King!

The figure raised his hands and approached the microphone stand again. The clamour quietened.

'This dawn will go down in history as the commencement of the day of liberation of our Island race. For today and tomorrow, through our actions, we will put the great back into Great Britain. We will turn the clock both backwards and forwards, my friends. We will reinvigorate this flaccid, idle country and institute a virile government under the League. We will unite the Empire under the Crown – and we will save the rightful wearer of that crown from the mediocrities of Westminster!'

The speaker raised his fist, offering a salute. The Blackshirts raised up their right arms, braced straight, their hands clenched into fists.

Kelly! Kelly! Kelly!

The sentry below Drabble threw up his own fist, and bellowed, his mouth straining open.

'KELLY! KELLY! KELLY!'

Drabble edged away from the rail and leaned back against the wall. He pressed his eyes shut and clutched his stomach. Holy Mother of God, he thought, his chest heaving. It was like the first time he actually laid eyes on the brutal, black face of the Eiger – those layers of rock and ice-fields stretched vertically into the heavens like the rows of shark's teeth. He felt a lump in his waistcoat pocket and remembered Harris' ring. He took it out and held it up, so that by focusing on it the fascists blurred into the background. He turned it in his fingers and saw a smear of blood on the inside of the metal loop. He licked the tip of his little finger and wiped it away. If nothing else, he thought, I'm going to get Harris out of here. The ruddy fool's only in this mess because of me – he bit the corner of his lip - and his own stupid curiosity, of course. Push come to shove, the Army – with ruddy tanks for all I care - can sort this lot of nutcases out, he thought. But I'm getting Harris out of it. Right now.

Drabble pushed the ring back into his pocket. He followed the maroon handrail along the circle of the parapet and reached the top of a stairway. He descended to a gangway, where Blackshirts stood, clustered, watching the proceedings on the main parade ground below. He glanced down – a line of soldiers had now formed up before the dais and the speaker was among them, shaking hands.

Behind, Drabble saw a door, set in one of the squared-off stone archways, and went over. Inside he confronted the bulbous black breach of one of the great guns. Either side of it, he saw more archways. He went left, passing into another gun-chamber, and then another. Finally he reached a bricked-up wall; an iron stairway, again painted maroon, leading down. Bending forward, he crept down and peered through the metal steps. A Blackshirt sat before a desk, leaning back, smoking a cigarette, and reading a newspaper. He was in his late middle age, bald with tufts of grey hair at the sides and a double chin which bulged over his collar and concealed the knot of his tie. Drabble saw that next to him on the green baize-covered table was a clipboard, a stack of buff paper files, and pencils. Beyond him were shelves of neatly piled grey blankets, cardboard boxes, and boots, tunics, trousers, and hats, all arranged by size. There's enough here to clothe

261

an army, thought Drabble. He looked down at the iron lattice work of the step.

Good Lord. *That's precisely what they've got.*

He cleared his throat and clattered noisily down the stairs. The man laid down his newspaper and looked up.

'Yes?'

'You must be the quartermaster?' Drabble beamed. 'The most important man in the building. Gate sent me over. I'm from the Cambridge branch – running late.'

The quartermaster looked at his watch.

'You can say that again.' He got to his feet and gave Drabble an abrupt look up and down, sizing him up. 'All right,' he sniffed and picked up the clipboard. 'Cambridgeshire, eh?' He turned several pages over, then nodded. 'You'll be needing a uniform obviously; boots, trousers, tunic, hat, brassard – you'll get your weapon at the armoury. I don't do firearms. We'll be sending the rations and mess kits up with the column, so you don't need those.' He ticked the sheet, 'Right.' He passed Drabble the clipboard and the pencil, which was attached by a string. 'Print your name and sign here. You look like a 40 medium. Right? Come, chop-chop, we've haven't got all day.'

At the top of the page Drabble saw the letters 'F.L.G.B.'. Between the 'L' and the 'G' was the cross and thunderbolts logo. The number next to the first blank space was 04236. Did that mean that 4,235 people had preceded him? Drabble made his mark and handed the clipboard and pencil back. The quartermaster studied the sheet for a moment, his brow forming a frown. He then covered it with the previous sheets and placed the clipboard back on the table.

'Size tens?'

Drabble nodded. He made a note on the pad and then set it down.

'Wait here.'

The quartermaster turned towards the shelf, muttering to himself, his fingers playing along the racks. He took down a black jacket, trousers, hat, and brassard and folded these in a tidy pile, surmounting the black boots he selected.

'Right,' he said, handing a tall bundle to Drabble. 'Change over there.' He nodded towards a cubicle formed by a green curtain and took out a cigarette. With the faint smell of tobacco in the background, Drabble dressed. For a moment he inspected himself in the mirror. He straightened the slouch hat so that the silver fascist logo was visible above his left eye. His eyes – his gaze hovered on the pallid, puffy bags beneath them, and the cut on his cheek was black against his ashen face. He raised his right arm and offered the fist-salute. Ruddy hell, he thought, I look dreadful.

Drabble pushed the green curtain to one side and emerged from the booth. The quartermaster placed his cigarette on the ashtray.

'You'd better get a wiggle on if you don't want to miss all the fun.'

'Right.'

'Keep going,' said the quartermaster, gesturing. 'Doorway beyond the staircase. Chop-chop.'

Drabble inched the door open and a pair of sentries turned and looked at him. He nodded and stepped into the courtyard, closing the door behind him. The speaker was in full flow. The assembly roared: *Kelly! Kelly! Kelly!*

Drabble frowned and stared at the small figure on the podium. His mouth opened slowly. It must be Sir Carmen Kelly, he thought; the Conservative MP who Hodgekiss mentioned. Drabble saw him approach the microphone, his outstretched hands moving up and down to quiet the audience. He smiled, revealing neat white teeth.

'This dawn,' said Kelly, his finger jabbing the air as though he were pressing a button over and over again, 'is the day we will all remember. This is the day that the Fascist League of Great Britain takes charge.'

Kelly! Kelly! Kelly!

Drabble looked over and saw the right arms of the sentries next to him go straight, the fists lifted high.

'Kelly!' they shouted, their voices falling into the general cry. 'Kelly!'

Drabble raised his fist and mouthed the word. The parade was as one.

Kelly! Kelly! Kelly!

After a few seconds Drabble dropped his arm and edged back. He looked over at the nearest sentry. He was skinny and small – no more than about five foot four, fresh-faced, and wore a puny toothbrush moustache. Drabble saw an intensity to his gaze, in the conviction of the mouth as it pronounced the syllables; the determined frown, pinched at the top of the nose; the swollen blood vessels in the forehead and temples, and the convulsion as he extended his arm each time he uttered the cry. These people really *are* fanatics, thought Drabble. Real ruddy fanatics. In a moment Cambridge burned in front of him;

Sidney Sussex ablaze: its Roman cement facade and Gothic crenellations falling from the Tudor brickwork beneath. His hand formed a fist. These people have to be stopped. Or they'll be burning books...

Drabble pulled his cap forward and followed the perimeter of the courtyard, exchanging nods with the Blackshirts as he passed. He reached a doorway and went in. It opened into a corridor that had green doors leading off it. Through the internal windows he saw rows of empty desks and filing cabinets. There were telephones.

He went in and hastily lowered the Venetian blinds, turning the cane to alter the pitch of the slats. He went to the desk furthest from the door and lifted the receiver. There was a flat tone. So far so good. He dialled: *one* – he glanced towards the door. The chrome rotary dial *click-click-clicked* as the device reset itself; *zero*, he breathed in and looked over to the door, his finger hovering over the dial. *Come on, come on...* It stopped clicking. He inserted his finger: *zero*. He watched the hole in chrome dial slowly revert to the grubby black nought where it had started. He heard a click.

'Hello, operator?' There was a pause. 'Yes, I'd like to make a trunk call, please. Victoria 2300.'

There were a couple of ticks and he heard ringing.

'Good morning,' said a man's voice, 'Houses of Parliament.'

'Mr Churchill's office, please.'

There was a moment of silence.

'It's very early, sir,' said the telephonist. 'I doubt there'll be anyone there to receive your call for another hour at least. Perhaps I could take a message?'

Drabble's focus moved from the dial to the window, the green door, and the metal door handle.

'Is there anywhere else I can reach him?'

'Mr Churchill, sir? I could give you the constituency office but I expect it'll be the same story. Why don't you telephone back at about 11.30?'

Drabble saw the blind sway. His heart pounded against his chest.

'Look – why don't you just *try* the office?'

'Well –'

'Come on, man,' he barked. 'Just do it. *Do it now.*'

He heard a hiss and then the line began to ring. The blind swayed and slapped against the glass. Come on, Hodgekiss, thought Drabble. *Answer.* He frowned down at the big black telephone. *Come on, come on.* He heard low voices from the corridor and turned to the door. He saw the door handle turn.

'Hallo?' said a voice on the line.

'HODGEKISS! It's Drabble.' He saw the door open and a hand on the outside handle. He turned away, his voice rising. 'The fascist plot is live, Hodgekiss. It's started. *Alert Churchill.*'

The line was dead.

'Hodgekiss?'

Drabble jabbed the ringer but there was nothing. He looked over. Three Blackshirts stood before him; one by the door raised his hand, showing the frayed ends of a telephone cable. The closest fascist put his hand to his hip. Drabble saw three pips denoting the rank of captain on his shoulders and sleeves.

'Hold it,' the officer said. He unclipped his holster.

'Get your hands up.'

Drabble's gaze left the fascist and drifted down to the telephone – and then back. He saw the captain's fingers locate the grip of his pistol and retrieve it. Drabble started raising his hands but was prevented by the brown wire of the handset, which stretched tightly across him. The fascist grinned and flicked the snub barrel of his pistol in the direction of the receiver. Drabble nodded, and slowly passed the handset from his left hand to his right and then down to the cradle of the black Bakelite phone on the desk. He kept eye contact with the captain throughout. There was a *ding* as the handset landed.

The fascist's focus shifted to the phone.

Drabble hurled the telephone, and dived. The receiver struck the captain's face – cracking against his jaw – and the main part of the device collided after. Drabble barged the man's chest and his gun clattered to the floor. The captain collapsed into the fascist behind and the trio tumbled into the grey filing cabinets that lined the far wall. The Blackshirt at the door fumbled at his holster. Drabble jumped up and swung at him. His right jab caught the man's cheek and his face span away – his mouth spitting blood. Drabble followed it with a left hook – the best he could manage – and the man collapsed, groaning. He seized the door handle but suddenly everything went black...

***

Drabble stirred. He tried to move his arms but found he could not. His eyes creased open and he saw they were tied to the arms of the chair. He tugged at his feet, but they were attached to its legs at the ankle. *Bugger.* He flattened his hands and tried to slide them back but the cords were too tight. *Double bugger.* He clenched his teeth as he became aware of throbbing pain at the back of his head.

His prison was a brightly lit, spacious, if stark, office. In front of him was a broad oak desk, behind which stood a luxurious leather swivel chair with broad arms. There was a pair of telephones on the desk, both black, a brass desk-lamp with jade green shade, and the backs of several silver-framed photographs. He also saw the necessary accoutrements of correspondence, including a large, leather-bound blotting pad. On the wall behind the desk was a portrait of the King in the military uniform of a Highland regiment Drabble did not recognise. Tartan was draped over his left shoulder, and elsewhere the Royal person was adorned with gold braid, medals, and decorations. The gilt frame stood out against the bare red brick walls.

Beside it stood a tasselled standard lamp, and two high bookcases which abutted the walls. Drabble scanned the shelves: there were leather-bound volumes of atlases, collected papers, essays, and letters: he saw Plato, Aristotle, Machiavelli, Locke, More, Rousseau, Marx, Nietzsche, *Mein Kampf* – and next to it, *The Bible*. Drabble scowled and tore his eyes away. On the wall to the right he saw a large map of the world. He stared at it for a moment. Something wasn't right. Then his lips parted. The map showed Britain and the Dominions - India, Canada, South Africa, and New Zealand - all tinted in a greyish-black, along with the Colonies, most noticeably the disjointed swathe of British East Africa, which sat at the heart of a inky landmass that dog-legged down the entire continent from Cairo to Cape Town. He drew breath as he saw the expanse of the Near East; Palestine, Transjordan, Mesopotamia – all painted that black. The same tint covered Germany, Spain, Italy, and their respective imperial possessions in North Africa. Drabble's eyes travelled east to Imperial Japan. Yes, she was black, too, along with her vast colonies in Korea and Manchuria. Drabble's stomach turned. The only significant exceptions were the United States of America, the Soviet Union, and France, of course. He closed his eyes; Good Lord. And when you considered the combined maritime strengths of Britain and Japan you might as well paint the seas and oceans black, too. *For good measure.*

He exhaled, squeezing his eyes shut. His head throbbed painfully. He stretched his head to the left and saw a black fascist banner hanging from the wall. He also saw a wooden table. He jerked his body and pulled to the left with his feet and arms. The chair made a small jump sideways. Drabble leaned forward, tensed, and then threw his shoulders up once more: the chair pitched forward and made an unsteady hop left. The small table was now in front: on it he saw Wilkinson's wooden box. So that was that, he thought. He heard a metal rasp and he looked over at the green door. It swung open and a Blackshirt - rifle hanging from his shoulder – stepped back against it, holding himself smartly to attention. Drabble saw a pair of black leather boots and black flared breeches sweep in. He looked up and recognised the man from the podium: Sir

Carmen Kelly.

'Ah, Professor Drabble,' he said, removing his tall peaked cap and handing it to the guard. He came over to the desk, laid down his swagger stick and yanked off his black leather gloves, finger by finger. 'How very convenient of you to drop in.' His hair was slicked-back and dark with the faintest hint of a parting down the middle. He also wore a precise, thin moustache that, at no more than a quarter-inch in thickness, resembled an exceptionally long eyebrow hovering above his mouth. On his shoulders Kelly wore the insignia of a field marshal - a silver crown above crossed batons set on a laurel, and ornate silver collar flashes on both lapels of his black tunic. Drabble noticed that the FLGB logo was embroidered on his right shoulder. Kelly retrieved the stick and approached, his hand squeezing the large silver pommel. 'I'm relieved to see that you have returned to the land of the living,' he announced. 'Welcome back.'

Drabble met his eyes and watched him walk past from view. He saw the broad double silver stripe running down the side of the Prussian-style breeches. Beyond, Drabble saw a second man arrive. He was a big fellow but dressed in a civilian suit. The guard pulled the metal door closed. The big man grabbed the back of Drabble's chair and pulled it around to face the desk. Drabble saw Sir Carmen lower himself into his seat, lean back, and place his booted heels on the corner of the desk.

'If you don't know it already, my name is Sir Carmen Kelly,' he said, addressing his comments to the ceiling. He met Drabble's gaze, 'And if you don't know it already, you *are my* prisoner. This,' he waved the pommel of his stick in the circular motion above him, 'is my fortress.' His tone rose, 'Arkwright.' He waved his stick. The burly figure appeared in the corner of Drabble's eye and set the wooden box on the desk.

'Thank you,' said Kelly. 'Now, be so kind as to fetch the Van de Graaf Generator.' He peered for a moment at the end of his boot. 'Arkwright.'

'Sir?'

'We'll also take tea – I'm sure Professor Drabble is parched after all his rope-assisted peregrinations.' Kelly rubbed the shin of his boot with the end of the stick. He turned to Drabble. 'You'd like tea, wouldn't you, Professor?' Arkwright moved away and Drabble heard the door close.

'I expect you have many questions to ask of me, Professor,' said Kelly, dropping his feet from the desk. He sat up and arched an eyebrow.

'I do, as a matter of fact,' Drabble crinkled his nose. 'Such as why you're dressed up like a Nazi clown?'

Kelly chuckled and rose from the chair.

'You don't like the uniform, Professor? My tailor charged me a hundred and fifty pounds for this sartorial masterpiece. The silver piping is Japanese silk. He'd be devastated to hear you.' Kelly moved around to the front of the desk. 'In any event *you* seem to have taken to it, rather.' He prodded the button flap on Drabble's tunic and leaned against the desk. 'I can say this - you'd better get used to it because you're going to be seeing a lot more of it.' He grinned but kept his mouth shut - an action which Drabble saw caused the ends of his moustache to turn down as it pitched around the corners of his mouth.

271

'Now, it is a matter of no small irony to me that for the last forty-eight hours or so, we've been doing our level best to eliminate you, but now that you're here I'm rather pleased about it. Why? Because I'm hoping you will address your considerable grey matter to a little historical riddle for me.'

He rapped the top of Wilkinson's box with the pommel of the stick. Drabble snorted.

'Why on earth should I help you, Kelly?'

Kelly cleared his throat and raised the swagger stick.

'I can think of a couple of reasons,' he said. Drabble heard the door and craned his head round. 'Say hello to the first of them.'

There was a shriek and Drabble turned sharply.

'*Kate!*'

Two guards hauled her into the room. She wriggled and the men grimaced as they held her.

'What are you doing here?' cried Drabble. 'I told you to stay put.'

'I did!' She glared at him, 'For the first two hours.' Kate stamped on the toe of the Blackshirt to her left. He snatched his boot away, as the other guard shuffled his feet to evade from her jabbing right heel.

'Miss Honeyand!' Kelly pulled on his gloves and approached. 'You are being hysterical. You will kindly settle down. There's a good *little* woman.'

Drabble saw her eyes narrow.

'Don't "little woman" me,' she hissed. 'And who the ruddy hell are you anyway?' She smiled resourcefully and Drabble saw a twinkle in her eye. 'If... if I wanted the telegram boy, I'd have sent for one!'

272

Kelly's chin rose and he stepped in front of her, his right hand formed into a tight fist. Drabble cried out.

Kelly's fist cracked against Kate's cheek and she broke free from the hold of one of the guards, collapsing to the floor. Kelly turned to Drabble, his eyes cold, hard, and shining. There was silence – and then Kate sobbed. When she lifted her head up, her right cheek was crimson. Her eyes were rimmed with moisture.

'You bastard, Kelly,' shouted Drabble, struggling against the chair to stand. 'You'll pay for this.'

'Oh hush, Professor,' Kelly wagged his finger and leaned back against the desk. 'You know,' he added, reflectively, 'it is so deeply frowned upon, but actually there's something curiously *freeing* about hitting a woman.' He tossed his gloves onto the desk and reached for the box of cigarettes. 'I don't expect you to agree with me.'

'I can't say I've any experience in the matter,' said Drabble. He glanced over at Kate, who was getting to her feet. 'You could always introduce me to your mother, and I'd be happy to explore the sensation.'

Kelly frowned disdainfully and lit the cigarette. A cloud of smoke, followed by a second, lingered in the air, and the door creaked open.

'Ah,' beamed Kelly, showing his regular white teeth, 'here's the machine.' He gripped his hands together. 'Yes, over there, Arkwright. Wire her up.'

Drabble heard a muffled cry and strained his head around. He saw the guards drag Kate, a black gag over her mouth, to a chair as Arkwright brought the device up to it. He saw the guards hold Kate down and tie her wrists and kicking legs to the chair. He looked back at the chrome-topped device and the straggling red wires that hung from it.

'What are you doing, Kelly?' he cried. 'Tell me!'

Kelly's gaze was passive. 'Nothing I wouldn't do to *your* mother, Professor.'

'You bastard!'

Drabble saw his eyebrows lift and the moustache straighten.

'Professor Drabble, kindly calm yourself. Nothing will happen to Miss Honeyand, if you cooperate.' Drabble heard the tinkle of porcelain. Kelly smiled. 'Here's the tea.'

A servant in morning tails, striped sponge-bag trousers and white cotton gloves brought a tray to the desk. He set it down and offloaded the tea things. The crockery was white and angular, with silver edges: the cups and saucers were hexagonal.

'Milk or lemon, Professor?' asked Kelly, with a gregarious flourish of the hand towards the tray. 'Arkwright, kindly liberate the professor's hands so he may join me.'

Drabble asked for milk and sugar – two lumps - as the cord straps were untied. He rubbed his wrists - they were raw – and then took the tea from the servant. The man withdrew. Drabble sipped some of the sickly sweet fluid and lowered the cup.

'So what is your historical riddle?' he asked, and took another sip of tea. Watching Kelly over the top of the cup, he met the pale grey eyes and saw them close.

'Professor, have you heard of a text called the

274

Pseudodoxia Epidemica, or in the vulgar, *Enquiries into Very Many Received Tenets*?' For a moment Kelly's gaze fixed on him. Drabble shook his head. 'No? Well, that is not surprising - I am the owner of the only known copy. Let me enlighten you: it was written by a philosopher, mathematician, and occultist zealot by the name Thomas Browne. He died in 1702 and was every inch as good as Newton – or so they say.'

He saw Kelly savour the end of his sentence and waited for a second or two to pass.

'I know of Browne.'

'Good.' Kelly took a sip of tea. 'In his treatise of 1698, in a chapter dedicated to the dark and arcane mediaeval art of alchemy, Browne alludes teasingly to "Cromwell's crown".'

'Cromwell's *crown*?' scoffed Drabble. He drained his cup and leaned forward, placing it in the saucer on the desk in front of him. 'What the devil are you driving at, Kelly? You know as well as I do that Cromwell never had a crown. He turned it down.'

Kelly set his cup down and stood up. He cleared his throat.

'I suppose you can't be expected to know everything, Pugh Prize or not.' He moved around to the side of the desk and perched on the corner. 'So, my dear fellow, *listen*. In the text, Browne is suitably evasive, but he does hint strongly at the actual discovery of the secret of alchemy - only to add that it has been lost from us.'

'How disappointing,' said Drabble, raising his cup and saucer. He watched Kelly get up and pace towards the map, the swagger stick gripped behind his back. 'I don't suppose there's a spot more tea in the pot, is there?'

Kelly turned around; his expression cold. Drabble lowered his cup and saucer.

'The good news for us,' continued Kelly, raising an index finger, 'is that Browne goes on to opine that, "He that findeth the remnants of the Lord Protector will stand a chance of uncovering the secret of alchemy".' The corners of Kelly's moustache lifted. 'Now, Professor Drabble, as you know, quite probably better than anyone, the body of the Lord Protector went into the mass grave at Tyburn, so,' Kelly raised his stick, 'it is our judgement that Browne could only be – and was - referring to the head, of the great man, since that is the only identifiable part remaining. Now, what I want *you* to do, Professor, is to examine the head,' he pointed the pommel at the wooden case, 'and see if you can shed some light on what Browne was going on about. And I'd like you to do that right *now*, if you'd be so kind.' He glanced at his wristwatch.

Drabble looked at the box and imagined what lay beneath its grainy mahogany surface: the rotten, brittle, blackened, and mummified skull of Oliver Cromwell. Could it really contain a clue to the secret of alchemy? Surely it wasn't possible? He looked over at Kelly. *The fellow was barking mad.* Drabble saw his captor's gaze linger at his wristwatch. He saw the grey eyes look over towards Kate and a diagonal crease form in the forehead.

'Come on, Professor,' he said. 'Or we'll warm up the Van de Graaff generator. I'll let you watch, if you want. The fun starts when the eyeballs start to glow like light-bulbs.'

Drabble looked over his shoulder and glimpsed Kate. She was gagged and tied to the chair, wires running from her wrists to the device. The guards had fallen in by the wall, their hands behind their backs. Kate caught his eye – she shook her head defiantly. But Drabble saw fear, too.

He turned to Kelly, and unclenched his fist. The man had been waiting for him. Drabble gave an infinitesimal nod.

'Very good,' said Kelly. His voice lifted, 'Arkwright.'

Drabble heard his footsteps approach. The man gripped the back of his chair and shoved him forward so that his legs went through the knee hole and he could reach the wooden box. Arkwright cleared away the tea things, the cups looking absurdly small in his hands.

'Now, Professor,' said Kelly, 'this is your chance to demonstrate your worth.' Drabble curled his lip and looked over at Kelly. 'And if you don't, I'll be forced to engage the Van de Graaff generator. As you may have noticed, the device is of, shall we say, *a size*.' He looked beyond Drabble at the machine and lowered his voice to a whisper, 'it can produce one million volts.' Kelly smirked, 'Of course we would scarcely require such a dramatic electronic profusion for Miss Honeyand.' He leaned back in his chair. 'Oh, I'd say about thirty seconds of charge would do the job nicely. Now, if you'd be so kind.' He gestured towards the head.

Drabble regarded the box, becoming aware that until this point he had not actually given it any close inspection. It was almost square – though just slightly taller than it was wide. On the top was a stout, hinged brass handle, rather like one would find hanging from the drawer of a Georgian chest. The lid was affixed by a clasp on the top, and hinged all the way along the opposite side in nautical style for additional strength. Drabble turned the box around so that the side with the lock was in front. Beneath the clasp he saw there was a fine crack, a close seal in the woodwork. Doors, he thought. He swallowed and lifted up the bar and drew the sprung clasp to one side; he gripped with his fingertip and lifted it back. From his seated position he could not see inside. He heard a flinty rasp and glanced up at Kelly over on the far side of the desk; dark smoke erupted from the end of a tan-coloured cigarette. Kelly saw and pulled out his long silver cigarette case: it flicked open, revealing a line of yellow cigarettes. *Just like a rank of Italian soldiers* would be Harris' remark, thought Drabble. He saw that each bore a tiny cross and lightning bolts of the Fascist League in scarlet at the filters. Kelly offered the case; Drabble shook his head and looked back at the box. He reached forward and gently drew back on the right-hand door – it was locked. He bit his lip for a moment, his gaze pausing on the join running down the centre of the panel. He ran his fingers along the inside of the top of the doors. His hand stopped. There: a horizontal bolt with a metal arm. He worked it back and forth and then slid it across; it clicked. The little doors moved fractionally apart. This was it, he thought. This was the moment I finally come face to face with Oliver Cromwell. He exhaled slowly, and parted the doors.

For a moment his expression remained impassive.

'What is it?' said Kelly, springing forward. 'It *is* Cromwell's head, or isn't it?'

Drabble looked up. He smiled.

'Of course it is.'

Before him was a skeletal face – but one fleshed out with dark brown and brittle-looking skin and muscle. He blinked; once, twice. I can't believe it, he thought. Oliver ruddy Cromwell. How do you do, sir? He nodded at the head.

'Look,' he said, indicating, 'this is the depression created by the heavy wart above the right eye. And here on the top are the small holes left by the trepanning process,' he looked over at Kelly, 'that was an important, well, actually an essential stage in the seventeenth-century embalming process.' His eyes flashed, 'and look at *this*: this is unquestionably the bulbous nose of the Lord Protector.' He rotated the box towards Kelly so that the face was shown to him, 'I'd swear that it's the same as you see in the death mask at the Bargello in Florence, or the Robert Walker portrait.' He saw Kelly's eyebrows rise and a lurid smile form on his mouth. Drabble continued, 'Take my word for it. It's him. Here,' his voice rose, 'you can see the remains of his moustache and small beard. I can't believe it. No, no, it's definitely him.' He glanced at Kelly and saw he was watching him. 'It's *definitely* him.'

Kelly drew on his cigarette: the end glowed red, and he threw it to the floor. There was a scrape as his boot extinguished the stub and then he rose wearily from the chair. He knelt next to Drabble, leaning his hand on the back of his chair.

'Very good, Professor,' he said. 'Now, we know it's Cromwell right enough. I can recognise the man, just as you can. But what about Browne?' Drabble heard his voice over his shoulder, his voice level and firm. 'What about Browne?'

Drabble glanced back as Kelly moved away, strolling around behind him and around the other side of the desk. He heard the slow grind of the leather soles of his boots against the concrete floor. Kelly completed a lap and then sat in his chair. He took another cigarette from the case. Drabble addressed his attention to the head, and heard the rasp of the lighter's flint. He saw wisps of hair above and below the mouth, the remains of that flowing beard and moustache; he saw tiny hairs, almost like spiny fossils, at the eyebrows. The head itself, though, was hairless. This confirmed to him that - as was the practice of the time – Cromwell's head had been shaved during the embalmment. The eyes were hooded heavily and there were dark, indefinable recesses where the eyeballs had once been. What could he find that Kelly and his people had not, he wondered? And what on earth did any of this have to do with alchemy? Surely Cromwell didn't even believe in it either? He saw that at the mouth, instead of lips, stiff-looking skin and the remnants of the moustache merged to form a jagged aperture. The lips had gone. They looked almost as if they had been torn off. He chewed the inside of his cheek thoughtfully, rolling the skin to and fro. His tongue caught a rough edge on a tooth and felt a sharp pain. He saw the dark crease that was the mouth of Cromwell. Was it possible? He frowned and pulled the base of the box closer. He leaned forward so that his eyes were level with the mouth and peered into the dark oral void. He looked over at Kelly. He saw him push the cigarette between his lips and raise the flame to it. Drabble reached out with his hand.

'Lighter.'

Kelly passed it. Drabble held the device to Cromwell's mouth. He stroked the flint. Suddenly light danced inside the mouth and Drabble saw the palate of the Lord Protector. And there – *there* he saw a little row of wooden false teeth, the very teeth that Cromwell had so bitterly complained about during his lifetime, even though they had been made in Paris by the best experts in the world. He hurriedly stood the lighter on the desk and placing his left hand on the cheek, reached into Cromwell's mouth with the first and second fingers of his right hand. He felt the interior; the blunt crenellations of the rotted teeth surprisingly pronounced. He gripped the top row and pulled gently, pushing them from side to side. He heard a sound – almost like the noise of bone tearing – and he felt the top row of teeth loosen from the jaw. He pulled it back from the mouth and several dusty pieces of skin from the jagged mouth broke away. Drabble laid the teeth and the semi-circular wooden frame that formed them onto the desk. He cleared his throat and reached deep inside. His fingertips felt the rough, brittle interior: cold ridges of bone and layers of skin the texture of sandpaper. He pushed his fingers further into the mouth, finding its roof. His hand halted. Drabble's eyes widened.

'What is it?' said Kelly, rising to his feet.

Drabble retracted his fingers from the mouth – between them was a tightly rolled parchment about an inch across, bound by blackened thread.

'Good God,' said Kelly. He placed the cigarette on the corner of the ashtray and reached forward, clapping

Drabble on the shoulder. 'Well done, Professor, well done indeed! Now,' he snatched the parchment packet and placed it on the blotter. 'Let's see what you've found,' he exclaimed, as he yanked out a drawer, from which he took a scalpel. Bending the desk lamp closer, Drabble saw him stroke the blade over the black twine, its threads frayed and parted. After a few seconds he scraped the blade across the surface and removed the last threads. Then he brushed the remnants away with his fingertips and opened up the stiff scroll. An inch deep, Kelly unravelled it like a tailor's tape measure, until it reached about eight inches in length. From one end to the other it was covered in tiny, spidery black ink - letters, numerals, dashes, and mathematical symbols. That was definitely not Cromwell's handwriting.

Kelly looked up from the parchment and grinned broadly.

'Congratulations, Professor,' he said, raising the black telephone to his ear. There was a pause. 'Get me Dr Hinterhoisser.'

Kelly replaced the handset and retrieved his cigarette from the ashtray.

'Arkwright, show the professor to his room.'

Drabble was pulled to his feet. A second guard snatched Drabble's wrists and cuffed them behind him, as a third undid the bonds that tied his ankles to the chair legs. Arkwright dragged him towards the door. Drabble looked over at Kate.

'Don't worry about Miss Honeyand,' said Kelly, calling after him. 'We'll take impeccable care of her.'

Drabble's feet skidded from under him as they hauled

him, struggling, into the corridor. He heard Kate scream. *Clang*. The iron door slammed shut. Silence.

The guards dragged him along the corridor, his heels scuffing lines in the dirt on the concrete floor. Occasionally they passed glass windows and Drabble saw out into the courtyard – there were two rows of parked coaches. In the front windows of each he saw white signs: 'LONDON' said one, 'PORTSMOUTH', said the next, then 'SOUTHAMPTON', 'DOVER', 'BIRMINGHAM', 'LIVERPOOL', 'MANCHESTER'...

At the far end was a pair of black armoured cars. He saw internal windows to his left, opening out into more offices. He saw a prim secretary typing as a man in Blackshirt uniform paced behind, his eyes fixed on the ceiling, his mouth moving and hand circling the air. Drabble heard the hiss, hum and rhythmic metallic beat of machinery and he looked left, seeing not a brightly lit office, but a vast, cavernous chamber, with printing presses and huge rolls of paper. Newspapers spilled from the end of the racks, where they were snatched up, rolled, and folded into bundles. From here men with trolleys sped the bundles away.

'Hey,' he yanked at the arm of the guard and struggled away. On the far side of the presses was a raised office area where men worked on copy. On the floor far below he saw a newspaper. He could not quite read the headline. He pulled away from the guard and lunged towards the glass to get a better view...

The last thing Drabble remembered was his name being shouted. Then everything went black.

Drabble collapsed, his knees giving way, and the two

guards either side took his weight. Arkwright slotted the truncheon back in his coat pocket and led away down the corridor. The Blackshirts followed, dragging Drabble, his head lolling, like a broken, outsized rag-doll.

CHAPTER TWENTY FIVE

Drabble opened his eyes. He was in darkness. He groaned painfully and rubbed the back of his head. *Sod*. He raised himself slowly, and then gagged, his head jerking in a convulsive spasm. He covered his nose and mouth with his hand.

'Ruddy hell!'

With his nose still firmly gripped, he looked accusingly around the room. Where *was* the terrible smell coming from? Light shone from outside in the corridor through a series of slits in the door and at its hinges. As his eyes adjusted, he saw faintly the walls of his prison in the gloom, at first fleetingly, like apparitions. There was a narrow table and simple stool by the door. He slumped back down on the bed. It squeaked loudly as it took his weight.

He, *they*, were in trouble, he thought, deep trouble. He shook his head and leaned his face into his hands. Kelly was on the verge, the cusp of insurrection, a coup, you name it. And if it were conceivable, he, Ernest George Drabble, was guilty of furnishing this lunatic with the long lost secret to alchemy. He shook his head and saw that the ceiling was coming into view as his eyes became accustomed to the darkness. Turning base metal into gold? It would never work. He gave a hollow laugh. *The fools.* The bunk squeaked as he got up.

But what if it did work?

He stood and clenched his fist. What if the map in

Kelly's study was a plan – what if it was going to come true? It was time for action. He had to raise the alarm. And now… Oh God. And poor Harris. The ruddy fool. He sighed. It was too late. Kelly, he recalled, had talked of the new dawn for Britain. A new dawn. He referred to his watch. Four p.m. Could the fascist attack already be underway? He shook his head slowly and edged back to the bed, lowering himself down onto it. He leaned back against the wall, staring into the darkness. It couldn't be true.

But suppose it was – and suppose the fascists *were* successful. Suppose they marched on London and the provincial centres, suppose the King sacked Baldwin and Kelly formed a minority fascist administration. And suppose they'd now also got the source of an unlimited supply of gold– which they could pass to their fascist friends in Germany, Italy, Japan and beyond. He swallowed. Well, there wasn't a chance in hell of Harris, Kate, or him ever seeing the light of day again, was there? *He had to escape.*

His gaze was drawn to the thin strips of light from the door frame. He went over and put his ear to the door. There was no sound. He got onto his knees and ran his hands over the floor – it was freezing beneath his palms and fingers. He slid his hands methodically over the rough surface from one side to the other, meticulously, as though he were mapping it. There must be something, he thought, as he patted and rubbed the damp and tacky concrete floor. There must be something. His search took him to the far wall, where the vile odour again caught at the back of his throat. His throat convulsed involuntarily as his stomach contracted. The smell grew stronger – his hand found a steel bucket. He moved it and it gave a metallic scrape against the floor: there was the delayed movement of a solid mass suspended in fluid, and a slop as some water danced over the rim. His stomach tightened and his mouth croaked open. He retched, and edged backwards, breathing hard until his backside met the bunk. He ran his hand underneath. There was nothing in the cell. There had to be something. There always was. He spat on his hands and rubbed them, digging his nails into his palms to remove the muck. He wiped the dirt onto his fascist trouser-legs. *There had to be something*. He sighed and moved towards the bed. He had an idea.

Dragging the flimsy mattress from the bunk, he pulled at the wire mesh beneath. The bindings were tightly woven steel.

'*Ow!*'

He flinched, sucking his finger. He shoved the mattress back and hooked out the stool from under the table with his toe. He plonked his weight upon it. The small seat gave a little – and *CRACK!* He tumbled backwards…

Cursing, he got to his feet, rubbing the back of his head. He glowered at the shattered stool. Sodding thing, he thought. He snatched it up. The legs hung from the seat limply. Useless, he thought. No wonder it fell apart. Sodding thing's only held together by nails.

Hang on a ruddy second.

He pulled one of the legs free and with his thumb located a long, powerful nail protruding from the wooden base. Who on earth built this thing, he thought. He knelt

287

down and tapped the nail quietly back upon itself against the floor. *Tap, tap, tap.* The flat head of the nail broke through the crust of the wood-coloured glue that capped it, and stood proud from the base. *Tap, tap, tap,* the remainder inched free. Drabble heard footsteps outside and yanked the nail out. He jammed the leg of the stool back into its splintered socket, and, pulling the other legs into line, stood the stool under the table. He heard a clang from the direction of the door and then a second quieter noise of a bar or bolt being shifted. He slid the nail into his watch strap and prepared himself to act. There was a scrape and then a shaft of light shot into the small room as a hatch swept open.

Drabble shielded his eyes from the dazzling beam. After a moment the intensity dimmed and he saw a head in the square opening; then there was a scrape and he was in darkness. He heard a clang as the bolt was brought across – and then the louder sound of a bar or heavier piece of metal grinding into place.

These buggers were leaving nothing to chance. He turned on the bunk and lay back, staring patiently into the darkness.

***

Drabble heard the clang of the bar being lifted and sprang to his feet. He snatched up the bucket and went to the door: there was the second scrape as a final bolt was shifted. Drabble squeezed his eyes and waited for the stinging light.

It came. He drew back the bucket and hurled the

contents at the hatch. There was a splat as the contents of the bucket struck the door - and the gaoler, who growled.

'You bastard,' he hissed. 'Alfred,' he shouted, 'Give me an 'and.'

Drabble stepped back as he heard another bolt being shifted: the door shot open and he saw the gaoler's head glisten with foul moisture. The man was big – fat but powerfully built - and he held a truncheon in his hand. A second man stepped into Drabble's line of sight behind him.

'You little fucker,' said the gaoler, his voice quivering. 'No one gets away with that in *my* prison.' He raised the truncheon and lunged for Drabble. He sprang from the gaoler's reach and parried the weapon with the metal bucket.

'GET HIM,' roared the gaoler, as he made another wild lurch. Drabble jumped back but found his back to the wall. The second man's hand was on his shoulder. Drabble threw the bucket at his head and dived at the gaoler before the man could lash at him with the bludgeon. They staggered back, the gaoler's face reeking of excrement. Drabble slashed at the man with the nail and he hurried back holding his face.

'You bastard,' he cried. Drabble saw the second gaoler glance over at the injured man and gather his wits. Drabble pounced, and bundled him over. They rolled into the bunk: the man striking the wall with the back of his head – *thud* - and he was out cold. Drabble got up and then buckled forward as the truncheon knocked him down. He turned and saw the gaoler, a bleeding gash across his right cheek, coming in to land another blow. He flung his right foot up, connecting with the man's groin. The gaoler's mouth formed an 'o' and he blinked. Drabble dived for the door and pulled it shut, turning the key in the lock. He shut the hatch and brought the final bar across.

CHAPTER TWENTY SIX

Drabble was at the end of a wide corridor with several metal doors leading off, either side. In the middle of the room was a desk, on which sat a telephone, a pack of playing cards and a metal ashtray. A sign on the wall opposite said, 'No Smoking'. He quickly went to the nearest door and started undoing the bolts to the hatch. He creaked it open and called inside.

'Hello?'

There was silence. He went to the next door. *Clang... click!* He looked inside. A faint glimmer from the skylight showed the room to be bare.

'Hello?'

He pulled open the next hatch and looked inside. There was another skylight and he saw a huddled figure seated in a chair, facing away. The man, his head bowed forward, talked in a low voice.

'F-flash'd all their sabres bare,
F-flash'd as they t-turn'd in air
Sabring the gunners there...'

The prisoner suddenly stopped and span around the chair, wailing; the soles of his feet pawing the floor, his hands raised protectively over his face. 'W-Who's there?' he cowered. 'Oh, Lord, oh, Lord...' He breathed fast, *'Please don't hurt me!'*

Drabble reviewed the meek specimen through narrowed eyes.

'Harris!' he said, at last. '*Harris!* It's me, Drabble.' He got to the bolts and started freeing them. Harris looked up; tears suddenly welled in his eyes.

'Ernest?' he cried, his lip buckling. 'ERNEST? You've come to save me?'

The door opened and he rushed in.

'Hello old man, nice shiner... we've got to -' Drabble cursed and covered his face. 'Lord, you ruddy well reek. Are you sitting in your own -'

'They tried to frazzle me with an electric generator,' sobbed Harris. 'I-I tried but they kept doing it. The bastards. And they beat me - and look, they cut off my -'

'Can you stand?'

Harris looked down at his feet.

'I think so; if you help me.'

Drabble got an arm around his back and lifted him up. Slowly, Harris rose, his knees knocking together audibly.

'There you go, old man.'

The tears rolled down Harris' face. He looked up at Drabble with pitiable gratitude.

'Ernest, thank you.'

With great effort Harris took a tremulous step forward, perhaps accounting for six inches. 'That's better. Thank you, old man. You're such a good chum. I knew you'd come for me.'

'Let's get away from here,' said Drabble, seeing the filthy bandage around Harris' left hand. 'Come on, buster.' He helped Harris achieve another shuffling step. 'That's it, old man, we'll be out of here in a jiffy.'

Drabble guided Harris into the corridor. He heard a thud against the door and the shout of the gaolers from inside the cell.

'Halt!'

He turned and saw a slim figure in Blackshirt uniform: her Luger was trained on them. At her side stood a dog, a beautiful black Labrador dusted with white at its muzzle.

'Who are you?' she demanded of Drabble, giving his dishevelled black uniform a rapid up and down. 'You're not the normal gaoler, where is he?'

There was a cry from inside the cell.

'That's the bitch that cut my finger off,' hissed Harris, his hands raised.

'Silence!'

She gestured with the pistol towards the open door.

'Back into the cell. *Now!*'

Drabble met her eyes: they were hard and blue. He puffed out his chest.

'No.'

Smith's eyes narrowed.

'I said, get in the cell. Do it.'

Harris started to move towards the cell. Drabble gripped his shoulder and stared hard at Smith.

'No,' he said. 'What are you going to do? Shoot me?'

She smiled and raised the gun to eye level, aiming it directly at Drabble's face. He swallowed. The barrel then panned across to Harris.

'No,' quivered Harris. 'N-not me.' His hands went higher.

'Silence - get in the cell.'

'Hold it, Harris -' Drabble seized his collar. 'What do you think she did with your finger?'

Captain Smith edged sideways towards the cell that contained the gaolers, reaching out to it with her free hand.

'I said move!'

He saw her slide the top bolt across. Only the bolt at the foot of the door now stood between them and two seriously angry gaolers. Drabble turned to Harris.

'I think we'd better do what she says. Go on.'

'That's just what I was thinking, old boy,' said Harris, his hands still held aloft. He stepped back towards the open door. '*HEY!*'

Drabble shoved him: Harris tumbled, arms flailing, towards Smith. She fired – as Drabble dived for the far side of the desk. The sound of the gun in the confined space was ear-splitting. There was a second flash from Smith's Luger and she crabbed sideways across the corridor, her gun trained low. Drabble crouched behind the desk, his mind racing. In the left-hand side, in a deep drawer, he found a drinks cabinet – there wasn't much to celebrate yet, so he began hauling out the slim drawers on the right.

Bingo!

Harris scampered to his feet, his bandaged hand raised. Drabble heard him breathing hard.

'Hold it,' said Smith. She was pointing the Luger at him. Harris eyed her and looked towards the desk.

There was a double click of a pistol being cocked. But it wasn't the Luger.

'Freeze,' said Drabble. He held a revolver aimed at Smith. Her eyes moved over and narrowed. 'Drop it,' continued Drabble. 'If you move an inch towards me, I'll shoot. And if you're stupid enough to shoot Mr Harris here, you'll be dead before he hits the deck. Place your weapon on the floor. *Slowly.*'

Smith regarded him, her blue eyes studying his expression. She swallowed.

'Very well,' she said. She crouched and laid the Luger on the floor. Harris retrieved it.

'Right,' said Drabble, moving forward and taking the Luger from Harris, 'where's Kate?'

'Miss Honeyand?'

'Yes,' said Drabble, handing his revolver to Harris. 'Do you know where she is?'

Smith nodded.

'Good.' He ejected the magazine from the handle of the Luger and counted the rounds. It clicked as he slotted it back into place. 'Take us to her.'

Smith nodded.

'Yes,' added Harris. 'And no funny business.'

He gestured threateningly with the revolver.

Gripping her arm, the barrel of his gun pressed into her side, Smith led Drabble and Harris along a corridor, the Labrador following behind. They entered the vast room where Drabble had seen the presses – these were now silent and in darkness. The workers had gone.

'Who's *Kate*?' asked Harris, from the corner of his mouth.

'Miss Honeyand. She's Wilkinson's secretary.'

Harris glanced over. 'You didn't mention her before.'

To the right, through the broad windows, Drabble saw the circular courtyard. It was now more or less dark. The buses had all gone. He saw the two armoured cars, and a Rolls-Royce, now parked to one side. Its Greek temple grille gleamed and a pair of Fascist League flags flew from each of the long black running boards. The flags were fringed with silver braid. It's started, he thought. Can Kelly really have deployed his troops? Will Hodgekiss have raised the alarm?

'So what's she like?'

Drabble grinned. 'Very bonny.'

Harris' eyebrows raised jauntily.

'Wonderful.' He stepped forward and pressed the barrel of the revolver into Smith's side. 'You see, Smith, every cloud has a silver lining.' He chuckled. 'Not just fascist flags!'

The corridor followed the great curve of the circular fort and approached the green metal door that Drabble recognised belonged to Kelly's office. A guard stood outside.

Drabble leaned to Smith's ear.

'Say anything, and you'll be the first to go,' he whispered. He raised his gun, 'Hands up!' Slowly, the guard moved his hands into the air. Harris went forward and tore the rifle from his shoulder.

'Right, Harris,' continued Drabble, not taking his eye off the man. 'Cover the guard with that Lee-Enfield rifle – put one up the spout if you have to. That way he and Smith will know you mean business.' He took the pistol from Harris and tucked it into his tunic. 'It's not loaded, old man,' he said, answering Harris' questioning look.

Drabble next referred to the guard, 'You - open the door.'

The man hesitated: he looked to Smith.

'Do it,' said Drabble.

Smith nodded in reply and the guard pulled the steel

bolt across. They went inside.

'Sit down,' said Drabble, pulling out a wooden chair from the wall. He pushed the guard into the seat and went behind him, snatching off his college tie. 'Harris – take off your tie and bind her hands together.' Drabble bound the guard's wrists behind the chair.

'Right, Smith,' he said standing in front her, his Luger pointing dead ahead. 'Where is she - *Miss Honeyand*? Don't mess us about.'

Smith contemplated her response.

'I don't know,' she said flatly, her eyes focused on the end of the barrel. Her tone lightened and she met Drabble's gaze. 'I *simply* don't know.'

Drabble growled and pressed the barrel of the gun to her forehead.

'You bloody well *do* know, Smith, and you're going to tell me.' He slid the safety catch off. 'Right,' he said, 'I'm going to count to three.'

Drabble's chest heaved.

'*One.*'

He saw Smith's eyes blink reflectively and a frown form around the muzzle of the Luger. Come on, you bitch, he thought.

'Ah… *Two!*'

Drabble looked over to the guard; he saw him avert his eyes fearfully to the floor. Still Smith's narrow mouth was contracted in a posture of defiance. Drabble raised his hand so that the Luger aimed down into her head and edged back.

'Thr -'

'*She's in the lab!*' Smith cried, tears forming at her

297

eyes. 'She's in the laboratory.'

Drabble lowered the gun as Smith bowed her head and sobbed. The muzzle of the Luger had left a pale circular impression on her forehead. He was grateful that that was all it had done.

Harris cleared his throat and tugged at his arm.

'Hey, Drab,' he said. 'I think you'd better see this.'

A copy of what was evidently the fascists' newspaper lay on Kelly's desk. Its front page declared:

'BALDWIN RESIGNS – LORD KELLY IS PM'
FASCIST LEAGUE FORMS GOVT.

'What's this?' he said, showing the page to Smith. 'It's not true!'

'Not yet.' She gave a haughty chuckle. 'It's tomorrow morning's news, Drabble. You're too late to stop it now.'

'We'll ruddy well see about that,' he said, striding over to the guard. He pulled out his handkerchief and stuffed it into the man's mouth. 'Harris,' he said; his friend looked up from his tobacco pouch. 'Forget your pipe, man, *we're leaving*.' He went over to the guard and raised the butt of the Luger, 'But not you,' he said. 'You're staying put.'

CHAPTER TWENTY SEVEN

They hurried along the corridor. Drabble gripped Smith's arm and pressed the gun into her side; Harris followed, with the Captain's Labrador trotting by his side. The trio went through a side door and down a maroon staircase. Their footsteps chimed on the metal rungs. Looking down, Drabble saw the flights of stairs zigzag away into the distance until it was impossible to discern what was what. Harris adjusted the leather strap of his rifle at his shoulder. Drabble noticed a fresh red stain on his grubby dressing.

'How's the hand holding up, old man?'

Harris removed the pipe; smoke tumbled from his mouth.

'It's been better.'

Smith curled her lip. 'You stink.'

'*Shut up* – or I'll shoot your little finger off.' Harris flashed a look at Drabble and whispered into his ear, loudly, 'This cow cut it off with a *pair of pliers*!'

Drabble winced.

'It was so painful,' continued Harris, in a hoarse tone, 'I *almost* passed out.'

'He *did* pass out,' corrected Smith, glancing over her shoulder at Drabble. '*After* he pissed himself.'

Drabble jammed the barrel of the Luger into her kidneys and she stumbled painfully.

'Button it, Smith,' he pulled her upright and turned his attention to Harris. 'They sent it to me, as a warning.'

'Sent it to you?' He looked over at Smith. 'In the post?'

'Delivered by hand, I gather.'

Harris shook his head gloomily.

'That's almost funny.'

At the metal landing Drabble glanced over the side. They were nearing the bottom. He checked above. He quickened his pace.

'I say,' said Harris, as he hurried to get back in step. 'Have you still got it?'

Drabble shook his head.

'I had to throw it away.'

'You threw it away?'

'I had to,' he said. 'It was getting whiffy.'

'Whiffy?' Harris frowned. '*That was my ruddy finger!* It's part of me. It's got my soul in it!'

Harris planted the pipe back in his mouth and puffed it grimly. They circled around another landing.

'Last flight,' said Drabble.

Harris was still miffed about his finger. He came muttering into Drabble's earshot.

'I can't believe you just threw it away.'

'Oh, come off it, old man. I had no choice – it was damned unhygienic. And it's not like it was any good to you. It never was.'

'What does that mean?'

Drabble's face cracked into a grin.

'I've seen you type. You only use two fingers.'

Harris plucked out his pipe, failing to suppress a smile.

'That's not the point. It's the principle. *It was my finger!*'

At the foot of the stairs they arrived at another passage: a solid concrete floor and dirty grey walls disappeared into the distance, illuminated by a series of single ceiling-mounted light-bulbs.

Drabble and Harris exchanged a doubtful glance. Drabble tightened his grip on Smith's arm.

'Where the dickens are you taking us?'

She gritted her teeth.

'The lab is contained in the fort's bunker and old magazine. It was built to withstand bomb attacks in the Great War – from Zeppelins and naval artillery.'

Harris adjusted his pipe and nodded to Drabble.

'Come on then,' he said, shoving Smith. 'Let's go.'

They moved off, their paces lengthening and footsteps quickening. Harris unshouldered his rifle.

'I kept your ring, by the way,' said Drabble.

Harris brightened.

'You did? Thank you.'

They took a few more paces. Harris had a thought.

'What did you do with it?'

'What?'

'The finger. You said you threw it away. Did you just toss it into a bin or something?'

Drabble smiled uncomfortably.

'Something like that.'

Harris regarded him with a hard look, but said nothing.

Drabble cleared his throat.

'I gave it a burial at sea.'

'*You what?*'

'I threw it overboard on the way here.'

'Did you say a few words?'

301

Drabble arched an eyebrow.

'Are you serious?'

Harris tilted his head to one side, and then to the other. He put the pipe to his mouth and inhaled.

'It's all right, old man,' he said, at length. 'I'm sure you did your best.'

The corridor turned sharply and they came face to face with a pair of fascists, standing guard at a large square grey door.

Drabble pulled Smith to him and raised the Luger to her temple.

'Hold it, you two,' he said. 'Put your hands on your head.' Harris brought the bolt of his rifle forward. The guards exchanged a glance and their hands edged up into the air.

Harris went ahead and unhooked their rifles. He slipped them over his left shoulder.

'Right,' said Drabble, addressing the men. 'Take us in. I want you to walk two abreast immediately ahead of Smith and me. Put your hands on your head. And no monkey business, or I'll shoot.'

On his friend's word Harris opened the door: Drabble felt a gust of air brush his face and he caught the breeze – it was acrid and bitter, like burning rubber. He glanced over at Harris who raised his nose, sniffing hard.

The cold, gritty concrete floor was replaced by a metal gangway and below them, a deep subterranean chamber was visible on their left. A sign on the wall read, 'No smoking'. Another declared, 'Inflammable materials'.

The convoy proceeded slowly. Drabble saw a warren of wooden benches, rows of smoking test tubes, and several large vats. The bitter smell strengthened. They continued in silence around the limits of the room, their shoes clanging on the walkway. On the level below, Drabble saw a large vat, containing a thick, dark fluid which was decanting into it from a tall copper cylinder. From the vat, the thick liquid passed along a raised, pitched duct and descended into a wide, shallow cooling tray. From there an overflow pipe fed a multi-layered glass spiral. Drabble saw the glass turn dark and the new mixture cascade into a long bath into which men in white coats poured buckets of dull, rust-coloured liquid. One technician, a bald man whose stomach stretched his white laboratory coat, stirred this mixture with a long aluminium spatula, rather like it was a giant soup. His face was pinched in concentration and effort. They turned the corner.

Sir Carmen Kelly leaned against the handrail, looking down at the laboratory, his gloved hand clasping the silver pommel of his swagger stick. He turned towards them and removed his spectacles.

'Ah! Professor Drabble and Mr Harris,' he said, his teeth shone in the strip lighting. 'Welcome to the world of Dr Hinterhoisser.' He grinned and slotted the glasses into his inside pocket. The black Labrador left Smith's side and cantered over to him. 'The man is a certifiable genius.' Kelly gestured towards a grey-haired man below, who looked up, braced himself, and straightened his arm to perform the Nazi salute. Kelly continued, 'He was sent over to me from Berlin. The man possesses an *uber*-intellect. Makes our chemists look like monkeys rubbing sticks together.' He snorted. 'Let me show you something.'

He started to move away-

'Hold it, Kelly,' shouted Drabble. 'We've seen enough. Where's Kate?'

'Don't worry, Professor, Miss Honeyand is quite, *quite* safe,' he said, 'She is perfectly unharmed - a state which will be ensured under the rule of the Fascist League of Great Britain, I can assure you.' Kelly dipped his chin and winked, 'Trust me, we need all the good genetic stock that we can get our hands on.' He coughed. 'We would not readily squander such a delightful specimen as Miss Honeyand. Come!'

He moved away, the Labrador obediently at his heels. Kelly led them down two flights of metal stairs and along a gangway. They passed the bath where the thick red fluid was being measured out and added to the acrid mixture. They then passed a tall rectangular glass and steel tank in which the red and grey liquids bubbled and broiled, with spouts and crests fizzing from the surface. The fluid splashed against the glass and slowly traced down it, leaving a thick greasy trail. Above, brown smoke rose listlessly from the tank and was sucked away by an extractor fan, its blades and engine producing a mechanical drone. A concertinaed rubberised silver and red tube snaked away along the wall, to a hole in the ceiling, into which several other pipes and tubes also fed. Kelly raised his voice above the sound of the motor.

'For the last five and a half years the good doctor has dedicated his life to a very important vein of research - a major experiment on sea water. Did you know, Professor Drabble, that seawater contains gold?' He chuckled, 'In minuscule quantities, of course, but it *does*. Oh yes. Every droplet constitutes a tiny gold rush.'

Kelly's hand brushed along the side of his head, flattening his hair.

'However,' he continued, 'not even a man of Dr Hinterhoisser's undeniable genius could alter the facts, and – indeed, even he will concede – while he managed to prove that it was both theoretically and physically possible to extract gold particles from the sea, there is in fact one insurmountable problem: scale. You have to process so much water that you may as well go back to first principles, by which I mean, employ people to dig the stuff out of the ground. So,' Kelly's white teeth flashed red in the reflected light, 'I was on the verge of mothballing this facility, and even sending the good doctor back to the Fuhrer, when I discovered the existence of the head of Oliver Cromwell just the other night. So, thank you, Mr Harris; your indiscreet slip to our mutual friend, Grubby Howse, was *most* timely.'

Drabble looked over at Harris, who averted his gaze.

'But,' continued Kelly, 'it was your intervention that made all the difference, Professor Drabble. Without you, we'd still all be at sea.'

He smiled - and moved. The guards, their hands still on their heads, started to follow.

Drabble stood still.

'Hang on,' he said. 'What are you talking about, Kelly?'

Sir Carmen turned to look back.

'Alchemy, Professor Drabble.' The moustache appeared to widen. 'This is about gold and power.'

Kelly moved on, but Drabble remained still.

'You're deluded,' he said, 'utterly deluded. It'll never happen.'

Sir Carmen gazed up to the ceiling and smirked.

'Never happen?' he said, looking over. Drabble saw the grey eyes swell. 'It already is, Professor. As we speak, my supporters are assembling in each of the major conurbations of this great island. At the stroke of midnight they shall seize the ports, airfields, railway stations, and town halls across the country – and for good measure we shall take control of the BBC installation at the Crystal Palace and in the small hours the King will broadcast to the nation and the Empire.' Kelly stroked his moustache. 'Yes, Professor. He has decided to call Baldwin's bluff, after all. In the morning the standard of the Fascist League of Great Britain will be flying over Downing Street. If you don't believe me you can read about it in the newspapers that you saw being printed earlier.'

Drabble scoffed.

'If you believe what you read in the papers, Kelly,' he said, 'then you're even more of a damned fool than I took you for.'

Kelly's eyes flashed angrily.

'I'm afraid that it is you who are the *damned fool*, Drabble!' He turned to leave, but stopped and looked back. 'I find it most dispiriting, Professor, that with your great understanding and appreciation of the past, not least of the seminal dictatorship under your beloved Oliver Cromwell, that you do not share my vision. This, after all, is what he would have wanted.'

Kelly strode away, the dog's claws clattering on the

metal floor at his side.

Harris glanced over questioningly. Drabble pushed Smith forward and pressed the Luger into her side. They followed. The narrow gangway opened up into a wider area, where there was a desk, several office chairs, and a pair of filing cabinets. A green telephone sat on the corner of the desk. On the wall behind, Drabble saw a portrait of Adolf Hitler. It showed the German leader from the chest up. He wore a tawny jacket with a bold swastika on the left arm. In the background were the sharp white Alpine mountains below a blue sky. Drabble recognised the angular, mean summit of the Eiger. Kelly saw Drabble's gaze linger.

'Herr Dr Hinterhoisser is *very* keen on the Fuhrer,' he said.

Drabble looked at him, 'Almost as much as you are, I dare say.'

There was a cry and Drabble turned: he saw Kate, her cheek blackened, struggling in Arkwright's grip. Her fists flailed uselessly as the man carried her under one arm. 'Welcome, Miss Honeyand,' called Kelly, leaning against the balcony. His arm performed a languid arc over the laboratory below. 'We are on the verge of a new golden age in the history of fair Britannia. Look!' They approached the handrail. Drabble looked down and through the steam saw a shimmer and a golden pool. He saw a small circle form on the surface: it bulged, then burst.

'Great Scott!' said Harris, his eyes glistening. 'It's gold - *it's ruddy gold.*'

'Ruddy gold indeed,' said Kelly. He smiled and

307

nodded towards Drabble. 'Mr Harris, you should congratulate your dear friend here on making it all so very possible. Professor, believe me now?'

Drabble stared down, his eyes fixed on the golden pool. It certainly looked golden, he thought. His jaw trembled and he swallowed hard. He turned away and saw the portrait of Hitler – he saw the intensity of the eyes. He remembered the map in Kelly's office. A shiver ran down his spine. He heard Kelly laugh. 'You should feel proud Professor, for your part in helping to make all of this happen. Really, you should.'

'You're a bastard, Kelly,' said Drabble. 'You've got to be stopped.'

'Is that so?' He arched an eyebrow. 'Men,' he addressed the two that stood before Harris and Drabble. 'Take your hands off your heads: you look stupid. Retrieve your weapons from Professor Drabble and dear Mr Harris. If either of them puts up a fight, Arkwright, shoot Miss Honeyand.'

Drabble looked over at Arkwright: the man reached for his gun.

'Stop,' he shouted, raising the barrel to the side of Captain Smith's head. 'I'll kill her if you move an inch.'

'So be it,' crowed Kelly. 'ARKWRIGHT!'

Drabble's focus flicked from the two guards, who stood centre ground, not knowing what to do, to Kelly, who stood beyond. Lastly he saw Arkwright, who was at the far side.

'HOLD IT!'

Drabble shoved Smith to the floor and raised his revolver, pointing it at Kelly's head. He pressed his finger to the trigger and met Kelly's staring face – the man's expression tinged with confusion. After a moment he frowned and inclined his head to one side.

'I'm unarmed, Professor. Going to kill me in cold blood?'

'You only have cold blood.'

Kelly's eyes travelled away from him. He looked back, smiled, and pointed over to the right.

Drabble glanced across. Kate knelt before Arkwright; his pistol pressed to the back of her head. Arkwright gripped her by her hair, close to her scalp. Drabble saw his knuckles whiten. Kate winced in pain.

'Drop it,' said Arkwright, cocking his revolver.

A glance told Drabble that Harris had his rifle at his side, trained on Smith. He thought fast. If this went badly they'd finish up with a dead Kelly, a dead Smith, and a dead Kate. After that it was anyone's business. There had to be a better way...

Drabble laid the Luger on the floor and stepped back, his arms raised. Harris, on his cue, threw his Lee-Enfield to the floor. Kelly nodded at Drabble slowly, a smirk developing on his face.

'How interesting,' he said. 'Funnily enough, I expected more from you. Now,' he fluttered his fingertips in the direction of the guards, 'you two, rearm yourselves. Smith, I'm very disappointed with you.' He pulled the swagger stick from under his arm and pointed to one of the metal chairs by the desk, 'Miss Honeyand, sit over there where I can see you. And Drabble, be so good as to place your hands on your head. If you move them, yours will be the first official execution under the new administration.'

Kelly referred to his watch. One of the guards kicked away the Luger – it fell into the laboratory below - and stripped the two rifles from Harris' shoulder; the second freed Smith's wrists. Arkwright picked up the phone and spoke into the receiver. Drabble saw Kate's eyes narrow and focus on Sir Carmen. From his angle the bruise on her left cheek seemed larger, more brutal. Drabble gritted his teeth and looked over at Kelly. There was a shout from below.

'Sir Carmen,' called a German voice. 'Come quickly. We have done it – *we have gold! Look!*'

Drabble saw a flash pass across Kelly's face. He sprang towards the handrail; the black Labrador yelped in pain, knocking into its master, and Kelly's feet skated from beneath him. The dog scuttled away. Kelly went down, arms flailing. Drabble dived at the nearest guard, butting him and kicking him to the floor. He snatched up his rifle, and stabbed the stock into his face; the man tumbled over and cowered beneath appealing hands. Drabble flicked the barrel towards the exit and the man bolted.

'Ernest!' Harris cried.

Drabble looked over and saw the second guard fumbling with the bolt of his gun – Drabble charged, swinging the rifle, and caught his head. There was a shot and the guard cried out, dropping his gun, and falling down clutching this stomach. Drabble span round and dived as Arkwright fired his pistol again. Sparks flew as the bullet ricocheted off the metal gangway beyond. Arkwright growled and fired. The bullet whistled past

Drabble and struck the concrete wall, showering Kate in dust. Drabble got Arkwright in his sights... suddenly the big man jerked and then coughed, blood spilling from his mouth over his bottom lip and chin. He collapsed to his knees. Drabble turned and saw a twist of smoke rise from the rifle at Kate's hip. He heard a wail – and saw Harris on his knees, his hands at his throat. Smith, above him with a maniacal look on her face, garrotting him with Drabble's college tie.

'H-e-l-p,' croaked Harris, his pleading eyes looking up at Drabble. '*H-e-l-p.*'

'ERNEST!' Kate screamed.

Drabble cried out in agony, his rifle clattering to the floor. He buckled forward – a hot, searing pain in his left shoulder. He turned slowly and saw Sir Carmen Kelly, a bloody spike of a sword stick in his hand.

'Valiant effort, Drabble,' said Kelly, inspecting the red blade. He kicked the rifle away, and it fell from the edge of the balcony into the laboratory below. 'But it's too late. We have gold and we have power.'

'Not yet you don't,' Kate raised the rifle and fired.

The bullet zipped by, grazing the handrail. Slowly, Kelly turned to her, his neat teeth gritted. Drabble heard her bring the bolt back.

'Miss Honeyand,' he said. 'I've had a just about as much as I'm prepared to have of you.'

He hurled the swordstick like a javelin. Drabble turned. There was a loud crack and he saw Kate drop her rifle.

'KATE!'

She looked skyward and for a moment her teeth

attempted to bite the air.

'Kate!'

Her hands went to her chest and just as they grasped the sword stick, they fell lifeless by her side. She slumped to the floor.

Drabble turned on Kelly. He saw the smile slowly leave his face.

'You bastard.'

There was a gunshot nearby and Kelly ducked as the bullet skidded past. Drabble charged. Kelly put his fists up but Drabble broke through his guard and stabbed the nail into Kelly's face. He growled and stumbled back, blood surging from the small hole in his cheek. Beyond him, Drabble saw Harris had broken free and was wrestling with Smith for a rifle, which now pointed to the ceiling. The barrel veered this way and that. Drabble glanced back at Kate. She lay on her back, the silver pommel of Kelly's sword stick protruding upright from her chest. She wasn't moving. He gritted his teeth and turned to Kelly.

'You bastard,' he said, glowering. 'This is it.'

Drabble brought his fist back and drove it into Kelly's mouth. His two front teeth stoved in and the head snapped back, sending him staggering backwards. But he was still smiling, thought Drabble. *I'll wipe that grin off your face you bastard.* There was a sudden glint of a blade and Kelly swung at him. Drabble swerved – and dodged a second wild left slash. Kelly over-balanced and Drabble pounded his fist into his gut. He groaned and lurched forward. A second blow knocked him back, stumbling. Drabble brought his right fist back and drove it squarely at

312

Kelly's jaw. He flew backwards and crashed against the handrail; the knife span from Kelly's grip and disappeared into the mass of cauldrons and tanks below. Drabble turned and saw Harris still locked in combat over the rifle. The remaining guard lay on the floor gripping his stomach in agony.

He heard the sound of laughter. It was Kelly.

'You can't stop me,' he said, his jagged teeth showing through his swollen, bloody lips, and spittle and saliva hanging from his mouth. 'More guards will be here any second. It's too late.'

Drabble looked over at Kate and he drew back his right fist.

'It certainly is.'

He punched up into Kelly's chin, sending him flying back, splinters of tooth showering through the air – then there was another crack. His shoulders jerked and Kelly's eyes opened wide. He reached out to Drabble, his mouth falling open as the handrail gave way behind him and he tumbled backwards, his arms wind-milling.

'Help!'

Drabble dived forward, reaching the edge in time to see Kelly break the surface of the molten, golden pool below, his shattered mouth forming an 'oh'. The metallic fluid absorbed him instantly, covering his head and face and trickling into the open mouth. After a second, just his outstretched hand was visible, the gold signet ring on the little finger glinting as it, too, disappeared into the bubbling cauldron. Drabble turned to the figures beyond, still wrestling over the rifle. Suddenly the barrel was pointing at him. The muzzle flashed and Drabble fell back, crashing to the ground, staring at the ceiling, gasping.

Harris looked over and then back to Smith.

'It's over,' he said, as the rifle swept to and fro. Harris looked down as the gun stopped, pointing immediately at his throat. Smith's blue eyes widened.

'Oh, Mama,' he wailed.

She pulled the trigger.

Click.

Harris raised his knee up sharply, connecting with Smith's groin. She cried out and he wrenched the gun from her grip. He kicked her sharply away from him and dashed her across the head with the wooden stock of the rifle. Smith slammed to the floor. He rushed over to Drabble.

'Ernest, old man, are you all right?' he patted his chest, 'Bugger – you did well, eh? I saw what happened to Carmen, what? You know what they call that in the City, don't you? *A golden goodbye!*'

Drabble breathed in painfully, wincing. Above him he saw Harris' face; it was pinched in concern and there was fear in his eyes. His gaze left Drabble's face and travelled down to his chest.

'Cripes,' he said, his bottom lip wobbling. 'Ernest, I don't want to alarm you, old man, but you're actually bleeding, err, quite badly.' Harris pulled out a spotted handkerchief from his breast pocket and pressed it to the bloody wound on his shoulder. Drabble cried out.

'Rest easy, old man,' said Harris.

'She's dead, isn't she?'

He saw Harris look over; his eyes narrowed. Kate was

perfectly still, lying on her back, the sword stick perpendicular to her torso. Harris' expression darkened and he looked back down at Drabble.

'I'm awfully sorry, old man.'

Drabble's face tightened and his bit his lower lip. Tears poured silently down the sides of his face.

'Oh, pal,' moaned Harris, 'it's my fault. If I hadn't been such a chump in that fight,' Harris looked over at Kate. 'If my hand hadn't been injured I would have been much more useful.'

Drabble nodded wearily.

'I know,' he said, his eyes closing. 'Just do one thing – *right now* - use the telephone. Call Winston Churchill. Get Hodgekiss. Tell him everything. Tell him that Kelly's dead.' He coughed, 'then we've got to destroy the lab. Come on, help me up...'

Suddenly there was a shout and the clang of boots on the metal gangway. Harris' face paled.

'Oh, *fuck*,' he said, his eyes widening.

The German doctor charged towards them, a cavalry sword held above his head.

'*Deutschland uber alles!*' cried the scientist, his ringing footsteps becoming louder.

'Do something,' croaked Drabble, trying to raise himself.

'*Der Fuhrer!*'

'HARRIS!'

'*Deutschland -*'

Harris got his hands on the rifle and fired.

Through the gun-smoke they saw the doctor stop dead – frozen mid-charge, his right leg raised partway through his stride, sword held above his head. Suddenly he toppled over backwards and crashed to the floor.

'Blimey,' said Harris, surveying the scene, 'That would have been a disappointment.'

Drabble heaved himself up onto his elbow.

'Come on, Harris,' he gasped. 'We've got to destroy the lab – and we must warn Churchill. Pass me your lighter…'

Just then, Drabble felt his last energy drain away and he was overcome by a powerful sense of sickness. His body was hurting. The noise and commotion of the laboratory seemed to quieten and he found himself fading into oblivion.

EPILOGUE

The six trumpeters gave a lengthy blast and Harris stood to attention, his chest out, his hands at his sides, his stomach sucked in. He wore an immaculate morning suit. As the fanfare faded, an attendant in the gold-embroidered uniform of a Royal Navy Commodore tapped Harris on the shoulder. He took two paces forward and planted his right knee on the red velvet cushion, which in turn was located on a red carpeted step. Harris bowed his head. Drabble, his left arm in a sling, stood at the back, behind some dozen rows of ornate gilt chairs filled with well-wishers. He saw the new King, dressed in scarlet army uniform, the blue sash of the Garter from his shoulder to his hip and his chest festooned with decorations and orders, raise the sword and touch Harris' right shoulder and then the left. After a moment Harris rose, bowed, and the two shook hands as they conferred. Drabble beamed. Across the room he saw Harris shake His Majesty's hand once again before being shepherded away by a second attendant to the side. Drabble heard someone clear their throat. He turned.

'Hodgekiss!'

They shook hands.

'How good to see you again, Professor,' he said. 'Mr Churchill sends his very best, sir.'

'That's kind.'

Drabble saw Harris walking along the aisle by the wall, grinning broadly. A silver, ruby, and blue cross

317

dangled from his neck on a short red and blue ribbon.

'Of course,' Hodgekiss continued, 'you should have been up there as well.'

Drabble looked at him.

'Not my cup of tea, I'm afraid,' he offered a smile. 'Though I am grateful. I dare say Harris will enjoy the privilege enough for both of us.'

'Good.' Hodgekiss nodded. 'Well, just so you know, we're all very grateful for everything you've done.'

It wasn't just me, thought Drabble. He noticed Hodgekiss' eye settle on the black band that he wore on his right arm.

'Mr Churchill also asked me to convey his condolences in respect of Miss Honeyand.' Hodgekiss' expression became grave. 'I'm very sorry,' he said.

'Thank you.'

Drabble coughed and turned away for a moment. He saw Harris reach the end of the aisle. He stopped and shook hands with a white-haired gentleman in a morning suit. Drabble saw the old man's mouth moving; he saw Harris nod slowly. Hodgekiss cleared his throat.

'As a matter of fact, Mr Churchill did ask me to ask you about Cromwell's head. Where is it, precisely?'

'I thought I told you on the telephone,' said Drabble. 'I've disposed of it. It's somewhere no one will ever find it.'

Hodgekiss looked down at his shoes. He leaned closer and said in a low voice, 'And what of the formula?'

'The formula?' Drabble raised his eyebrows, '*What formula?*'

'*The* formula, Professor. *Alchemy?*'

318

'Oh, that,' Drabble's tone rose. 'It was destroyed in the fire along with the laboratory – not that I'm sure it worked anyhow.' He coughed into his fist. 'Sorry.'

Hodgekiss met his gaze. His brow was knitted.

'You're sure of it?'

'Definitely,' said Drabble. He smiled as he saw Harris approach, but he addressed Hodgekiss. 'And no one need worry about it. That ghastly secret has been lost for ever – if indeed it was a secret worth having in the first place. I mean, no one's really sure if it worked, are they?'

'How can you be so sure?' Hodgekiss exhaled nervously. He gripped Drabble's arm. 'And what about the mad German scientist and his staff - and there was the scroll…'

Drabble patted his hand.

'Hodgekiss, don't worry. I told you, the scientist was killed,' he performed an involuntary glance in the direction of Harris, 'and as for his staff, none of them was in possession of all the facts. If any of them was so minded, it would take them more than a lifetime to piece it all together. I can assure you that no trace of it survives. The Lord Protector's wishes, such as one might be able to discern them, have been followed to a T.'

Hodgekiss exhibited the signs of fretting. He looked over to a small group who stood just a couple of yards away.

'But, Professor, what on earth were *his* intentions?'

'His intentions, Hodgekiss? Well, it's obvious: he was a pious, puritanical man; a genuine public servant who didn't care for, nor desire, the trappings of power or wealth, be they material or otherwise. But he was no

319

fool.' Drabble frowned. 'It is my belief that, possessed as
he was of a great moral zeal, he decided that *he* and *he*
alone could be trusted to hold the secret of alchemy, it
possibly having been discovered, and that before he died
he had come to the conclusion that he could not trust
anyone else with it. After all we lesser mortals would end
up destroying ourselves and would take his godly republic
with us. Therefore, he did the decent thing and saved his
successors from themselves. Thus, as I said, I feel we've
followed his wishes.'

'Sorry, I don't think you understand, Professor. We
couldn't give a fig for the Lord Protector's wishes.'

'Oh, come off it,' replied Drabble, eyeing him
playfully.

Hodgekiss shook his head, and his tone changed.

'Now don't forget, Professor, Mr Churchill was
responsible for expunging those very nasty charges
against you.'

Drabble raised an eyebrow.

'Hodgekiss,' Drabble offered his hand, 'we shall part
as friends. I think Harris could do with rescuing.
Goodbye.' They shook hands and Drabble moved away
towards his friend. He paused and turned back to
Hodgekiss. 'Do send my very best wishes to Mr
Churchill.'

Drabble moved slowly into the knot of well-wishers
who had surrounded Harris, who was grinning excitedly.
He broke free from the crowd.

'Who was that?' he asked, craning his head to see over
Drabble's shoulder.

'Chap who works for Churchill. Sends his

congratulations.'

'Ah,' sniffed Harris. He looked over, peering along his nose. 'The mysterious Mr Hodgekiss I'll be in no doubt. Hmmm. He could have ruddy well said thank you in person. After all, it was *me* who burned down Kelly's laboratory – and, don't forget, I dragged *you* out of there, too.'

Drabble smiled at his friend.

'Ah, well,' he said, 'I shouldn't take it personally, I think he had to dash off. And so should we.' They started moving towards the exit. 'So, what does it feel like? *Sir Percival.*'

'Oh, shush,' said Harris. 'Don't call me that. Sounds like I need a round table.'

Drabble laughed.

'All right,' he patted his shoulder, 'I'll call you *Sir Harris* then.'

Harris nodded thoughtfully as they reached the white and gold door. A footman stepped forward and opened it smartly.

'You know,' said Harris, nodding to the servant as they passed, 'that could just work.' They entered a long gilded corridor and the door closed silently behind them. 'And now,' said the journalist, 'I think Sir Harris could do with a spot of lunch.' He pulled a gleaming golden coin from his trouser pocket, flicked it into the air, and caught it, 'My treat.'

AUTHOR'S NOTE

The germ of the idea for this novel was inspired by *Hurrah for the Blackshirts*, a study of fascism between the wars in Britain by the social historian Martin Pugh, who once upon a time also taught me at Newcastle University. In his compelling study, Martin touched upon the Abdication Crisis of December 1936 and discussed the possibility of some twenty to forty Tory MPs, who were sufficiently pro-fascist, actually serving in a right-wing minority government under a figure such as Sir Oswald Mosley. Indeed, Pugh makes the point in the book that many were keen for the King to call the bluff of the Prime Minister, Stanley Baldwin, and the leader of the opposition, Clement Attlee, and to stand firm in his choice to marry Wallis Simpson.

Very transparently, Mosley's British Union of Fascists provides the inspiration for this story's own right-wing cell, the fictitious Fascist League of Great Britain: likewise Kelly's group was coloured by other small fascist groups, such as Arnold Leese's decidedly barmy and thankfully niche Imperial Fascist League.

The story's villain, the dastardly Sir Carmen Kelly, is clearly modelled, albeit superficially, on Mosley – they're both baronets, they're both strong supporters of Edward VIII, and they share appearances: the spiv moustache, the dark, slicked hair, the military bearing and the uniforms. Kelly, however, is a Conservative, whereas Mosley was originally a Labour MP, and our baddie is half-American, whereas Mosley's background was Anglo-Irish. Furthermore, Kelly comes to his fascism through a belief that democracy has failed the country's elite and weakened it; there was a stronger dose of working class sympathy in Mosley's motivation.

Additionally, the BUF's real lightning bolt logo inspired the motif of Kelly's political organisation in the book. Furthermore, the pro-Edward VIII slogans chanted by BUF supporters in the book are true (thanks again to Pugh). Of other characters, it's worth noting that Captain Smith is modelled on one Valerie Harkell-Smith, a fascist supporter and BUF member, who assumed male identity (and military rank, in her case 'Major') and bigamously married several women before being exposed in court.

Many of the details of the Abdication Crisis, not least the timescale of events from December 6 through to the actual abdication on December 12, are true, not least the various visits of, among others, Winston Churchill, Baldwin, and the Archbishop of Canterbury, to the King's house in Windsor Park, Fort Belvedere.

The story of Oliver Cromwell's posthumous beheading and the fate of his detached cranium as detailed in chapter one, is all, for the most part, true.

The Lord Protector died in 1658 and his corpse was dug up in 1660 following the Restoration of the Crown. His body (and those of two others, including his son-in-law and fellow Parliamentarian Henry Ireton) was exhumed – it spent the night at the Red Lion in Holborn, and was duly hanged, drawn, and quartered before being gibbeted at Tyburn. It did indeed require six strokes to detach the head, which then spent twenty years on top of a spike on the Palace of Westminster before being blown down in a gale and spirited away by a soldier, who did indeed hide it in his chimney. It then passed through private hands, ending up in a travelling circus and ultimately in the hands of one Canon Wilkinson. Where my story deviates from reality is that – as far as I know - Canon Wilkinson did not live on Dartmoor (rather in Suffolk), nor did he meet an untimely end. He did keep the head in a wooden box, however, and allowed the historians Pearson and Morant to examine it in 1935 (this study is referenced by Drabble when he first examines the head in Kelly's office, and did indeed conclude that the skull did belong to the Lord Protector). And while Wilkinson is said to have refused permission for the BBC to film the head in 1954, he was known to show the head to local children – once again, a detail I have co-opted for the story. Another change I made, for purely practical reasons, was to make the Wilkinson of fiction a general practitioner; this allowed for him to seem somewhat less historic, and also to have a convenient medical supply on hand if, and when, required.

When Wilkinson died the head was kept in a bank vault in Woodbridge, Suffolk. It was formally offered to Sidney Sussex College, Cambridge, (Cromwell's *alma mater*), on February 12 1960, and accepted by the College Council. It was re-buried almost 300 years after it had been dug up from Westminster Abbey and now rests somewhere within the ante-chapel at the college. The precise spot is unmarked to ensure that it is left in peace. I must acknowledge Lady Antonia Fraser's magisterial *Cromwell, Our Chief of Men* for furnishing the story of the exhumation and the unusual journey of the head, and providing a photographic source of the head itself.

Where my story reacquaints itself with reality is with Sidney Sussex and my decision to make Drabble a Fellow of that college – precisely because that is where the head ended up in real life and could therefore provide a convincing final resting place for it. The central 'McGuffin' – as Alfred Hitchcock would have called it - of the book, that the head contains a secret formula, is needless to say complete fiction and came to me after enjoying too many historically inspired mysteries.

The setting for the finale of the story – Goodwin Fort – is modelled on Landguard Fort in Felixstowe. Landguard Fort is indeed circular, being in the main a Victorian castle built around a Georgian one and topped off with a couple of less attractive Second World War ramparts.

For those familiar with such surroundings, you can possibly guess that the real life inspiration for the Granville Club, the gentlemen's establishment at which Drabble stays during his visits down from Cambridge and the setting for the opening of the book, is the Royal Automobile Club, whose opulent interior, layout, and snooker room, I have borrowed for the occasion.

Finally, the back story of Drabble's climbing accident is broadly consistent with the facts. Since 1858, when the Eiger was first climbed along the western side, the treacherous North Face was widely assumed to be impossible to climb. However in the thirties there were the first serious attempts on it by daring, often mixed-nationality groups of mountaineers: and these claimed victims in 1935 and 1936 – the second and third serious

ABOUT THE AUTHOR

Alec Marsh was born in Essex in 1975. He graduated from Newcastle University with a first class degree in history. Beginning his career on the *Western Morning News* in Cornwall, he went on to write for titles including the *Daily Telegraph*, *Daily Mail*, *The Times* and *London Evening Standard*.

In 2008 he was named an editor of the year by the *British Society of Magazine Editors*. He is now the editor of *Spear's Magazine*, a title focused on luxury lifestyle.

He is married and lives with his family in west London.